The best things come to those who wa[it] *Lucy*

WAITING ON JUSTIN

ROAD TO LOVE SERIES, BOOK 2

LUCY H. DELANEY

United States, 2017

:

To the students of the Wenatchee Valley Tech Center JAG classes of 2011-2013, this book is as much yours as it is mine. Each one of you left a lasting mark on my heart. I love you all.

To Dr. David McDonald and the AHS staff of 1992-1995 who believed that a kid like me could grow up to make a difference and keep kids safe. Thank you.

And to my Justin, thanks for the title. I owe you.

CHAPTER 1

I FELL IN LOVE WITH JUSTIN when I was seven years old, and I have loved him ever since. I knew him my whole life, but before that night he was nothing more than a really cool big kid. He was eleven, and at my young age of seven, an eleven-year-old is pretty much an adult. I suppose he was in my life even before I knew how to make a memory because as far back as I can go in my mind, he's always been there, protecting me, loving me silently.

Justin was the most amazing boy I had ever known, even before I decided I loved him. Some people said he was worthless and good for nothing, a loser and a punk. Clayton, Justin's dad, even said he wasn't worth the oxygen he breathed.

His hair was dirty blond and usually a little too long. I remember once my mom cut it into a raggedy mohawk and then never kept up with it. Eventually the sides grew out, and the top and back were so long I almost couldn't tell he ever had a mohawk until he turned his head really fast; then the top hair would fly up and the shorter sides were obvious. Honestly, it looked ridiculous, but he liked it and kept it that way for a real long time.

When I look back at his fifth grade picture I can see how young he was. His chubby cheeks, his uncombed hair, and his favorite Power Rangers shirt all showcase his youth. But I swear, when I was a kid I couldn't see anything but a grown-up when I looked in his green eyes. He was a man, and he watched out for me.

We knew each other before we fell in love because our parents ran in the same social circle. By that, I mean that they partied and drank with the same people, and occasionally got high. I know now that it was more than occasionally, but when you're young, hours, days, and weeks are stretched out, and it feels like forever is between them.

I'm not sure exactly how it happened, but his parents split up when I was in kindergarten. Clayton kicked her to the curb, and that's when our parents got together. I don't know what Clayton and Karina's love story was all about—that's their story to tell—but I'm sure in their addicted, co-dependent ways they could have loved each other at one time. But love is never enough, and their love ran out. And so did my dad. I don't know anything about him except that by the time Karina was gone he was already ancient history. The only thing my mom ever said was that he was no one I needed to bother knowing, so I never bothered, and neither did he.

Justin's mom and my mom had been friends since they met in high school. They liked to go to grown-up parties, and they got into grown-up kinds of trouble. My mom was the good one, I guess you could say. Karina, not so much. She started sleeping around in high school and got knocked up her sophomore year by Clayton. My mom felt sorry for her, and they both agreed Mom was practically the only friend Karina had who didn't desert her when she decided to keep the baby and left the regular school to finish at the alternative high school. She dropped out before Justin was born, though. Clayton graduated the summer before Justin was born and went right out to get a job to feed the kid. He started his career mudding, taping, and sanding drywall and worked his way up to painting by the time he and my mom got together. For all I know that's what he does to this day. Our moms stayed close, and when I came along four years later, the young mothers let their kids play together while they partied and Clayton yelled.

Karina was kind of mental from what Clayton says; I don't remember too much about her. She got into heroin and started shooting up and chasing the high. Clayton wanted nothing to do with someone who stuck needles in her arms (and legs), and that's why he got rid of her.

After my mom and Clayton got together, Karina would sometimes find them and ask for a place to crash or money for "food." If the parents were feeling benevolent, they would let her couch it for a day or two until she started fiending again, in other words, she wanted the high more than anything, even her son.

Justin loved it when she came. He tried so hard to be good when she was there, as if he could be good enough to make her want to kick the habit for good. It kind of creeped me out the way she would fold him up into her skinny pock-marked arms and hug him, rocking him for too long until it was awkward for us all to watch. Even when he was bigger she talked to him like a baby. "Mama loves you so much, honey," she would say, swaying him back and forth, or grasping his face between her hands, usually before she bailed again.

She always took off after a day or two. She left the same way every time: we would leave for school, and when we came home she was gone. No note, no good-bye, just gone.

I think it made my mom feel bad for Justin and guilty about being a lousy mom herself because she would be real good to us for a long time after that. On the days Karina bounced, my mom would be waiting in the car at the end of the road when the bus dropped us off after school. Clayton had a pick-up he drove to work, but Mom had a rattly black Accord with rusted fenders. It was barely street-worthy, but it got us around. We kept the inside clean—Clayton hated it dirty—but the cleanliness didn't hide how broken down it was.

Mom only met the bus when Karina disappeared, and over the years we got used to the pattern. I got in the habit of watching Justin's face. He tried to hide it, but I could see it there plain as day, something that said, "She left me again." I felt sorry for him but happy that we got to go out to eat. Mom usually took us to McDonald's, where my friend Lizzie and I would play on the playground while Justin sulked.

That's when my mom was the best kind of mom. I would stop playing long enough to see her rub her hand down Justin's arm to comfort him. Sometimes he would pull his shirt up to his cheek and wipe away a tear or two. He could take a hit from Clayton easy, but take away the kid's mom and he was mush. I guess Mom tried as hard as she could in her own way to make it better for him. For days after that she would be way too happy and meet us at the door after school. She would turn on MTV and dance and sing to the videos with us. She would ask for the book Justin was reading, and we would sit at her feet and listen to her read it. I liked it when she read to us because she did the voices, something Justin refused to do. It was goofy and ridiculous, but it helped Justin forget that his mom didn't want him. I thank my mom for that, and I thank Clayton for mostly not yelling on those days.

My mom and Clayton never dated or had a love story that I know of; they just kind of merged together. One day Mom and I were living in a tiny, cramped Section Eight apartment, and the next we moved into Clayton's place. It was a surprise, but then again, so was everything back then. My mom never told me what we were doing or how my life was about to change; she just did stuff, and it changed how I lived. I rolled with it; I was resilient like that. I had to be prepared for anything because sometimes Mom and Clayton could go for what seemed like weeks being normal parents around the house, then BAM! they were off and partying, and we were home alone for a day or two. Once it was three days in a row—Labor Day weekend, if I remember right.

It didn't bother us. Justin and I preferred being alone. We were better at playing house without our parents there to ruin it for us. Justin liked to fix all the broken things when his dad was gone. He never dared to do it when Clayton was home, and he made me promise not to tell. When I asked him why, he told me that one time when he was tightening a table leg Clayton accused him of stealing the screwdriver and thumped him good for it. There was another time too: my mom's car had a flat tire and he tried to change it for her, but the bolts were too tight and he couldn't loosen them, so she went inside to tell Clayton. He came out laughing, but he wasn't happy—he was mad and drunk. He pushed Justin out of the way hard and told him that boys shouldn't concern themselves with a man's work, and that he was sick of him trying to be the man of the family. So Justin learned to keep a list of things to fix when Clayton was gone. If Clayton or Mom noticed what he did, they never said a word.

I was the chef when they were out and would make breakfast and dinner with whatever food we had. That was another good thing about them: they always made sure we had something to eat. It wasn't a lot, but it was food. Sometimes I think they must have planned ahead of time to leave but didn't tell us because the only times we ever seemed to have Captain Crunch in the cabinet were the mornings they didn't come home. When I was really young I made mostly cereal and sandwiches, but as the years went by I got quite good at a number of breakfast dishes. Omelets were my specialty, though, and still are to this day.

It didn't scare me when they didn't come home; I honestly preferred it. We could watch whatever we wanted on TV, listen to the music we wanted, and play however and wherever we wanted. But the best part was the quiet. We didn't have to worry about Clayton getting mad and yelling at us. There was no blaring music unless we wanted it up like that. The house was still and empty and free of stupid people doing stupid things. Peace came in and filled the rooms, only disappearing when they came back home. If we could have bought our own food I don't think I would ever have wanted our parents to come home. Of course as a kid I didn't think about all the other things they were also providing us, like clothes and lights and shelter; I only thought if we could get our own food we wouldn't need them.

Night was no less scary for me without them there. When they were gone I knew I couldn't be woken up by their fighting or Clayton's raging over some dumb thing my mom said or did. Justin would tuck me in with a story, he read to me almost every night of my life, but he read longer when they were gone. I wasn't afraid of being home alone because I had him, but he didn't have anyone. I think he was afraid and reading was an excuse for him to stay with me longer. Eventually I would fall asleep, and if I woke up first I knew I would find him not in his bed, but on the couch, with his bat in his hand.

I don't know how Justin felt about it, especially after he started partying with them, but I really didn't like it when they brought the party to our house. That happened often enough to be more than a novelty. It seems like it was at least a couple times a month, but maybe it was less than that. Let's just say it happened so frequently that it was common to find hungover idiots passed out on our couch on any given weekend morning. Some kids wake up on Saturdays to pour their cereal and watch cartoons; we did the same thing, only we had to maneuver around vomit piles and sleeping ogres, too. Clayton, thick, stocky and muscular was sociable with his friends, a real party animal, and he liked to invite people he and Mom knew, from the bar and work and who knows where else, to come over to our place.

Once, on New Year's, some guys got into a pretty bad fight right after the ball dropped. Clayton made them take it outside. It was my "Uncle Jon," who wasn't really my uncle, and this punk who thought he could take him. It stands out in my mind because it was the first time I had seen a fight in real life. I remember the sound of fist on face; it surprised me because it wasn't like the sound effects in the movies, like celery breaking crisply. It was flat, dull and deadly.

They kept fighting, hitting, punching, bloodying each other with blow after gruesome blow. People were cheering, and somehow it stopped being a vengeful fight and turned into a fun, bloody-knuckle boxing match. They took breaks to chug beer and slam shots, laugh, talk crap to each other, and have the blood wiped from their faces; then they went back at it. I don't remember how it stopped, but when those good old boys were done, a couple more stepped up to fight. It was horrible and wonderful all at the same time.

I couldn't stop watching, but I stayed away from the crowd and watched from my perch in Justin's room. His bedroom, on the southwest corner of the dumpy double wide we called home, overlooked the driveway, and his window sill was just wide enough for me to balance on. I could see everything. Had I been in the mix I would have been lost behind knees and big butts. Justin wasn't in the room with me; he was outside with the guys, right in there with them. He wanted to box so bad, but they wouldn't let him. I don't think he was even ten then, or they probably would have let him. I saw them taking bets and trading money. I heard the laughs and cheers when a man went down. I saw the guys who got knocked out get pulled into the grass and watched as they gradually came to and got up. I saw it all and took it in. It was my life.

Someone in the neighborhood must have called the cops because they came. I don't know which neighbor it was—we were pretty tucked away from them all—but the noise was probably going on for too long. Nothing bad happened to my parents or anyone really. I saw the first police officer on scene, arms crossed and stern looking, talking to Clayton, who was swaying like a tree in the wind. He had fought and won, but his cheek was busted open and still bleeding a little. He was trying to laugh and play it cool.

I couldn't hear the words, but knew he didn't want to get in trouble and was saying whatever they wanted to hear. It worked because no one went to jail, and after an eternity, the two cop cars finally left. Everyone must have stashed the illicit stuff—I know there was at least weed and probably coke too. Either they hid it well or the cops didn't look too hard because it was New Year's, and even adults were allowed to get crazy sometimes. They probably thought we only had parties once a year.

Before they left I heard the big policeman tell everyone to quiet down, leave if they were sober, and let the neighborhood have its peace and quiet again. That was the only time I ever remember the law coming over—until I was older and they were coming for me.

No one called the cops when the parental units didn't come home. No one called when Clayton and my mom fought. Maybe they didn't hear those fights because they were inside, but I don't see how anyone couldn't hear. That man could scream like a drill sergeant, even though he got kicked out of the Army for conduct unbecoming of an officer—a nice way to say his excessive partying made the Army look bad so they let him go. If he would have stayed in, I'm sure he would have become their best drill sergeant; he would have been great at it. Yeah, he could yell . . . and yell . . . and yell. I hated it when he got going because nothing could stop him— certainly not the weed he said mellowed him out. He would only stop yelling long enough to light up, but it didn't calm him down; it just gave us a momentary reprieve from the lecture. I wished the drugs would have relaxed him, but I don't think they ever really did.

We knew when they were getting high like we knew when Karina left: they did the same things every time. They went into their room to do it, shut the door, and put a towel under the crack, as if a towel could keep the smell from seeping out.

When they came out of the room, their eyes were red and it smelled like skunk, but Clayton was not more mellow. If he was in a mad mood when he went in, he would pick up right where he left off when he came out. I felt like he would yell more about everything and then broaden the targets of his anger from just us to the whole world: the governor, the president, the Iraqis.

But he would always bring it back to us to wrap it up; he was gifted in the art of trash talk like that. He would chastise me for laziness, first getting up in my face, then into my mom's because she birthed me. He would go off on how disrespectful Justin was and thump him in the chest. Then he would circle back, complaining about how dirty we were, how dirty the house was, how pathetic our lives would be because we didn't listen to his sage wisdom, how pathetic my mom was for being so lazy and not teaching us how to be anything but slobs. When it was really bad he would scream right into my face, only an inch away, and if I moved, he would follow me, leaning into my face, twisting his head to match mine move for move. His spit flecked my cheek and sometimes splashed into my eyes, that skunk breath of his invading my nostrils.

Believe it or not, I preferred the skunk breath to the booze breath. When he was drinking, I was liable to get slapped or spanked if I turned my head or closed my eyes, so I guess maybe the weed did chill him out after all. If he was yelling at Justin, it was no big thing for him to hit him. His favorites were sucker punches. I think he liked those best because they didn't leave bruises.

We learned to take his rants just like the soldiers in the movies we would watch together as a raggedy family. If we stood there strong, stiff, and stoic, looking straight ahead, he would eventually tire out and leave us alone. We never yelled, "Sir, yes, sir!" like they did in the movies, though. That would have not fared well for us.

I guess it's OK with your neighbors if you fight with your girlfriend and slap your kids around as long as you mostly keep it inside where they can't hear. I wonder if anyone would have called if Clayton took it outside more often. I can't blame our neighbors; they probably thought our life was as normal as theirs. We didn't bother them and they didn't bother us.

My favorite neighbor, Justin's too, was Mrs. Diaz. Mom called her an old bag; we called her Gramma Diaz, even though she wasn't anymore our grandma than Uncle Jon was our uncle. She was as persnickety as they get. She went to church every Sunday and Wednesday, and she smelled like old flowers. I liked that smell. She displayed pictures of her family in golden, gilded, gaudy frames all the way down her million-mile-long hallway. I always seemed to find my way to the hall. I loved to stare at all the happy people behind the glass in her frames. None of her people held beer bottles or pipes in their hand; they smiled just because they were happy.

Mrs. Diaz never asked us what happened at our house, and it never entered my mind to tell her that sometimes my parents left us alone or let people party until they puked. I did ask, once, where her bar was. Every house I had ever been in had a bar or liquor cabinet or something. She chuckled, exactly the way you would expect a chubby grandma with silver-gray hair to chuckle, patted my head, and said, "Oh honey, not everyone needs alcohol to have a good time."

I loved to go over to her house. One step inside and I was consumed by a cloud of warmth and love. We ate her cookies; she baked them fresh for the neighbor kids every Wednesday before church. It was a ruse: get us in, sugar us up with sweets and invite us to church. How could we say no? Our parents were only too happy to let us go since it gave them one night a week they didn't have to deal with our snotty noses.

Gramma Diaz went to a church that was exactly four songs away. I still remember every single word to each song on the cassette tape she would play. We would go to AWANA as they called it; we called it game night. We played games, memorized Bible verses and got fake paper bucks to spend on goodies like sunglasses and erasers. Whenever I thought of heaven it always resembled the AWANA store, full of good things I wanted but could never reach.

Like I said earlier, our neighborhood was kind of spread out, not like the new developments nowadays. We lived at the end of a long dead-end road with six houses on one side and five on the other. I could only see the Diaz house from the street, and even theirs was barely visible because it was so far back. Our bus would drop us off at the beginning of the road, where Justin, Lizzie, and I would get off, along with two other kids, Michael and Kim. We saw other kids' parents wait in cars for them at the front of their roads; my parents almost never did. Clayton worked, and Mom was usually drunk by three or had a headache—and besides, we were old enough to know where home was anyway. So we walked home from the bus unaccompanied.

The road was long enough to keep the houses spread out. Maybe they really didn't know and couldn't hear what happened at our house. I know trees blocked one house from another, so I'm sure no one could see into our house to see the fighting and drinking just like no one could see mischievous kids prowling houses that weren't theirs. I'm not going to lie, once or twenty times we walked down my neighbors' driveways. Once or twenty times we opened their locked doors, ate their food—just a little bit, like innocent mice—and left before anyone knew we were there.

Our house was the last one, a half a mile or so from the beginning of the road and far away from the other houses. Clayton bought it before I was born from an old-timer he used to work for after school, right after the Army sent him packing and he went back to doing drywall. That's why he got it when he and Karina split: because he bought it and because he kept Justin, the courts thought he was better for Justin than his mom. It made me wonder what his mom was really like for anyone to consider Clayton the better parent.

Our home—or rather, Clayton's—was down a rutted, gravel-less, brush-lined driveway of its own. Maybe that's why no one saw, heard, or said anything about what happened there. I think if I were a neighbor of that ramshackle double-wide down the road, I could have heard the yelling. I think I would have called about it. Yeah, I would have.

When I was a kid growing up in it, I didn't realize how bad it was. I thought it was normal. But other people must have known that wasn't normal. Maybe not Clayton and Mom—maybe they were so broken they thought it was fine—but the neighbors? All of them? They had to know, at least some of them, like Gramma Diaz and the young couple in the pea green house. They had to have heard—at least in the summer when the windows were open. I swear Clayton would yell louder in the summer because his voice didn't stick in the house the way it did when they were closed. It was like he thought he needed to be louder for us to get the point that we were good for nothing. The old man with the huge hearing aids all the way up at the front of the road—I can accept his not hearing us. But there were nine other houses that could have. I still do blame them, I guess, and I need to get over it—*accept the things I cannot change,* right? But I can't quite accept it yet because if I could hear their music and barbecues, they must have heard Clayton yelling at me, Justin, Lizzie, and Mom. I don't know what good it would have done to call the police; maybe they would have taken me to Aunt Aerin sooner, or maybe they wouldn't have done anything. But if I were my neighbor back then, I would have done something to save a kid like me from a life like that.

In the summertime Clayton played his music louder too. I could hear it from far away in the woods where we would play. But I could still hear his voice over it—not the words but the yelling—when he was mad at Mom. The music blasted outside but inside it was so loud I could barely think; their Friday friends liked it that way. They only had big parties every now and then, but they had friends over most weekends if they weren't out at the bar themselves. We would play outside with the other kids who had parents like ours. We took them to the woods where we had climbing trees and forts and freedom. That was the nice thing about their Friday friends, a lot of them had kids too. The grown-ups would be inside listening to AC/DC, Queen, and Duran Duran, while getting wasted, and we would be outside pretending to be real adults in wars and houses. We would stay outside as long as we could to avoid the noise and the noise makers, spilled beers, and nonsense.

Like I said, my mom was lucky: she had a man. In their social circle, Clayton was actually a pretty good man; he came home almost every night, he kept a job that paid the bills, he even cooked us dinner most weeknights while watching reruns of *The Honeymooners*, which I hated. Yeah, he was a great guy. Ha! All he expected in return was a clean house (which my mom could never keep clean enough), a stocked bar (which he accused us of stealing from), and kids who kept their mouths shut. Because of Clayton's awesomeness, Mom didn't have to work like most of the women we knew. She could stay home, which was a good thing because her drinking habit would have gotten in the way of a real job. She had the shakes almost every morning when we left for school (that's if she wasn't blacked out from the night before), and she was drunk or on her way there by the time we got home, yet she still contributed financially by babysitting Lizzie.

Lizzie's mom, Brenda, was one of my mom's drinking buddies who liked to listen to the loud music too. She wasn't lucky like my mom—she was single, and busted her butt to make ends meet. Lizzie's dad was a three-time loser, back before they even had three-strikes laws. He was locked up for something—murder, I think. He was a biker, I guess; Lizzie doesn't talk about him, and I know better than to ask about bad memories. She really doesn't like to talk about the past unless it's about the good times.

So anyway, Lizzie's mom, Brenda, raised her alone but needed help. She worked as a residential house cleaner until she failed a drug test; then she took anything she could find for a while. She was a cashier at a grocery store, then a convenience store; she worked at a mill doing something, but I don't know what. She always worked on the swing shift and got welfare to cover the difference—and the child support the locked-up loser didn't pay. Later she found her true calling as a dancer, but that's Lizzie's story to tell, not mine, not really. I'll save it for when it comes in to play. All that matters for now is that Mom helped Brenda out by watching Lizzie and because of Brenda's schedule she stayed the weekends with us and almost all the weekdays too, and Brenda paid her for it. I don't know how much, but I think she and Clayton relied on the money to make our own ends meet.

I'm pretty sure Brenda and Clayton slept together. I don't know if it was an affair or only a hook-up thing they did when Mom was passed out, but I'm almost certain it happened. Clayton was the kind of guy who wouldn't let an opportunity like that go; Brenda had a reputation for sleeping around, and she was indebted to us. She gave my mom money for watching Lizzie, so she had to be paying Clayton with something too for him to put up with another sniveling brat hanging out around his house all the time. Sex is all I can figure she gave him for his kindness to her daughter. Justin and I would never talk in front of Lizzie about what kind of a woman her mom was.

Justin got into plenty of fights over Brenda's reputation. People talked about what Brenda did after she started dancing. The guys probably talked about it because they got dances from her themselves. Kids at school made fun of Lizzie for it too. If Justin caught her crying because of something someone said, he would find out who called her mom a name and beat him up. It worked out well for Lizzie but not so much for Justin. Whenever he got suspended for fighting, which happened all too often, Clayton would let him have it.

"You like to fight, huh, boy?! Fight me then, and I'll show you what's up. Fight me, punk!"

"No, Dad," Justin would always say before Clayton would give him a famous sucker punch, sometimes knocking him to the floor.

"You like it? You like fighting?"

"No, sorry."

"You're right, you're sorry! Is it going to happen again?"

"No."

"You sure about that? 'Cause this isn't the first time. When are you going to get it through your thick skull that you can't be fighting in school?"

Justin never cried or showed weakness, but Lizzie did, her big brown doe eyes would pool with tears that spilled over onto her pink cheeks when Clayton bellowed at him. Clayton only allowed him bread and butter on the days he stayed home, telling him that's all he would get in jail if he kept it up, so we would save bits of food from our dinner and take it to him afterward. I don't know what Justin did while we were at school, but on the days he was suspended, Lizzie and I always knew he would be there at the bus stop to get us when the yellow doors opened.

CHAPTER 2

BEFORE I GET TO THE NIGHT I fell in love with Justin I have to share a little more about us when we were kids. Back then it was three of us—me, Justin, and Lizzie—for life. We would get off the bus together and walk the long dead-end road to the house.

The two other kids on our street were brother and sister. They were spoiled losers who called us poor because our parents couldn't put us in designer clothes like theirs did. We didn't talk to them much at all. They ran in a different circle, one for the "cool kids." We weren't good enough for them, and I knew it. I hated Kim for her perfect hair and her mom who brought cupcakes to class on her birthday. I had tried to make friends with her in first grade, we had the same teacher, but a week later she told another classmate I got my shoes at the Goodwill, and it embarrassed me. I knew my shoes weren't new, they showed up one day and Mom said she found them for me. I thought they were nice. I had no shame about them until Kim made fun of me. After that I hid them in my closet and said they were lost. The only other shoes I had were jellies that I wore until it was too cold, as if wearing summer shoes in winter was somehow better than used tennis shoes. It worked though: I got another pair of shoes from Payless, brand new, for $9.95; Justin scored a pair too on a BOGO deal.

"How do you lose a pair of shoes?" Mom asked me the day she finally took us. "You've gotta be some kind of an idiot to lose the shoes off of your feet. I just got those for you, Haylee. They fit you fine. You think we have the money to get you shoes every month?"

It was easy getting yelled at by Mom. Clayton was harder, but while he was dribbling spit in my face I squished my toes into the soft padding of my new Pro Wings and smiled on the inside. Yep, it was worth it.

The only other time we talked to those spoiled kids was once when Justin heard them call us losers. It was the last time he wanted to hear it. Justin was smart about it, he waited until the bus was out of sight, then ran right up to an unsuspecting Michael and kidney-kicked him from behind.

"You ever call us losers again and I'll beat your face in; you got that?" he yelled in a fashion I'm sure Clayton would have been proud of. Michael tried to look tough but complied.

Sometimes, after that, we would kick a pine cone between us, and of course we all played nice at Gramma Diaz's house on cookie Wednesdays, but we weren't ever friends with them. Other than those two, the only other kids on our street belonged to a youngish couple who drove an older Volvo and a minivan, and they were too young to go to school. And so the three of us played alone together. Clayton and Mom called us the Three Musketeers, but we didn't know who they were.

We were left to ourselves most days after school. Mom didn't care what we did as long as we left her out of it, and Clayton never got home before dark and usually after a long layover at Brewer's, his favorite bar. We liked outside best because it was away from the parents, but there was more to it than that. Outside, in our secret places, we traveled the world through time, space, and history.

Justin was amazing at building things: forts, toys, wooden guns, furniture, bunkers, and contraptions for any number of schemes. He was a creative genius, and Lizzie and I were his helpers.

We had this perfect shack of a hide-out in the woods not too far from the house. It was hidden under years of overgrown ivy, sticker bushes, and rotting leaves, and we were certain no one else knew our secret place. The adults probably knew about it, but they never spoke of it in our presence, and neither did we. Inside the safety of those rotten plywood walls we would pretend to be cops having a shoot-out with bank robbers or hijackers, pioneers in a covered wagon, Native Americans in a teepee, travelers stuck in a sandstorm hunkered down in a Bedouin tent, or adults living in our own house (OK that was me and Lizzie, but every so often Justin would allow us to play a girlie game like that). Most of the time, we would pretend there was a war and that we were hiding from the Nazis or Japs or Charlies, shooting out Justin's windows and snipe holes. I didn't get the names but played along for fun. We could disappear for hours, and no one cared. When Mom or Clayton called us for dinner, we had to stop everything and run home as fast as we could, hoping to avoid trouble for being late.

When I was in first grade, Justin started fourth, and our make-believe games were forever changed. His teacher, Mr. Sanchez, introduced the class to science fiction. Female teachers read Beverly Cleary during story time, but Mr. Sanchez read H.G. Wells, Heinlein, and Bradbury. Justin said during science Mr. Sanchez would talk about sci-fi inventions that people were actually creating right then. Computers, Justin told us, had been science fiction, and now almost every workplace used them. Communicators people carried with them were make-believe, but real-life inventions were making them reality. It changed him. Justin got lost in the possibilities of time and space travel and all things science fiction. I know now it was his escape from our pain like he was mine.

Despite Justin's bad grades, he always had a book checked out from the library from fourth grade on. He had always been a good reader, telling Lizzie and me stories from books all the time. After Mr. Sanchez, though, they went from *Hatchet* and *White Fang* to sci-fi and alien thrillers. He read them to us in our shack and it magically turned into whatever space we needed to imagine the story into real life. Time travel and teleportation stories were his favorite. Where once we were content being police or soldiers in bunkers, we transformed almost overnight into scientists in lab coats, mad geniuses inventing true teleportation machines in secret labs. We invented a teleporter of our own and named it the BTTF24, Back to the Future 24. We pretended it was our 24th try and we finally had success. We would transport ourselves to other places: the desert, the future or past, New York City, or Mrs. Diaz's kitchen on the next Wednesday. We would run to our machine to escape danger just in the nick of time. It was really just a bunch of rusty metal scraps, wires, and buttons we glued and stuck into a three-by-three piece of peg board, but in our imaginations it was pure science. I swear I really went to the places we programmed in our fake machine. It didn't feel pretend to us; it was real, and to this day Justin is dreaming up ways to make teleportation through space or time— or both—possible.

Though we avoided being inside as much as possible, our part of California wasn't always warm and sunny in the winter and we had a real problem enduring the cold. Our teleporter was great for imagination, but we didn't know about insulation. That's when we had to get creative.

It was Justin who first had the idea to sneak into Mrs. Diaz's house when she wasn't home. It was winter—I remember because the slightest amount of slush covered the road and driveway. Justin said we should stick to the ruts to cover our tracks. It felt like a grand adventure to Lizzie and me, so we obeyed. We were cold, and neither the BTTF24 nor home was a welcoming thought, but the Diaz's place was; who wouldn't want to leave our sorry lives and teleport into theirs?

Our excuse to do it was to see if she had any more cookies left over from the Wednesday before, but it was as much to have fun as anything. Justin, ever the creator of our fantasies, said we needed to teleport there and had us stalk into the bushes before the driveway. I think he was really holding us back while Michael and Kim disappeared down their own driveway. He was like a cat burglar, only a good one. He used one of those fake credit cards they send in the mail, he had tons of them in his wallet, to pick the lock. We used to play with those too, pretending we were rich and were buying anything we wanted, but that day it was a key to a secret world.

The Diaz house had an anteroom that Gramma Diaz called the mudroom. It was never locked; Mr. Diaz used it as a holding place for his muddy shoes and plastic grocery bags. The floor was worn and wooden, but Gramma Diaz kept the mat that lay in front of the locked kitchen door fresh and clean. When she invited us over for cookies she would have us wipe our feet on the hard bristly rug outside the mudroom then come into the room and take our shoes off while sitting on her old wooden bench. She told us her granddad had made it with his bare hands and she didn't have the heart to get rid of it.

She was fair and gave all five of us, we Three Musketeers and the two rich brats, a chance to be first in the kitchen. After our shoes were off, our feet weren't to touch the dirty floor, no, no, no! Instead she insisted we stand up in a line on the bench like little ducklings, and hop, hop, hop, one after the other, from the top of the bench right smack onto the clean floor mat in front of the kitchen.

"That's the way," she would say to each of us respectively. Her house always had Jesus songs playing. When we were little they were fun little kid ones, but as the years stretched they were more like what we heard in church when we went with her, which we did every now and again.

When we snuck into her house, we obeyed the same rules. They fit perfectly into our teleportation fantasy anyway. Justin was first with his wizard key-card. He made a fantastic whooshing sound effect as he opened the door and transported himself inside. Next was Lizzie, then me. He didn't have to tell Lizzie and me to keep it secret. Even though Gramma Diaz let us in when she was home, we knew better than to go in when she and the old man were away.

Once we were in, Lizzie and Justin scoped out the kitchen, looking for the cookies, but I inevitably found my way into the hall. I wanted to fill up on smiley-faced pictures more than cookies.

"C'mon, Haylee, it's time to go," Justin said that first time, coming around the corner with a cookie in his hand for me. I didn't want to leave; I wanted to stay right there with the happy people forever, but I knew it would be bad to get caught.

We left the way we came and pretended to teleport from their mudroom straight out into the woods. Really all we did was run like the wind (in the ruts of the driveway) from the slamming mudroom door to the tree line, but in our child's minds we were floating on scientific waves of greatness.

We never took anything but food, I swear, at least not from Gramma Diaz. It was just fun to go in and pretend we had normal lives. For two or three winters we broke into their empty house when it was cold, but we never got caught—not even when we started to get brave enough to stay longer. We liked watching their TV. Justin would kick his feet up in Mr. Diaz's chair, and Lizzie and I would snuggle together in Mrs. Diaz's. We loved staying warm and feeling safe at their place. We were careful to put things back the way we found them and only take food that wouldn't be missed. Justin must have known their schedules and when to expect their return because there was only once we had to rush out a back door to avoid being found out. Justin said they were predictable; I didn't know what that meant for a long time, but now he uses the same word to describe me.

One day we went into the mudroom and found an unbreakable deadbolt on the kitchen door. As hard as he tried, Justin couldn't unlock it like the regular door lock. Still, it wasn't a complete loss; Gramma Diaz had some cookies on a plate on the bench, and there was a heater keeping the whole space warm. That next Wednesday she told us she was leaving the leftover cookies and food in the mudroom for the hungry raccoons that were getting into her trash cans. Back then we believed her, though now it's obvious there was no way she would have had three leftover sandwiches almost every day for raccoons that could somehow get into a shut mudroom.

I know now that they had to have found us out. I wonder how long they had known we were hungry and cold and were sneaking into their comfort for reprieve and why they never said anything. Did they know that was all it was, or did they suspect us of something more sinister? And why, if they knew, didn't they stop us? After that we still crept to their door step but were forced to stay in the mudroom, which we did for long spans of time. We almost always ate the sandwiches but nibbled them the way we imagined raccoons would do and left bits of the sandwich bags torn up to trick them. We only took one or two cookies to split between us and hoped they wouldn't realize it was something bigger than raccoons eating their food. We really thought we were getting away with it. We were so young and naive.

After the deadbolt went on, Justin started watching the other neighbors. He said they were all unpredictable, but that didn't stop us from visiting some of their homes too, doing much of the same things; snooping, interloping into lives we wished we had but could only dream of. The alcohol in people's homes is what surprised me most, I think. That's when it started to dawn on me that we were different from everyone else. Our house practically contained a liquor store: vodka, whiskey, scotch, wine, beer, rum, mixers, we had it all, or had empty bottles or cans of it overflowing the trash.

None of the neighbors had as much as we did. The Diazes and the Volvo couple never had any. Most of the neighbors had beer or a bottle of wine or two loafing somewhere—on a shelf, in a fridge, or in the man cave—but never like our stash.

The house next to Michael and Kim's had an impressive collection of wine bottles high up on a rack, and that made me feel like we were a little more normal until I realized that they were dusty bottles that never seemed to be moved, few were ever missing, and only occasionally would a new one appear. The same bottles sat on the shelf, unopened, visit after visit while at our house that many bottles were consumed and replenished weekly. I didn't understand what it meant, but that's when I knew for sure that our house was definitely different.

I don't know what I would have done if Justin hadn't been there. He was special, and our love was unique, the kind that can only grow under the rarest of circumstances. It was real, and like so many other things between us, it was clearly understood but unspoken. We knew we weren't brother and sister. Mom and Clayton never called us that, and when people asked if we were, we never even pretended to be. We lived in the same house, our parents slept together, and I called Clayton my dad, but Justin never called my mom his mother, and we certainly never identified ourselves as siblings. We were always together though, sharing the same experiences, hearing the same fights, feeling the same hopelessness, avoiding the same sad reality of our existence by pretending we were anything but two kids with lousy parents.

We were together so much we were friends by default and did everything young friends did. I don't remember ever fighting with him the way siblings fight with each other; that's why I don't think I ever thought of him as a brother. Once Lizzie was old enough to tag along, they fought, and Lizzie and I fought, but Justin and I never did. It was like even then we were so much a part of each other that to fight with him would have been akin to arguing with myself.

And then came the fateful night everything changed and my friend became my hero and the love of my life. If there had ever been a time for the transporter to be real, it would have been that night. If I could have closed my eyes or switched a button to end up anywhere but where I was, I would have—but then again, if I hadn't been there, I may never have fallen in love.

Our parents were having a raging party, the kind I talked about before: loud music, drunken idiots, towels under doors, the kind of fun all kids dreamed of having happen in their house. There were a few other kids there too, so we were being sociable at first.

Justin snagged some whiskey from the bar and drank it with two other boys. They got almost as stupid as the grown-ups. I was disappointed but curious all the same while I watched them put the liquid in their bodies. They wouldn't let Lizzie or me try it; they said we were too little. I cried, and Justin promised that when I was ten they would let me. He said it would mess with my body too much until then.

The boys were running around with light sabers having some kind of Jedi fight, and Clayton caught them. He sent Justin to his room without so much as an angry look. *"Boy, don't let me see you again tonight, ya hear?"* was all he had said. I didn't know why he was so nice about it. Was he being cool because everyone was there? Was he saving his wrath for later? Or was it something else, like maybe he didn't care if Justin was drinking? It wasn't like Clayton to be cool like that, but maybe the audience kept him in check.The other boys were sent off to their parents' cars, and the adults laughed the whole thing off and went on with their revelry. It was late when the boys got busted, but the party was just getting started. We knew there would be strangers in our house who would be up until dawn before finally crashing, or rather passing out.

There was this funny glass mirror with white powder residue on it that would show up on the bathroom counter on big party nights and disappear the next day. We didn't know what that was all about for the longest time—and then one night we did. That night the bedroom was used so frequently the towel didn't even get stuffed against the crack, and a low-lying, pungent, blue-grey smoke hung in the air, swirling in dazzling circles when someone would walk past.

The music played on and on, and we Three Musketeers found ourselves hovering together away from the chaos after Justin's fun ended for the night. Lizzie and I went to his room to stay with him. It somehow felt better to be together than alone. Since Lizzie's mom was there, high as all get out, we knew she was staying the night. Justin told us it was time for bed at some point and ushered us into my room. He tucked Lizzie into bed next to me and read us both a bedtime story, talking louder than normal to be heard over the music playing outside the door. I noticed that his words were slightly slurred and knew it had something to with the stolen whiskey. I fell asleep before the first chapter was over.

I don't know how much time had gone by, but I woke up to man standing over me. I watched him, silhouetted in darkness, waiting for what was next, not knowing what it would be but feeling like it might not be good. Stevie Ray Vaughn was singing "Pride and Joy," and I imagined my mom dancing, letting her straight, stringy hippy hair, that was a little darker brown than mine was, fly this way and that to the beat, swishing and swirling the smoke as she swayed. The song still takes me back to that night, to that man. I hate it.

He wanted something, but I didn't know what. I knew who he was: his name was Brad, and he hung out with Clayton every now and then. I think they may have worked together. When he came over, he would look at me funny and pay more attention to me than most of Clayton's friends ever did, but he was a grown-up so he didn't exist much in my world.

In the darkness of that night I barely saw him put his finger to his lip to silence me and nod toward Lizzie, who was still asleep beside me. He leaned down and whispered in my ear that if I did what he told me to do, he wouldn't tell Clayton that Justin was in my room. His sour liquor breath spilled out of his mouth invading my senses, before he stood again and pointed to the floor. I followed his finger and in the dim night light I saw Justin asleep beside my bed, using my stuffed elephant for his pillow. Clayton would have been mad that he was sleeping in my room, and Brad and I both knew it. Justin was already in enough trouble with everyone all the time; I didn't want him to get busted for anything else. So when Brad told me to get out of bed and go with him, I did.

Years earlier, Clayton had made doors in both my and Justin's rooms that connected to the main bathroom so he didn't have to see our faces after he sent us to bed. It was to my bathroom door that Brad led me. He shuffled to the music, and motioned for me to shuffle too, so I did. He walked into the bathroom and held the door open for me. I walked in, and he smoothed his hand over my hair as I passed him.

"Mmmm," he growled, low and deep. It sent a burning shiver up and down my spine. He shut the door and locked it, muffling the music, but he kept dancing as he locked the main door and checked to be sure Justin's was locked too. He took out a baggie and cut a line on the bare counter, and at last the mystery of the white powder was solved. The music blared and I heard people hooting and hollering while he snorted it with a rolled dollar bill. Then he looked at me and smiled. I smiled back, still unsure of my role or what he wanted from me. In the fluorescent light his glassy eyes yearned for something, but I was too young to understand it was me that he wanted.

He stood, pinching his nose between his thumb and index finger, then reached down and unbuckled his belt. My heart started fluttering. It sounds stupid now, but all I could think was that he must be getting ready to use the bathroom and was so wasted that he forgot I was there, or forgot to care that I was there. I was embarrassed for him and turned quickly to give him privacy,

"Oh, no you don't. Look at me," he said, the hunger in his eyes reflecting in his voice too.

I turned back to look at him, bewildered that he wanted me to watch him go to the bathroom. I had never seen a man's parts before. Baby boys', yes, and Justin's once or twice when he peed outside and I came around a corner too quickly, but never a full-grown man's. Fear spread through my body. He didn't turn to the toilet when he unbuttoned his pants; instead, he came toward me, reaching inside to withdraw himself. I knew something that wasn't supposed to happen was about to happen; his predator eyes told me so, even though he tried to keep the smile on his face. I didn't smile back this time, but I couldn't for the life of me figure out what was going on. I didn't think I was in trouble with him—whatever we were doing was keeping Justin from getting in trouble, so I didn't think he was going to hurt me—but why would he need his pants off? I was confused and afraid and wanted to be rescued from what was about to happen.

For some reason the person I wanted most in the world at that moment was Clayton, and just as I wished for him, someone knocked from Justin's bathroom door.

"Hey...!" It wasn't Clayton, though. It was Justin.

"Busy, bro," Brad answered, but was quickly putting himself away and fixing his pants. Hunger was gone, his eyes suddenly wide and worried. I don't know if he knew it was Justin or not.

"Is Haylee in there?"

No answer. Brad shook his head at me, telling me with his eyes to be silent.

"Haylee, are you in there?"

I couldn't stay quiet. Something bad was going to happen, and I knew it; I could tell by how quickly Brad startled at the knock. This was my chance to escape. Since Justin wasn't in my room anymore we could lie about his being in there, so I no longer felt obligated to do what Brad said. I was rescued, just like I wished. I answered Justin loudly enough to be heard through the door and over the music, "Yes! I'm here."

"Let her out, you sick prick, or I'll tell Clayton you're in there with her. You hear me?"

It was enough to scare Brad into listening to a boy. I guess even adults were afraid of Clayton's yelling. He finished buttoning his pants and as he buckled his belt, I watched dumbfounded as Justin's door flew open. I saw that there was something bulging in Brad's pants, but I didn't know then what it was. I was so young and everything was happening so fast. When his belt was fixed, he grabbed the baggie off the counter and made for the main door.

Justin blocked him in a flash of a second. He was saving me from a bad thing I couldn't comprehend.

Justin was more than a foot shorter than Brad. And while he was no match in size or strength, he stood up to him, chest out, fists clenched, ready to fight like a man, to the death—for me. I didn't know what it was all about, but I could tell by his anger, his posture and his defiance to Brad's authority that Justin did, and he knew Brad would have to submit to him. Justin stared him down while looking up into his face. He called him names I'd never heard and threatened to kill him if he ever touched me or Lizzie. Justin understood full well what Brad was about to do and that being caught once wasn't enough to stop a man like that. Like always, Justin faced trouble to keep us safe. All I knew at that moment was I loved him. He was my hero. He had saved me.

And that's how fast it happened. I was his for my whole life after that, even though there would be times I tried to deny the truth of it.

Brad was pissed. Those glassy eyes of his shot darts at Justin, but he was the loser; he stormed out of the main bathroom door and slammed it on his way out. I told Justin I wanted to use the teleporter to get away from the house. He said he did too. That's when I noticed he was shaking all over the way Mom did in the mornings. I thought it was from the alcohol, not knowing what a rush of adrenaline could do to a human body.

"Yeah, OK, that's a good idea. Let's get Lizzie and some blankets and go to the teleporter."

We woke Lizzie, and we Three Musketeers chucked blankets out my window which faced the back yard and hopped out of the nightmare house and into the safety of the BTTF24. Justin made a fire inside the fort, in our fire pit. He had read a book about Native Americans and teepees and learned that we needed a smoke hole not long after the Diazs' door was deadbolted. We had fires in there often after that, mostly on the weekends when we played outside all day long. We kept an impressive stash of wood that we scrounged from the forest regularly.

We camped out all that night, the three of us, alone, together. It was the most wonderful night of my life up to that point. Justin slept up against the fort wall with a comforter around his shoulders, legs out to the fire. I laid my head on one thigh, Lizzie on his other, with our blankets wrapped around us. Every time he stoked the fire we all shuffled and woke, but we didn't mind.

Between sleeping spells, we pretended to transport to faraway places. He always picked Washington State, which never seemed like much of an exotic destination to me. He liked Seattle because of Nirvana and Boeing. Boeing, he told us, was a place that invented planes, and he loved planes and flying, the faster the better. He was determined to make a real teleportation device someday, and he knew they were the company to do it. He liked the woods of

Washington too because Sasquatch was supposed to live there. He wanted to be the first man to find him, and he liked hiding in the woods anyway, and he thought Washington had the best woods from the books he read. He was sure someday when he was old enough he would move there and have a good life far away from our house. I played along, even though I would have preferred teleporting to somewhere more fun like Disneyland.

He deserved to disappear to anywhere he wanted to go that night, so I let him take us to Diablo Lake in the North Cascades. We must have had a dozen pictures of the Cascades posted in the fort along with a thousand other pictures of places we teleported to. He showed me different pictures of the Washington forests all the time, so I knew what they looked like, and we went there in our imaginations with the flip of a BTTF24 toggle switch.

POOF! One second we were in a cold dark fort with make-believe buttons and wires inside it, and the next we were warm, safe and happy looking out the windows of our mansion-cabin with a stunning view of the lake.

"Do you hear that, Haylee? I think Bigfoot is out there. I've got my rifle in case he comes out and I can shoot him. Watch for him."

"I'm hungry. I want some cake," I said

"Oh, that sounds good. Let me have some."

I handed him a fake plate with a fake slice. Lizzie wanted some too.

"Sorry, you were sleeping so we ate it all. You don't get any," Justin teased her, ruffling her thick black hair.

"Have some of mine," I offered.

She took a bite off of my fake cake and we were in heaven, or as close to it as we were ever going to get. Lizzie fell asleep again, and that's when I told him. Maybe it was a mistake, but I told him I loved him.

"I love you too, Haylee. You'll always be my girl," he said. "Now go to sleep." He smoothed my stringy hair, but instead of scaring me the way it had when Brad did it, it reassured me that I was safe. He had a notepad he was drawing on, I think it helped him stay awake, and he would tear off the pages every so often. He folded one page up and shoved into his pocket but crumpled most of them up and tossed them into the fire. The noise would startle me out of my dreams momentarily, but I would fall right back to sleep, safe with my hero on guard.

CHAPTER 3

AND THAT'S HOW LIFE WAS FOR US. Me and my drunk mom and Justin and his crabby dad living miserably together and taking Lizzie along for the fun of it. They had their party weekends at home or away, and we had our shack in the bushes that would teleport us anywhere we wanted to go.

I honestly thought we were happy for the longest time. I thought our lives were normal, that everyone had parents like ours and a lifestyle like that. I couldn't imagine a house without yelling or parents that didn't disappear for days on end. I had fun with Lizzie and Justin, and it never dawned on me that other kids went to birthday parties at roller-skate decks and petting zoos while we hid in shacks from perverts. Other kids had parents who helped them with spelling and math and made them snacks after school, but we learned fast that it was best not to depend on our parents for much of anything.

I was too young, I didn't know life could be different, so I didn't know we weren't happy. We smiled, we laughed, we danced with my mom when she was in a good mood to the music Clayton blasted. She would tell Lizzie and me what to do when she wasn't passed out, and she was actually pretty fun before she got too drunk. She would put make-up on us and let us dress up in her old dresses and be show girls or cowgirl line dancers. She had lots of dresses we could pick from, and we had real fun. I don't know why she kept all her old clothes around; we all know they were, like, fifty sizes too small for her. She had grown to be a large woman over the years. But she would tell us about the dancing she used to do 'back in the day' and show us her moves. She would even say, "Who needs $100 dance lessons when you got a mama who can shake it like me? Right, Haylee?"

She said stuff like that a lot, making sure I knew we didn't have the kind of money to do things other families did. Aside from our neighbors' lack of liquor, those comments from Mom were my first clues that we were different. We learned that we were poor because Mom and Clayton told us we were.

It's hard to explain, but I didn't feel poor. And even though they told us we were poor, they would insist they gave us everything we could possibly need.

Our poverty was something I learned to recognize and despise as I grew, though. I hated to bring up my needs to Clayton. If I slipped and said the wrong thing, like the time I asked for $8 for a field trip, he would remind me that I never went hungry and claimed that should be good enough.

He would rant that my good-for-nothing, loser, sperm donor father ran off and that he was footing my bill out of the kindness of his heart. All he got out of the deal was a whiner baby who couldn't even pull her own weight around the house and a heifer for a woman. He would tell me I was lucky I was a girl because if I was a boy he would knock some sense into me, and if he was smart he'd do it anyway.

His tirades were long and loud—not blaring music loud, but Clayton loud. They were arguments. Not that I was allowed to argue back. The "ungrateful-for-what-you-have" lectures were some the worst kinds.

"You think you have it bad, but missy, you don't know how bad it can be. My parents were poor; we didn't have nothing! You've got everything: a roof over your head, clothes, food in your belly... You ain't starving, are you? You ain't needy, are you?

"I'm not sending that school of yours a single nickel. What do you think my tax money pays for anyway? You want to be like the rest of the girls at school? You know what they are? Whores, little whores in training! You want to be like that, you go find yourself some other sucker to pay your bills 'cause I ain't raising you to be like the rest of them girls. I'm raising you to be a lady who knows how to take care of herself and her family. Now make me some dinner! You think I'm going to work all day and make myself some food? You lazy sack of wasted life. Get out of my sight... Now!"

Face in my face, red with anger, beads of sweat so close I could stick out my tongue and lick them. I had to stare straight ahead or it would get worse. If I looked him in the eye, he would slap me and say I was being defiant and questioning his authority; if I looked away he would slap me for not paying attention to him. If I sat there and took it, it would eventually end before too long.

Usually he sabotaged himself. He'd get rolling, yelling so loud and long that he choked on his own words. It was absolutely not OK to laugh or look sorry at him when he went into a coughing fit. So I stared straight ahead, waiting for him to retreat to the bedroom to smoke up, or to the bar to drink up, and then I would slip away to the teleporter to some other time or place, even if Justin wasn't there.

Sometimes I would do the dishes or make Clayton dinner before I left the house to calm him down first, then I would run to the fort and pretend to disappear to somewhere safe. There, in my secret hideaway, I was allowed to feel sorry for myself. I cried so many tears in that place over the years, but they would always dry up, and I knew I had to go back. I would tell myself to suck it up, in a fashion not unlike Clayton's, and go back to the place I called home where I thought I was happy.

I suppose my stories make it sound like we had a horrible childhood, and we did, but Lizzie reminds me that it could have been a lot worse. She gets mad when I only bring up the bad stuff. She's like Pollyanna to this day, always looking on the bright side of everything. So to honor her, let me reflect on some of the good times we had in the middle of all the bad.

My favorite childhood memory of our parents is when I was nine or ten and Clayton taught Lizzie and me to ride bikes. Granted, he had to get good and hammered to have the patience to teach us, but it was truly fun. One day he came home from work with two bikes, one pink and one red. It was summer—I know that because it was still light for a long time after Clayton got home. Justin already had a bike, but neither Lizzie nor I had one yet. Clayton proclaimed that they were ours, and it was about time we learned to ride. To this day I don't know where Clayton got them, but he was happy and smiling and wanted us to learn to ride them that day, and for one afternoon we got to be normal girls with someone who wasn't either of our fathers pretending to be a dad and showing us how to pedal and balance.

Justin must have known to not interfere because he rode in wide circles around us but didn't interrupt Clayton's lesson even once. I remember the beige paint on his white pants and the brown beer bottles he held in his left hand while the other balanced my seat or Lizzie's. He still yelled, but it was happy yelling, and it was wonderful.

We both learned in one day, and after we got the hang of it we raced up and down the street with Justin until it was dark. Clayton stayed right there, cheering us on. I think he had fun too. When we got back inside Mom had dinner made, and we all sat down in the living room together to eat. I felt like we were that family on *7th Heaven* with Jessica Biel. But we didn't watch them; we watched *X-Files*, which was just about as good.

Lizzie wouldn't appreciate it if I mentioned how, a while later, Clayton ripped her a new one for leaving her bike where he couldn't see it. When he ran over it as a result, we all had to take that lecture. Nor would she want me to bring up the time we got yelled at for being out too late riding our bikes and had to endure his tirade about being good-for-nothing kids out looking for trouble. So I won't.

The other best thing I remember is the year the Salvation Army adopted our family as their token poor family for Christmas. That was the Christmas of my sixth grade year, by then I was so in love with Justin I was thinking I might give him a kiss for Christmas, but I completely forgot about it in the excitement of the day. Mom or Clayton must have filled out a form with everything they thought we wanted that year because, I swear, we got everything they ever complained about us asking them for.

The people brought food too—bags and bags of it, enough to fill the cabinets and fridge until after the new year. I don't know what they thought when they saw the stocked bar but mostly bare cupboards, but that food made me as happy as the CD Walkman did. We smuggled some of the non-perishables out to the shack to have for emergencies when Clayton and Mom weren't paying attention. Yeah, that Christmas was happy.

There were other good times too. Once my mom took us to the movies. That was nice. Then there was another time when Lizzie and

I had a Veterans Day presentation at school and both our moms showed up to watch us. Even though it was the middle of the day, they were there. I felt like all the other kids with parents who cared and gave my mom the biggest hug I could when I ran off the stage.

And once during a middle school conference, the teacher told my mom about all the things I was learning, and I heard my mother say I was a bright girl. I knew that meant she thought I was smart, or at least she was willing to lie to my teacher for me.

Lizzie is absolutely right: there were some good times, a few happy memories. It wasn't all bad; it could have been worse. But it wasn't good either, and no matter how optimistically Lizzie tries to remember it, there's no denying it got worse the older we grew—or maybe we just became more aware of our depravity.

As the years passed I was learning slowly that what the three of us had was not a normal life; it was, in fact, downright abusive. I can share the happy memories for Lizzie's sake, but if I said it wasn't bad I'd be lying.

Between their partying and Clayton's yelling we never stood a chance at a happy, normal life. Mom became as deaf to his yelling as we did. We had to listen, but eventually we stopped hearing what he said. He made me feel worthless, but it had to be a million times worse for my mom. What he said to her made what he said to me seem like mountains of praise.

At least he wasn't a hitter. By that I mean he didn't hit her every time he was mad, which was all the time. He saved it for extra special screw-ups on her part, like the time she was passed out when I tripped on the way home from the bus and broke my ankle. We screamed and screamed for her to come help, but she couldn't hear us because she was out cold. By the time Clayton got home I had managed to get inside with help from Justin and Lizzie. We had my ankle bandaged, and I figured I'd be in for it when he got home. I just knew he was going to yell at me for being stupid and clumsy. To my surprise he didn't yell at me at all. Instead he beat my mom up so bad. He must have slapped her ten times to wake her up; then he grabbed her by the back of her head and twisted her face to look at my bruised and deformed ankle.

"What kind of a sorry excuse for a mother are you? You're so drunk you can't even wake up to take her to the hospital?! You're pathetic. I ought

to kick you out right now, but she'd probably end up dead. Drink up, lush, while I take your daughter to the hospital. Clean up this cesspool while I'm gone. We're gonna have the state out here after I tell them her mom left her to deal with a broken ankle by herself because she was passed out drunk!"

Mom looked pitiful, bleeding from her lip and crying like she was. I didn't feel sorry for her, though; I was mad at her too. I knew she loved vodka more than me, but I really needed her, and she wasn't there for me. I can't say I liked seeing the blood, but I was glad she got hers, and I was glad I didn't get yelled at. It would have made the pain so much worse.

On the way to the hospital Clayton told me what our story would be. I would tell them everything just the way it happened except I was supposed to say that Mom was out grocery shopping; that was why it took so long to get to the hospital. He told them he brought me because my mom was too upset to drive.

The story worked. They didn't ask any questions, and they didn't follow up—or if they did, we never knew about it. Clayton was so nice in the ER. At least he knew how to pretend to be a good dad even if he wasn't one in real life.

I have to admit, that broken ankle scored me big points. Clayton hardly yelled at me about cleaning or cooking for a month. I loved the crutches; I was famous at school. Kids had to carry my books, and Justin would pack my stuff all the way down the road. I was ten then. He was in high school and was the first of us to take the big-kid bus home. Like an angel, he was always there for us an hour and a half later when our bus dropped us off. When my ankle was broken he would give me a piggy-back ride all the way home, and we let Lizzie goof off on my crutches.

That's when I first noticed his smell. He was no longer a boy— not that he ever had been to me—but was fast becoming a real man. It was sweat and pheromones, cheap cologne and deodorant, and I couldn't help but breathe him in. I imagined if I breathed in hard enough he would become part of me and could never leave. I would hug my cheek into the warmth of his neck and take him in.

By then I was old enough to understand what Brad had meant to do to me that night long ago. Life has a way of sucking the innocence out of unfortunates like us, and I was growing up fast. I think at ten I still shouldn't have known what he meant to do, but I did.

By then I'd seen the movies my mom watched with Clayton. Some weekends Clayton and his buddies would gather around our thirty-six-inch TV and watch them together, whooping and hollering and being vulgar with their lady folk. When Justin was there, he would keep Lizzie and me safe in the fort or in my room. He made me promise to stay in my room if they ever put the movies on when he was away. He showed me how to lock my door with a one-by-four board under the doorknob.

We found the board on one of our scavenges, and it was to stay hidden under my bed, out of sight, so Clayton or Mom wouldn't ask about it. I was also supposed to use it any night Brad or another creeper was in the house. I could spot the creepers easily; men shouldn't look at girls like they looked at women. When I saw one who looked at Lizzie and me funny—I mean it wasn't funny; it was creepy— we would lock ourselves up in my room or hide out in the fort. I don't know how to describe the look, but I know now that any female who's lost enough innocence can recognize it. When we saw it peer out at us, we locked my door or stayed close to Justin. I guess it worked because no one ever touched me after that night with Brad. I hope Lizzie fared as well, but something inside tells me she didn't.

The paradox and irony of lust was mine alone to ponder; I thought about it in my room in the darkness of the night but never told anyone. Even though I knew what a creep was and what they did to girls, I wanted Justin to want me like that and look at me the way they did. I wanted him to because that's the way I wanted him. I remember the exact day I wanted things a woman wants from him. It was more than love—well, maybe I shouldn't say that. It wasn't more than love; it was different from love, but just as strong. I suspected he felt the same way, but I didn't know for sure. I wanted him to touch me, or at least kiss me like in the movies—not Clayton's movies, just the regular love story movies, but he never did.

I tried to kiss him once, the year after that missed Christmas kiss. Lizzie was watching TV, and we were in my room alone. He liked to play my mom's old guitar, and he played it like a heavy-metal rock star. I knew he would be famous for it some day. He was playing "More than Words" by Extreme, a classic (at least for us), and ever our song. He was working the strings trying to get it right and singing in his sweet, squeaky voice. His hair hung down enough to almost cover his eyes, and he would look up every so often, just long enough to look at me and melt my heart into his. I loved him, and I loved watching him.

His fingers were busy on the strings, moving over them like a magician, tricking them into melody and harmony. The muscles in his arms mesmerized me as they flexed and twitched, drawing lines of strength from wrist to elbow in time with his finger movements. He was becoming a man in front of my eyes. I touched his arm, and it stopped him. He flipped his hair up and looked at me, green eyes smiling. He must not have known what I was thinking or he would have looked at me differently, I'm sure. He must have thought I was going to tease him about his pitch or playing, but that wasn't it at all.

"I want to kiss you," I said, and then he knew. The look said more than words, just like the song, and I wanted to show him how much I loved him.

"Why?" he asked.

"Because I love you...and...I want you to be the first boy I ever kiss. I want to know what it's like; I want you to show me."

"So you're planning on kissing more boys?" he teased almost brotherly.

"No, just you."

He saw I was serious. He was kind and gentle with my heart when he could have been mean. He was already in high school, and I was still just a dumb sixth-grade kid. Instead of laughing at me, he was sincere and honest and left me with a promise to soften the rejection he was about to give me.

"Then you can wait until you're grown up."

"I don't want to wait; I'm ready now." I wanted to cry. He was breaking my heart. I was embarrassed and suddenly painfully aware of how much younger I was than him. It didn't seem fair that I could love a boy this much and be too young for him to want me back.

"Haylee, I wish you were. Trust me, you have no idea how much I wish you were. But you're not ready."

"Just this once; then I'll wait."

"No, it's not right. Trust me." He caught the tear from my eye, his thumb warm on my face. His hand dwarfed my little ones as they raced up to catch his and keep him close to me. He was big; I was small; it made me feel even more like a child. I couldn't argue with him.

"Cheer up, kid."

"I can't. You don't love me."

"Haylee, I never said that! You know I love you." He reached his hand around my neck and pulled me closer, resting his lips on my forehead before letting me go so I could look at him again. "I will kiss you someday, I promise. But not yet, OK?"

"When?!" I was so excited to realize that he thought about kissing me too that I forgot to be disappointed about the rejection anymore.

"I'm not going to tell you. It'll be my surprise."

Then a thought struck me, and I had to know the answer.

"How many girls have you kissed already?"

He smiled and shook his head.

He wouldn't tell me, but it didn't matter. Even one was too many. I was jealous and hurt all over again but for another reason. I must have looked crestfallen because his fingers caught my chin and lifted it up until I had to look back into those green eyes of his whether I wanted to or not.

His eyes penetrated me, told me he loved me too, made me believe him.

"Wait for it, Haylee."

"We really can't kiss now?"

"No, you're freaking eleven years old! What are you thinking? Get over it!" He teased and ruffled my hair like I was a pet, then pushed me away, "You gotta grow up, kid. I want to kiss a woman, not a girl."

"So it'll be your first kiss too?"

"It doesn't matter. It'll be yours."

"But you won't tell me when."

"Nope. Wait for it. Now let me practice. Is your homework done?"

"I don't want to do it; it's stupid."

"Doesn't matter. Go get Lizzie and the two of you need to start in on it."

I obeyed and retrieved the tag-along, grudgingly. He played all afternoon, rehearsing the same chords over and over again, searing them into my soul. He would only stop if Lizzie or I needed help with a word or math problem.

Clayton was actually right about one thing: Justin didn't apply himself in school. But that didn't mean he wasn't smart. I know he was. He was the one who helped Lizzie and me with our school work. Sometimes my mom would try to explain something to me, but I was too stupid to understand it when she taught me, so she would send me out of her sight. I eventually stopped asking her for help and started to ask Justin instead. He always knew how to do the work and explained it in a way I understood. Even though he helped Lizzie and me get good grades, his were bad—except in science. It wasn't that he was stupid; it was that the teachers made him mad, and he didn't like what they taught. If the school would have offered classes in guitar, skateboarding, time travel or fighting, he would have had straight As.

It was weird how hard he made Lizzie and me focus on our school work. He told us we had a chance to make something of ourselves and we needed to apply ourselves and not miss our chance like he had. Sometimes he took out a book and made notes or did a project of his own, but not nearly as often as he made us do it. He usually practiced chords and songs on the guitar while we figured out multiplication or sentence structure. I still don't know why he did school like that. Maybe it's because everyone already pegged him as a loser and no matter how hard he tried to prove them wrong it wouldn't matter, he would always be Justin Parker the troublemaker. Any school work we did catch him doing was always for science. I loved the way he could get lost in science papers: his eyes would sparkle when he talked about the possibilities and promises the sciences could offer. It was all that space and time travel that intrigued him, and he used any excuse he could find to study it, especially teleportation.

Even though he was a "bad" student, he always had a book to read. He would keep it hidden with all his undone work until we both said we were finished with our own. We couldn't lie either because he would check us to make sure we completed the work and got it right. After he was sure we were done, he would pull out the book of the day and continue reading to us where we left off the day before. Sometimes we read a chapter; sometimes two or three. We were getting too big to make-believe in the fort, so his stories were becoming our grown-up escape into another time and place, and we could get lost for hours in the words he read.

I can't remember which story we were reading that day. I guess my brain only had room for the song and the promise that my kiss would come. If they hadn't been before, that afternoon our fates were officially sealed together. He loved me, and I loved him. He wanted me and told me to wait for him. I couldn't trust anyone else in the world, but of Justin I was sure. I could bet my life on him and never be disappointed. I slept that night dreaming of our first kiss and woke up to the hope that he had dreamt of it too. From then on, I knew someday our time would come, but not until I was older; he promised me that. I believed him. I was so tired of being a kid and wanted to be grown up already, but I wouldn't be grown-up enough for him for another two years.

I hated that everyone else thought he was such a loser, because he was my everything. Justin took a lot of flak from Clayton so Lizzie and I could think we were happy. The older I got, the more I saw the price Justin paid for that: Everyone, I mean *everyone*, thought he was a punk, his teachers, his dad, my mom, even the other kids he went to school with. And probably to a lot of people he was, but not to me or Lizzie. Clayton complained of his attitude, laziness, stupidity, suspensions, fights, and bad grades any chance he got. Truthfully, Justin did fight a lot, but it always sounded like the other guys had it coming.

Justin made my childhood happy. He was always there— always. He did whatever he had to do to watch out for me, even when it seemed like he was being mean—and even when it felt like he was abandoning me.

He started driving before he got his license and got a job at a clothes store in the mall. He worked as much as he could after school and almost every weekend, leaving Lizzie and me to fend for ourselves. Clayton let him use the Accord to get there but told him if he got pulled over he'd tell the cops he didn't have permission to be driving it.

My mom didn't hardly go anywhere by that time; she mostly stayed in bed or on the couch, getting up only to get more vodka. Come to think of it, I don't know why Clayton put up with it.

Justin saved up every dime he could until he could pay for driver's ed and get a real license. I missed him when he was gone, but I knew he was doing what he had to do. In the end it was worth it because once he finished driver's ed, he could take me and Lizzie (when she was there) to school. Taking us meant he was always late for his own classes but he didn't mind. Michael and Kim still had to take the bus and I got to smile and wave smugly as Justin drove us right past them. He was seventeen then, old enough to drive and work and be a man.

He was seventeen, and I was finally old enough to be kissed.

CHAPTER 4

I STILL FEEL THE WARMTH of his lips on mine from that first time. I remember everything about it. It was my thirteenth birthday. Justin started the celebration first thing in the morning, waking me up with French toast and giving me a pair of hoop earrings. My mom was sleeping and Clayton had already left for work, so the house belonged to us.

"There's one more thing," he said, smirking, retrieving something from a cabinet. "Unwrap it; you'll like it. You've been asking for it for a long time." He handed me a gift-wrapped shoe box. I really thought it would be the shoes that I wanted from his store, but I was wrong. It was too light in my hands to be shoes. I opened it, and inside there was only tissue paper and a card that told me to go to the BTTF24—our childhood teleporter, almost forgotten.

As I looked at him quizzically, his eyes sparkled back at me, his smile and lifted left eyebrow hinted of an adventure I couldn't yet imagine. I ran outside and he followed close behind.

He had been there already because the bushes and stickers were cleared away enough for us to squeeze inside the door, which seemed much smaller than it used to. Once inside, two things struck me simultaneously: the daylight filtering through blackberry stalks and green, corrugated sheeting cast a light green glow inside the fort, and there, in the far corner, shadowed in the sea-green dimness, lay his guitar—waiting, like I had been, on Justin.

"Sit down," he said, motioning to one of two folding beach chairs. He must have set them up ahead of time because we never had chairs in there when we were kids. If I hadn't known him so well, I wouldn't have noticed his mood and his subtle attempts to cover up his nervousness.

I obeyed—what else would I do? He was going to sing me a song for my birthday. I was so dumb I guessed that maybe he had a cupcake hidden somewhere and I would have to make a wish after he sang the birthday song like when we were kids.

But I was wrong. It was so much more. The song was an old love song I knew by heart. It was our song, and I realized it within the first few notes.

Apparently the teleporter still worked: one minute we were together in a childhood play fort where we used to share make-believe trips to faraway places, and the next I was sitting on my bed two years earlier, listening to him play our song for the first time.

I didn't have to flip one of the pretend toggles to go there; the chords and his eyes took me back to that afternoon instantly. His smile was delicious—I wanted to lean in as soon as I knew what he was doing and kiss him—but I listened and waited just a little longer, knowing the time had finally come. His voice was warm honey, no longer awkward and squeaky, but deep and the slightest bit raspy and pure perfection.

In all my life there has never been a first anything that compared to my first kiss.

When he looked at me I knew this was the day he had been waiting for too, and I was suddenly afraid. Doubt hit me: could a seventeen-year-old boy with lips like that and a voice that weakened my knees really have waited for me all these years? It was impossible; it wasn't realistic; I knew enough about boys by then to know there was no way he had waited for me. This would not be his first kiss; what other firsts had he beat me to? Would we have anything to save for "our" first?

But in the next minute, all my doubt was gone. He had never promised I would be his first kiss, only that he would be mine. It was not the time to worry about how many girls he had kissed. This moment was all about me: he was giving me *my* first kiss, and I wouldn't have wanted it to come from anyone else. I had been waiting on him to decide I was old enough, saving my first kiss for him, and the moment was upon me. I tried to push the doubt, jealousy, and worry away and focus on his words. The last note of the song hung in our shack, holding the silence at bay.

"Haylee, do you remember?"

"Of course," I whispered. My voice had disappeared.

"It's time for me to keep my promise." He laid the guitar on the dirt floor and motioned for me. The shack didn't have high enough clearance for me to stand, so I had to lean down as I came to him. Hunched over, I knew there was no way I could make it look sexy (not that I had a clue how to look sexy anyway), so I moved as quickly as I could from my chair to his lap. I was afraid I was going to ruin the moment, but he wouldn't let me.

He pulled me close, wrapping his big, strong arms around me, and looked at me. He was warm, so I snaked my hands into his jacket, touching him in the same places I had a million times before, but this time everything was different. I really felt him: his breath expanding his chest under my cold little fingers, his heat warming them. He was broad-chested, and sitting there with him made me feel so small, so safe, so completely wrapped up in everything that was him.

I must have looked ridiculous, but he didn't say so. He looked up into my eyes, lifted his hand, and stroked my cheek with his thumb, just like he had done that day when he wiped my tear away. My neck grew a million goose bumps, and I forgot how to breathe. It was startling: I had been breathing my whole life without even thinking about it, and now I had to will my lungs to move. I tried to play it cool, like I did this every day, like I wasn't afraid and excited and freaking out inside all at the same exact minute—but I felt like I was breathing too slow and fast and fake. He knew—how could he not?—but I refused to admit it. I told myself to be cool.

My heart was beating like a hummingbird's wings; it was going to fly out of my chest before he even touched my lips. I couldn't take my eyes off of his. He held me captive. He smiled. He smelled like maple syrup and Eternity by Calvin Klein. I thought I already loved him, but I had never known love like this, mixed with lust and desire and curiosity for the unknown. It was intoxicating. He was what I wanted more than anything.

"You understand now, don't you? We shouldn't love each other like we do. I'm too old; you're too young; we're almost brother and sister."

"No, we're not."

"I know, but it doesn't matter what we think. Clayton will freak; your mom will freak. They can't know."

"I know, I won't tell."

His hand pulled my face down closer to his. We were going to touch; our lips were almost together. *Breathe, breathe!*

"Wait, Justin!" I stopped him, my hands flying from his sides to push back on his chest, "I don't know how."

I think there was relief in his smile. "Good, I'll show you."

That was it. He pulled me down, put our lips together, and touched mine with his tongue. It was warm, wet, and strong. I had no idea what I was doing, but it didn't matter. My eyes closed instinctively, and my hands—limp noodles that they were—somehow managed to rise slowly from their resting place on his chest and trail up to his neck. I had to touch his skin.

It has always amazed me how at that minute nothing else mattered, not the cold or the time or the fact that my left leg was going numb. All I knew was him and his body by mine and in mine.

As his tongue pierced through my lips, I hoped for the slightest second that my chapped lips didn't feel rough to him. That made me think of his, and I paid attention to them all over again as if his lips hadn't been what stopped time in the first place. They were full and soft—surprisingly soft considering that just above and below them his skin was scratchy with whiskers, a contrast that made him feel all the more magnificent.

I stroked his neck, moving my fingers up into his coarse, heavy hair. He found my tongue, and I startled. I could tell he noticed because I felt his lips curl up into a smile; then his tongue trailed my teeth. We both opened our eyes, still connected, and he lifted his other hand to my face. It was easier to breathe with my eyes closed because as soon as I opened them I had to think about taking breaths again. He moved back a little, separating from me, but just barely.

"Don't be afraid, Haylee."

"I'm not."

It happened all over again: the lips, the tongue, the touch, my eyes shutting, shutting out everything but our bodies coming together. This time I didn't pull back. The first thing that came to my mind, honestly, was that his tongue didn't taste like anything at all. I don't know why that struck me—I never imagined that a tongue would have a flavor—but I was used to tasting things with my tongue, so to have something in my mouth devoid of flavor perplexed me. Despite that, he was delicious and beautiful, and he overwhelmed me in all the right ways. I felt his tongue stroke and play with mine, twisting and turning, pausing to play with my upper or lower lip before sneaking back in. His mouth held mine, and I wanted nothing more than to stay like that with him forever.

I felt him other places too, his neck and hair in my hands. I touched his cheeks with my thumbs like he was doing to me. His were hard, firm and rough, the opposite of my own soft little ones. In a split second I realized that his was the only other face I could ever remember touching. Our bodies were together, and even as we made out my leg was going dead, but I didn't want to stop the kiss.

All I could do in that moment was smell him and feel him. I don't remember a single sound or sight. It was as though my eyes and ears weren't allowed to be a part of that first kiss, like it would have been too much for them.

His scent was all over me. I knew his cologne well; he had bought some from a store in the mall a year earlier, and it was as much a part of Justin by then as the sound of his voice was. If I was somewhere and anyone else had it on, I turned, expecting to see him, as if he was the only person in the world who was allowed to smell that way.

That day—that moment—was all about eternity in my heart and in my memory . . . eternity and maple syrup. I knew where he sprayed the cologne, but even while we were kissing I wondered where the syrup smell stayed hidden. I have never been able to figure that out, or how the smell of French toast can magically teleport me back to that morning even after all these years.

He made his hands behave themselves for that first kiss. It must have been hard, but he was giving me this one thing, letting the kiss and only the kiss dominate the moment. I was sure he wasn't innocent like I was, but he let the memory stay innocent, pure, just a kiss—the most wonderful kiss known to man. And it was only a kiss, but it was mine.

I don't know how long we stayed there kissing and falling more in love than we already were, but by the time we were finished, my leg was dead to all feeling. He ended it as sweetly as he started it. One last little peck, soft and warm on my lips, a "Happy birthday," and a smile.

"Um, I can't move," I laughed, putting my forehead on his. "My leg fell asleep."

"Your leg?"

"Yeah, the whole thing."

"Why didn't you say anything?" he asked me.

"I didn't want you to stop." I shrugged, blushing.

He kissed me again, short and quick but amorously nonetheless.

"We can't stay all day. Wake that leg up!"

He shuffled me back to my chair, and we waited for feeling to come back. I bellowed as the blood rushed back into it and filled my leg with pins and needles.

"Ow!" I hollered. He laughed and flicked it to add to the discomfort. "Jerk!"

When feeling resumed, we took off in the Accord, but we didn't go to school. He had better plans for us.

Believe it or not, even back then I really think his greatest love in life was learning; he just didn't learn the way most people do, sitting down at a desk. He was a hands-on learner and found things out by trying and failing until he eventually succeeded—hence our teleportation machine, our ventures into the neighborhood houses, and his ability to keep the Accord running even when Clayton said it was a lost cause.

His favorite things to learn about were science, mechanics, guitar, and flying. He never outgrew his love for science and was always trying to figure out ways to make teleportation and time travel real. But as we grew up, time and space flight gave way to an obsession with real flying. He learned about all kinds of flying things: jets, planes, space shuttle propulsion, prop engines, helicopters—you name it, he wanted to know how it worked. He was especially fascinated with zeppelins and airships for a long time—not just the tragedy of the Hindenburg but the feasibility of zeppelin flight in modern times. Elsewhere in the world, people were working on making zeppelins viable forms of transportation, and that's when he started thinking about flying for a living. At first it was all about flying the zeppelins, but reality sucked him in. Zeppelins, like teleportation, were too far out of his reach. But he decided he wanted to be a pilot even though Clayton—and pretty much everyone else—told him he wouldn't amount to anything in life except a bum on the streets.

That's why he took me where he did for my birthday. The day was for me, but somehow we found ourselves visiting a place he always wanted to go: the Planes of Fame Museum in Chino. He wouldn't tell me until we were on the road. It's funny how an hour can seem like forever in the daily monotony of life, but when you're with your first love on your first drive after your first kiss, it races by. We drove from home, around the mountains and into the cities. They weren't too far away, but we never went there. It was a whole different world. He had saved up his money for gas and the day for I don't know how long, and now it was time.

We had to go a long way to get there, but by the end we were right where Justin and I both wanted to be: he was looking at planes, and I was looking at him in a whole new way. I wanted to kiss him every chance I could, and he gladly obliged me—after all, it was my birthday.

There was so much more to take in at that museum. I think his decision to take me there was his attempt to be cultured and civilized. To be honest, I couldn't have cared less about them, but he knew everything about all of them. I'd never seen him so passionate: he knew the make of all but three planes by sight and told me how they worked and what their specialties were.

He was in his element, but he never let go of my hand, taking me into his fantasies of the future. He'd pull me along, my little hand in his, sometimes raising them both up in the air with his finger extended to show me a feature of the model he was looking at. I loved seeing his eyes twinkle and hearing him know all the right things to say.

An old veteran came over and asked Justin if he wanted to fly, and of course Justin said yes. The man, wrinkled and wise, had a habit of tipping the bill of his WWII veteran hat when he looked at the hanging artifacts. He walked with us around two or three of the planes and competed with Justin to see who knew more about them.

When we got to a picture of a bomber plane, the old man was teleported back in time to his fighting days. He told us about the tail gunner he knew who died and about the many soldiers he knew who were shot down or shell-shocked during the war. He was impressed with Justin's knowledge of the "birds," told him about the schooling he needed to become a pilot, and encouraged him to join the Air Force. He also recommended that if Justin liked working on engines, he might want to consider becoming a mechanic as a back-up plan—a good field for a young man like Justin to get into on the off-chance flying didn't work out. Some people were color-blind, he said, and when their dream of flying was shot down they gave up on life.

The old man didn't know that where we came from, Justin was considered a lost cause, a delinquent who would end up in jail instead of holding any kind of job. Sometimes distance is all you need to get away from your problems, and we were more than a million miles from ours that day.

But all good things must come to an end, and so did our perfect day. We had to be home before Clayton got back. My mom didn't care about anything, but Clayton cared about everything, and he would want an explanation why we were gone when he got home.

We came up with our story on the way back: I had detention, and Justin had to work late, so he picked me up. It was enough to appease the beast. Justin didn't have to remind me that we were not to let Clayton or my mom know about us and we didn't bother to remind them that it was my thirteenth birthday.

It was hard for a long time after that to see Justin and not want to flirt with him. I knew it would get us both in trouble, but the risk made it all the more exciting. There were nights when he would come in, like he always had, to wish me sweet dreams, and if we were sure Clayton was preoccupied, we would sneak a kiss or two. It made life around the homestead a little more bearable, but oppression is hard to bear even when you're in love.

Later that spring, not long after our first kiss, Justin got fired from the store. He didn't like being told what to do, and the boss told him what to do for the last time. Justin told him where to go, and the boss told him to not come back; then, just to bring it full circle, Clayton told Justin he always knew he was worthless and couldn't believe he had held on to the job as long as he did in the first place. Clayton used it as an excuse to blow up and go off on us, especially Justin. He raged and screamed and got right up into his face and bellowed that he wasn't allowed to drive the Accord after that unless he paid for the gas himself—which was a stupid thing to yell at him because Justin always paid for the gas himself anyway. But Clayton needed to yell, and those were the words that came to him. Not surprisingly, Justin still had money for gas. I think I know where the money came from, but Justin never told me for sure, and I didn't want to come right out and ask. It was enough for me to know we still had wheels; I didn't care how he got the money to keep them.

Although there was no love shared between father and son, Justin tried to be cool with Clayton when he could. I think it was because he knew Clayton would beat him good if he got too out of hand—and probably also because even though Clayton was angry and demented, Justin needed to learn the man stuff from someone, so he had to stay on Clayton's good side to learn it from him.

There were plenty of times he got on Clayton's bad side, though. He always took Clayton's rage away from me, which meant he took the beating or lecture if he could. If Clayton was pissed and Mom was out of it too early, Justin would make us dinner or help me make it. But if Clayton was going to be mad no matter what, then Justin would act up or get him worked up about the president or taxes or something completely irrelevant so he wouldn't be mad at us.

I don't think he planned it that way, but that's how it happened more times than I can count. He never got really disrespectful, but he put the attention onto his bad behavior so Clayton looked at him and not at me or Lizzie. Justin didn't like guys getting too close to us, even Clayton. When I was younger, Clayton always got right up in my face, almost nose to nose, to yell. The older Lizzie and I got, the more it bothered Justin. He said it was bad, that it was only a matter of time until he took it too far. I knew he meant either Clayton would go too far and hit us like he hit Mom every now and then or he would go too far and touch us in a different way that was just as bad, maybe worse. Even when Clayton and Justin got closer, Justin still tried to keep us from his father's wrath.

Their relationship changed dramatically after Justin lost his job. I'm still not sure why, but it was almost as if Clayton liked Justin more as a for-real failure than as a kid trying to make something of himself. The first time I noticed the change was the day after Justin got fired, the day after Clayton reminded him that he was nothing but a loser with no future. It was hot, and Clayton came home with a case of ice cold beer and threw one to Justin like it was nothing. Justin looked up at him in shock; Lizzie and I did too.

"What?!" Clayton smiled through his yellow and brown teeth, "It ain't like you never had one before; don't lie to me, boy."

Justin was stuck: he couldn't say no, and the truth was he had been hammered plenty of times before then, and we all knew it. So he cracked it open and drank it down with his Old Man, and another . . . and more.

Within an hour, he was pretty much in the bag. He sat on the couch right next to Clayton, slouched and chill. I think he felt cool, accepted by his dad in a way he never had been before.

From then on, Justin got to drink with him and Mom, and he was invited into the bedroom from time to time and sucked on skunk weed with them too. It bonded them—the drinking and drugging and being losers together—and I was glad Justin had a dad for once. Don't get me wrong, Clayton still yelled and screamed at him, but he also hung out with him, too.

Meanwhile, Justin and I got closer than ever and he continued to watch out for Lizzie and me, deflecting Clayton's wrath when needed. But now he could do it in different ways. He told us what they did in the bedroom and how it felt to be drunk or high.

That's how Lizzie and I learned the most about getting high—by then we already knew about the drinking from our own experiences, but we listened to everything he had to say about weed so we knew what to do when we tried it. When they smoked it they put it in a pipe or bong and lit it on fire and sucked it up and coughed. Justin said their lungs burned but only for a while, and then it felt good.

I'd only seen the bad side: the smells; vacant, blood-shot eyes staring into nothingness for no apparent reason; the tripping and slurring; throwing up and blacking out. I couldn't see good in it, but he said it made him feel good, and I did like how I felt when I drank, so I took him at his word. Like Clayton, he said the weed made him calmer, but I'm pretty sure he got in just as many fights as he ever had. I also noticed that he got stuck on guitar chords more when he was high and played it less. Before he started drinking and smoking with Clayton, he would play every day. Guitar was his therapy. He would play and make Lizzie and I do homework. We would study and listen to him learn his own things.

I missed his playing the old way, where he would find a song he liked and obsess over it until he got it right. Once he started drinking and smoking all the time with Clayton, he would quit when he got stuck on a hard spot or was too hammered for his fingers to work. He still played what he knew—and played well—but I didn't like what using did to him or Clayton, and certainly not what it did to my non-existent ghost of a mother. I swore I would never let weed or booze change me the way it changed Justin. Turns out that didn't work too well for me.

After they started drinking together, Clayton hit Justin a lot more—and probably a lot harder, too. It was like being drinking buddies gave them the right to fight like men, even though we all knew Justin wasn't allowed to fight back—ever. Once, not too long after that first beer, Clayton came home in one of his moods, where nothing could make him happy. Justin was acting up to keep him from being mad at the rest of us. I think he was throwing a tennis ball at the wall or something annoying like that.

"Knock that off before I knock your head off, you hear me?!"

"Yeah, I hear you Old Man. Everyone can. All you do is *yell* all the time."

Then, BAM! Just like that Clayton flew across the room and sucker-punched Justin in the gut. I know it was hard because I heard all of the air go out of Justin's lungs. It reminded me of a kazoo, a funny-sounding noise for something that was anything but laughable. Lizzie and I stared in horror. Clayton backed away the slightest little bit and stuck his finger out, pushing hard on Justin's chest.

"This is my house, boy! You ain't got no place here, you understand me? You keep it up and you're out of here."

And then the words came out, the real reason for the anger: "Don't think I don't see how you look at her." He nodded to me.

It was true that we were hopelessly in love, but I couldn't believe Clayton figured it out; we had tried to be so careful. I was afraid and mortified all at the same time, but I didn't know why I cared so much if Clayton knew Justin and I cared about each other *like that.* Justin stood there and let the truth show on his face. He took the hit like a man: he didn't fall to the floor but stood hunched a little and sucked wind, trying to catch his breath. I was afraid Clayton would kick him out, but it was another dry threat, like most of what he yelled at us. But after he lost his job, any trouble Justin got in—including at school—was a guaranteed gut hit at the hands of the Old Man, as though that would teach Justin not to fight. Clayton rubbed it in Justin's face that at least when *he* was in school he had passing grades. Clayton didn't see what Justin was trying to prove by staying in school. I don't think he was trying to prove anything; he was just too young to know he could choose not to go. But then again, maybe there was a reason he didn't drop out—two reasons, in fact: me and Lizzie. Justin wanted us to be something, and he knew school was the only way.

CHAPTER 5

ALTHOUGH JUSTIN WANTED LIZZIE AND ME to do well in school, it wasn't for me any more than it was for him. It was easier for me to daydream in class than to pay attention to a teacher droning on about crap I didn't care about and would never need to know. I counted the days until I could be at the high school with Justin. At least then I'd have something to look forward to.

High school was a whole new world. We had made it to the big time; Lizzie and I said goodbye to childhood and hello to the halls of Serrano High. On the first day of school I felt like the queen of the campus. Lizzie and I rode in with Justin, who already owned the school—this was his senior year. We had shared our first kiss in the late fall of my eighth grade year, and by the first day of high school we were a known item to everyone but our parents, so I walked up the halls under the arm of the baddest troublemaker in the building, and no one would touch me.

Lizzie was smart like Justin, but unlike him, she tried hard in school and had the grades to show for it. All through elementary school she was honors and straight As. I'm sure the teachers couldn't understand how a girl with ambitions like her could be friends with the likes of Justin and me. When I went to middle school in sixth grade, they let Lizzie start too—not because she knew me but because she was "exceptional" and had promise, and the teachers probably figured if they could keep her interested and challenged in school, she might not turn out like her stripper mother. So we both started middle school together, only she had the "smart" classes, and I had the ones for the mediocre kids. That meant that even though she was a year younger, we started ninth grade together, too.

Lizzie was mostly a saint, and because of her personality and grades, she had a better reputation than either Justin or I ever did. She fit right in too, but in her own way. We Three Musketeers were becoming a mismatched motley crew: the teachers liked her, and she didn't get into nearly as much trouble as we did, but we managed to stay close . . . at first. The dark history we shared united us in a special way that even high school drama, as crazy as it can be, couldn't easily separate.

Lizzie was old enough to stay home by herself by then, but old habits are hard to kick, so instead of going home to her dumpy apartment she usually came home with us. Her mom stopped paying my mom, and we all heard Clayton complain about her being there, but it didn't stop her from coming with us. She was one of us.

Lizzie was everything Justin and I weren't, and she was growing into the most beautiful kind of girl, inside and out. She was smart and nice, and even with best friends like us, she managed to be popular with the cool kids. School was made for her, or she was made for it, or something like that. She took as much pride in her straight As and perfect handwriting as she did getting the curls in her jet black hair just right. It sure wasn't going to be her mother who recognized her for her talent, so Justin and I made sure we did. We were so proud of her. She was going to make something of her life— we knew it—and we did everything we could to help her and encourage her.

Justin showed us where all our classes were and expected Lizzie to get to each one on time. I think he and I probably skipped more classes than we attended, but there was one class I hated to miss, thanks to Mr. Reyes. His class was called JAG. It was where they taught high-risk kids how to get jobs and stay out of trouble. It was the perfect class for kids like us, and wouldn't you know it, Lizzie and I were picked for the program right away.

When Justin showed me the JAG room, he told me he was supposed to have the class, too, but hardly ever showed up. They kept putting him in it every year anyway. He didn't like it because the teacher was too nice and he figured there was a catch. I thought it was a stupid reason to skip class—not that he had to give me one in the first place.

The first day of JAG I knew what Justin meant, though.

"Good morning, ladies and gentlemen. Those of you who have been in here before already know me, but for the rest of you, my name is Mr. Reyes, and this is JAG. Miss Newton, you want to tell the newbies what JAG stands for?"

"Ummm," the sheepish girl with light blue eyes said, "I think it's like Jobs And Graduates? Right?"

"Nice try . . . not quite. Melissa, wanna help her?"

"It's Jobs for America's Graduates."

"Bingo! What's your poison?"

"You got any Anne Rice?" Melissa asked.

"I knew you'd ask for her! But of course!" He moved to a stack of books piled on top of an overflowing bookshelf, scanned them with his finger, pulled one out, and shouted, "Heads up!" before throwing it across the room into her waiting hands.

"Justin, I found some for you, too. You gonna be here to earn them this year?"

Justin shrugged. "Maybe."

"If I have to come, so do you," I mumbled to him.

"I like you!" Mr. Reyes said walking over to me. He extended his hand to me. I shook his hand back and looked at the books on the shelf. I always wondered where Justin got his books; the mystery of some of them was solved.

Mr. Reyes proceeded to tell us who he was and why he did his job—something about it being his duty to help make the world a better place, and this was how he was paying it forward. It was cheesy, seriously, but the kids who knew him seemed to really like him, and he was cool with them. Some of Justin's friends, also known as high-risk kids, were in the class, too, and told Lizzie and me that Mr. Reyes was chill. My first thought was that it was a decent class, but like Justin, I kept waiting for the catch.

I wanted to know why Mr. Reyes cared, why he didn't seem to change his opinion of us the way other teachers did when we were bad. He challenged us to be better, but he never saw the bad in me, always the good. He made me feel good about who I was, and no grown-up had ever done that before. He also taught me how to make a résumé and how to handle myself when I got mad. He said it was better to be bold and speak up in a kind and respectful manner than clam up and run away from a situation. I said he didn't know Clayton.

I liked him, and I couldn't find the catch. I told Justin to show up for the class and he did most days, and Mr. Reyes let him in without a lecture about the days he skipped. For once in school Justin and I weren't bad kids—and the best part was we were there together. Mr. Reyes made us all stand at the front of the room and tell everyone what we wanted to do when we grew up. Justin said he liked planes and wanted to fly, and if he could make anything it would be a teleporter like on *Star Trek.*

Mr. Reyes kept him after class that day. I stayed behind to hear why. He told Justin he needed to talk to an Air Force ranger about getting into the military. I remembered the veteran at the plane museum had said the same exact thing. Mr. Reyes said Justin could fly planes, fix planes, study space, and—he could even be in NASA if he wanted.

"Yeah, OK, that sounds cool."

"Do you know where to find an Air Force ranger?"

"Nah."

"You can call up a recruiter, or there's a recruiting office on Bridge Street."

"OK, I'll check it out," Justin said. I knew he was lying.

We knew we were losers then, and planning for our future outside of school was not high on the priority list, but Mr. Reyes didn't drop it. I swear, every day for the next two weeks he asked Justin if he had called yet. Justin always said he'd get to it but never did. Finally, Mr. Reyes held him back after class again.

"It's time for you to man up, Mr. Parker."

Justin looked at him. Maybe Mr. Reyes didn't know the look, but I did—Justin was ready to fight. He stood there waiting for the catch. Mr. Reyes didn't say anything, but after a minute, he turned the phone on his desk around and gave Justin a card.

"The recruiter's name is Sgt. Stallings. He's expecting your call. Go ahead, give him a call right now."

"Uh...," Justin stammered, taking the phone in his hands and looking at the card like it was a crypted number. I giggled, and Justin looked at me defensively.

"Here, you wanna make the call?" he asked me.

"No way, I don't know what to say."

"Thank you, Miss Howell. You can wait outside now."

"Wait, why?!"

"Because Justin is capable of doing this without you in the room."

"I won't say anything . . . "

"Outside, Haylee. He'll be done in a minute."

I left and waited impatiently outside the door. I did peek in the window and saw them practicing the call, making fake phones with their hands, Justin nodding his head when Mr. Reyes talked. Then Justin picked up the phone and dialed. He looked afraid but proud and serious all at the same time. It must have been a short conversation because the next time I looked he had already hung up the phone and was smiling and talking with Mr. Reyes, who clapped him on the back.

By the time he came out of the classroom and put his arm around my shoulders, it seemed like Justin had grown an inch. He told me the recruiter would be coming to talk to the class the next week, and he did. From then on, Justin's dream was the Air Force—all he had to do was wait a couple more weeks, until he was eighteen, and he could sign on.

Justin worked harder to get better grades after that. He had more than a year's worth of classes to make up, and suddenly it mattered to him to pass them before the end of the year. It wasn't that hard for him—all he had to do was try a little, and it showed a lot—he even got extra work to make up for past failed classes.

Justin finally had a plan. He was going to fly. Up until then, we didn't know what we were going to do or how we were going to do it. We were unwanted by our parents and teachers alike; all we had was each other and dreams of a better life but no idea how to get it. Mr. Reyes gave Justin a plan, and I went where Justin led me. For a while, life was about as good as it had ever been for us: we got to be together at school and at home, and we had a dream to plan our life around. But it only lasted a little while. Our world turned upside down forever the second semester of my freshman year—and it changed everything.

Justin never graduated from school. He almost made it . . . almost, but not quite. He got himself expelled. It was a stupid reason, too. I think the principal just wanted him gone once and for all—really I think everyone wanted him gone except me. He got into yet another fight, this time with a guy named Drew.

Drew had it coming if you ask me (not that anyone did). He was a jock with a grudge and a death wish, and he had been Lizzie's boyfriend of the day. She changed them almost as often as she changed her clothes, and just like the others, when she was done with Drew, she dumped him and moved on. She didn't sleep around, I don't think. She never said anything about having sex with any of them, so if she did she didn't tell me, and I don't see why she wouldn't. She was just picky: she knew what she wanted, and if a guy wasn't it, she moved on—and fast.

Drew wasn't having it though. He was kind of a possessive, sore loser, or—I don't know—thick-headed idiot, and he started to follow her around school. He turned into her personal stalker before long and wouldn't take the hint to leave her alone.

When Lizzie told Justin and me about it, we didn't take it too seriously at first. I hate to admit it, but the three of us were growing apart. She was better than us, and I guess we didn't want to corrupt her—or maybe she wanted to fit in with people who wouldn't like our kind of people hanging around. That's why we didn't notice Drew's behavior when she first broke up with him. But after a couple weeks it was too obvious for anyone to miss. Drew would follow Lizzie to and from JAG, and Justin and I would try to get him to back off in all the right ways. We would tell him to give her space and tease him about being insecure. We weren't the only ones, either. Her other friends were noticing too and trying to get him to leave her alone, but he was stubborn and wasn't listening to any of us.

One Friday he followed her to her bus and insisted that they get back together, yet again. I was there and so was Lizzie's friend ShamRae. We were all walking together, ShamRae on one side and me on the other. I was trying not to roll my eyes as they talked about a school project they were working on. I didn't understand how people could want to talk about a school assignment for fun. Then Lizzie sucked in her breath like she had seen a ghost.

"Oh no, there he is." ShamRae and I followed her eyes to the side of the bus. Drew, with all his five feet ten inches of brawn, was waiting for her. "Why can't he just leave me alone?"

"I can give you a ride home," ShamRae offered.

Before the words came out of her mouth, I already knew Lizzie would say no. As bad as my house was, it was a palace compared to Brenda and Lizzie's dive. Brenda was not the kind of mom to keep a clean house. That's a nice way to say their apartment was a one-bedroom dump, a nasty mess in a bad part of town, and Lizzie was always embarrassed by it.

That's part of the reason Lizzie preferred our house: at least we could see our floor. Being the mother, Brenda got the bedroom, of course, and it was the worst part of the apartment, but the rest wasn't much better. Lizzie had a bed and dresser in the living room, and her clothes were piled high everywhere, clean and dirty all mixed into heaps of mystery. Lizzie would sniff them and if they smelled clean, she wore them; if not, she threw them into another pile. I can't really judge her for her cleaning habits; Brenda never taught her anything different.

Even though Lizzie didn't know how to clean her house, she knew enough to be mortified to ever have one of her "popular" friends take her home.

"Leave me alone, Drew," she said as he approached.

"Yeah, stalker, she doesn't want anything to do with you," ShamRae threw in.

"Not until we talk," Drew answered as Lizzie tried to move around him to her bus.

"We don't have anything to talk about. We're done. Leave me alone."

"No, you need to listen to me." He reached right between me and ShamRae as we were trying to block the two of them and grabbed Lizzie's arm. I could tell it hurt because she winced and tried to pull back but couldn't.

"Let me go!"

"I said I want to talk to you. I just want to talk, and you keep shutting me down. Just listen to me."

"No! Leave me alone."

"Mr. Risher, do we have a problem?" It was Mrs. Huerta, our vice principal.

"Yes," Lizzie answered, "he won't let me get on my bus."

"I was just trying to talk to her," Drew lied, holding his hands up in surrender. "She can go if she wants to."

"Come take a walk with me, Drew," Mrs. Huerta said and escorted Drew away from the bus.

I don't know what she said to him; I wish I'd had a bit of stalker in me and had followed them instead of staying with ShamRae to calm Lizzie down. Maybe Mrs. Huerta was onto Drew and was telling him to knock it off, or maybe she was telling him to give Lizzie time, giving him a pep talk to help him feel better about getting dumped but still making it clear that he needed to leave Lizzie alone. To this day I wonder what they talked about—it's one of the little things that eats away at me on days when it's rainy and I get nostalgic.

Lizzie looked at both me and ShamRae desperately.

"I can't take it anymore." She leaned into ShamRae for a hug and started to cry. I felt out of place, unnecessary.

"I could have Martin tell him to give you space. Maybe he'll listen to him," ShamRae said. Martin was her older brother and was on the wrestling team with Drew.

"Yeah? Maybe . . . I don't care anymore; I just want him to leave me alone."

Neither Mrs. Huerta's nor Martin's talks worked. Drew was back at it on Monday.

"You're such a douche, Drew; leave her alone," I yelled at him when I saw him outside the JAG classroom. I was being bold like Mr. Reyes said to be, but he wasn't scared of me at all.

That's when Lizzie and I told Justin to do something about him—and he did. Even though we weren't as close, we both still loved Lizzie and Justin wasn't about to let her be bullied anymore. She was our prize possession, and neither of us wanted her to have her shot at life squashed like ours was. Somehow we both believed it didn't matter how bad our lives got if we could keep her safe from pain. We tried to help make her life perfect. In a lot of ways, we felt responsible for her like parents should. Justin, like an angry father, was now responsible for taking care of Drew.

CHAPTER 6

THE NEXT DAY WAS A TUESDAY. Funny how I remember the day of the fight that got Justin expelled but can't remember the day my mom died.

Justin skipped his second period class to catch Drew before he could creep on Lizzie again. I know he skipped because we were together at Smoker's Corner—that was what everyone called our hide-out in the woods. It was a couple minutes' walk from the school, close enough to get there in time for the next class after smoking, but far enough to stay unnoticed.

We were waiting together, buying time the best way we knew how–by making out, of course. We never did any more than that, even though I wished for more all the time. Just as we waited for our first kiss, Justin said we had to wait to have sex. *Age ain't nothing but a number*, I would say, trying to tempt him. He countered, insisting that the number could get him kicked out of the house or worse, depending on Clayton and my mom's mood. So instead, we just stole kisses where they wouldn't find out.

We weren't saints; Justin was just a gentleman like that. It was one of the things I loved most about him. I would have given up my virginity to him the day we first kissed if he asked, probably before. I knew he knew it too—he knew I was his body, mind, soul and spirit—but he didn't push me. He didn't even ask. It was always him who kept us from getting carried away.

I knew everyone assumed we were already doing it, and it didn't bother me at all. I liked people knowing I was his. Since I had no plans to be with anyone else, it didn't matter to me if they thought we were having sex. Justin wasn't going to let them think otherwise either. It was no one's business what we did or didn't do, but it wasn't exactly cool for a guy *not* to have sex with his girl. I guess we didn't think anyone needed to know we were being old-fashioned. It seemed like no one our age waited, but we did, and probably there were others like us who hid it too.

Clayton, my mom, and my age all mattered to Justin, but aside from all that, he wanted it to be right, like our first kiss. For as stubborn and mean and quick-tempered as he appeared to be, he was incredibly patient. I think he thought it would ruin me to have sex too early—that I wasn't old enough to handle it or appreciate it. He was wiser than his years.

The last time I argued with him about it had been a few weeks before the fight with Drew. We were in the car making out, and as usual, I wanted more. I wanted to know what it was like. He said pretty much the same thing to me about having sex as he did about our first kiss, only I think it was harder for him to stick to his guns about it.

"I want to make love to a woman, not a girl."

"I'm woman enough now; trust me," I teased, straddling myself over him on his seat. I kissed him good and long and pressed into him, onto him, running my hands right under his shirt, enticing him.

He grabbed my hands and pushed me back gently, breathing hard. I felt the proof that he wanted me too, and I smiled. I liked making him want me. He closed his eyes, leaned his head back on the head rest, and thought about it. But then, once again, he denied me: "Not yet."

"Why not?" I pouted, flopping myself back onto my own seat. "Don't you want me?"

"C'mon, Haylee, you think I really don't want you?" he said, turning to look at me again. "It's not the right time yet. Sex is so much more than our bodies coming together," he said as he reached over to kiss me. "You're not ready... I'm probably not ready. It's going to be a metaphysical bond that traverses time and space; we'll be one forever. Everything that is you is going to become part of me, and . . . "

"Blah, blah, blah..." I said and shut his mouth with mine and reached between his legs. I had heard all his supernatural, mumbo jumbo excuses before. He was convinced that sex was a soul collision and it would change everything. He had all these theories about how it would connect us forever. I had my own theory, it was that sex with him would be the best thing that would ever happen to me. "I want you now." I pouted, "I'm ready now. Let's traverse time and space right now . . . please?"

"Not yet," he repeated kissing me softly. He pulled my hand up, put both of mine together and kissed them, then looked at me while he stroked them with his thumbs. Though his decision was final, he held me like that, with his eyes and hands, for seconds that felt like hours.

"When?" I conceded the loss.

"In time . . . Haylee. I love you, and I want you more than anything." His stare penetrated deep into my soul; it was so strong I had to look away. "And I'll have you. Just wait." He let go of my hands and traced my nose with his finger, then finished the moment with a peck on my forehead while he held my head in his hands.

"Wow! You can totally reject me and still make it romantic; how do you do that?"

"It's a gift," he shrugged and smiled a devious crooked smile.

"Um hmm," I said, and kissing him again asked, "But seriously, when? I feel like I can't wait."

"Of course you can. Wait, Haylee; just wait."

I didn't push him after that for a long time. In my heart I wanted it to be as perfect as he seemed to think it could be. I knew it couldn't be this amazingly, unforgettably wonderful first-time experience if I lost it in an awkward moment in a car, or when we were trying to do it and worrying about whether Clayton or my mom would catch us at the same time. I didn't want to wait, but I would.

My reluctance to wait didn't come into play at all that morning at Smoker's Corner. In the winter, in inland California, there's not much a young horny couple can do exposed in the great outdoors, even if they wanted to. I was snuggled up into his jacket to suck up his heat, and we were doing a good job of keeping each other warm with our not-quite-innocent touches. My hands were inside his jacket, reaching in as far as I could get them. His hands were doing about the same thing, only he would sneak them out into the cold to smoke from time to time. Back then, he chain-smoked when he was anxious. He finished a cigarette and hugged me close—so close I could feel the wrinkles in his shirt against me. I loved that he wanted me; I felt powerful knowing I could make this big, strong, tough guy go weak and vulnerable with a simple, purposeful move of my lips—or my hips. When he would groan, it was intoxicating—it made me want him; it made him mine; but I also knew he would never let it go too far. Oh, how I loved him then!

We never knew when other wayward souls would come down to Smoker's Corner, and when they did, we would take breaks and separate. I liked to collect the dead leaves and make bouquets with them while we hung out with the others. Sometimes, mostly before first period, there could be fifteen or more of us there, deciding together if we wanted to show up to class that day or not.

That morning, when other kids stopped by, the talk was about how Justin would beat Drew's face in. One way or another, Justin was going to let Drew know it was time he moved on. We all knew a fight was imminent; I just didn't think it would be Justin's last high school fight.

Right before we left, some guys from school, Pablo and Edgar, showed up and interrupted one of our trysts that wasn't going to end anywhere climactic anyway. I bowed my head onto Justin's chest, and we laughed. I looked at the boys smugly. I was caught. I tried not to look like I cared as much as I did.

"Awwww, busted! You gonna finish this, Justin, or what?" Pablo joked.

"Not now," Justin answered back with a smile.

"Whoa!" Edgar shouted, grinning and nodding.

The boys came to get high, and we knew it. They were stoners. So was Justin, and by that time, so was I. There were no words spoken; we didn't need them. We knew what they were doing, and they knew we wouldn't narc on them. In our classes the kids drew their color lines if seats weren't assigned—the whites with the whites, the blacks with the blacks, and the Hispanics with each other—but the lines were more fluid outside of class, especially when weed was involved. Our school was small enough that as long as we stayed cool with people, we were all willing to share our toys. Only now that we were older, instead of Matchbox cars, lizards, and dolls, our toys were smokes, beer, weed and leftover boyfriends and girlfriends. The rules were known, even if we didn't post them on walls like teachers did. The rule here was "share and share alike." It wasn't like we hadn't smoked them out before, so the expectation was that we were automatically invited to get high with them if they brought it out. Pablo passed the pipe to me; I took a hit and passed it to Justin, but I knew he wouldn't smoke it. He was going to fight soon, and he liked to be clear-headed when he fought.

"I'm good," he said passing it back to Edgar, "You know Drew Risher?" Justin asked the boys while I exhaled.

"He's with Lizzie, right?" Pablo answered.

"Not no more he's not. She's done with him, I'm about to beat the facts into him to make sure he gets it."

"Nuh uh, when?"

"After second period. He turned all OJ on her. Dude's going psycho, following her everywhere she goes. It ain't cool, man."

"I hear you, I hear you," Edgar said, nodding.

If it would have happened nowadays, we all would have been texting, Snapchatting and messaging what was about to go down, but we didn't have that technology then. The amazing thing was, we didn't need it to get the message across. Kids found out about stuff just as fast even before we had cell phones.

Lizzie—the good girl, the honor student who never skipped— had been telling everyone her childhood friend, Justin, was going take care of Drew that day. The rumors started old-school style, with whispered words in the halls that morning, when teachers weren't around. Teenaged hype took it from there, and before the first-period class bell rang, everyone was on high alert, there was going to be a fight.

Pablo, Edgar, Justin and I stayed together, making small talk and wasting time, until a few minutes before the bell rang. Usually we would have waited for the bell to help us decide to go or not, but today Justin wanted to be at Lizzie's class when it let out. Unless Drew chickened out because of the rumors or because he grew a brain since the day before, he would probably already be there, too.

The four of us walked up to the school together. Justin and I walked hand in hand until we got to the sidewalk; then we weren't a couple anymore. It was time for him to be strong and mean. It was not time for him to be seen as weak. I knew the rule and let go even before he unconsciously pushed my hand out of his, as he had done in the past before a fight. It was amazing to me how this boy I had loved as long as life itself could be so soft, gentle, and kind with me and then turn in a moment into a monster I didn't recognize. He wasn't one to mess with when he was pissed; too much of Clayton's rage was bottled up inside him, waiting for an excuse to get out. I didn't like seeing him mad. It scared me.

I think it scared him, too, because he was the one who made the rule to keep me safe. He wasn't mad when he said it; that's why I knew I had to listen and obey. He was making the rule to save me from himself.

We had been lying on the couch together watching *Star Trek TNG*. It was a hot, almost-summer night. Clayton and Mom were still gone from the night before, and we were spooning, but he curled me in his arm and turned me to face him. I readjusted and rubbed my hand across his chiseled chest. As he looked at me, his eyes, like they always did, told me he loved me, and his fingers ran lightly up and down my arm. He had gotten suspended the day before for fighting and had the busted face to show for it. He never said if he won or lost that one; I wasn't at the high school yet and I didn't need to know.

"Haylee, don't ever get in the way when I'm fighting, you hear me? I don't care if I'm winning, losing, or you think I'm a fool for fighting, or I'm fighting for you—stay out of it, all right? You can be there for me, but don't get in my way."

I didn't know how to answer, so I nodded. And every time I saw him fight after that, I obeyed the rule. I still wonder what made him say it. Had there been a girl at the fight getting in the middle of it? Did the other guy have a girlfriend messing the fight up? Did he hit a girl who got in the way during the fight? He never said. I never asked.

He walks faster when he's mad, and it was hard for me to keep up with him after I let go of his hand. I lagged behind Pablo and Edgar too, knowing it could turn into a brawl if Drew had other guys with him. I didn't want to be caught between them or hold them back while I scrambled out of the way.

Part of me didn't want to be there at all for the fight. I had seen a million fights by the time I was in ninth grade: Justin's fights, other friends, Clayton and his buddies on Friday nights. I hated fighting but it was like watching a train wreck: I couldn't walk away. Some dark place inside me was drawn to the carnage.

It wouldn't be good for Justin if I bailed either. He didn't want me in fights, but he wanted me there while he fought, the way Rocky needed Adrienne. He never told me that; but I knew it was true. All men need their girl by their side; it's how they're wired.

And as much as he needed me there, I needed to watch. We were part of each other, so for me to walk away from his fight—this one especially—would have been wrong. I never worried about Justin losing because he never did, except when he let Clayton hit him. More often I felt sorry for the other guy and worried that Justin wouldn't stop before he really hurt him. There were times watching him fight that I wanted to cry out and tell him enough was enough, but I didn't want him to yell at me, so I kept my words in my mouth. Truth be told, I liked him strong. What girl doesn't want her man to be the toughest guy around? I didn't need him to fight to prove it to me, but he needed to prove it to himself.

Justin didn't fool around in a fight. It was never like the movies where the guys would talk about the reason for the fight and circle each other a dozen times before the first blow or kick; no, Justin went right for the knockout. Some guys really didn't want to fight; they tried to talk and reason with Justin to get him to back down. In those cases Justin was the automatic winner, and everyone gathered around knew it. I hated it when he beat them down anyway; I told him that once, when we were alone after one particularly bad fight with a boy from another school.

"You already knew you had him, Justin; why did you do that?"

"I had to. Everyone was watching."

"You didn't have to. He was scared; he was begging you like a baby not to fight him. Everyone knew it."

"I had to make my point."

"You did. He even admitted it—he said he didn't want to fight 'cause you would mess him up. You shouldn't have done it."

"What do you want me to do, look weak?"

"No. Look like you, just don't . . . be like that."

"Like what?"

I didn't want to say it, but he needed to hear it: "Like Clayton. You're better than him; don't be like that." We were sitting together on the couch that time too, watching another afternoon rerun of *Star Trek TNG*. Since we were alone, it was safe to be close. His hand, bruised from pounding the guy's face in, was holding mine until I said that. He let go quickly and pretended to be suddenly focused on the conversation Captain Piccard and Jordie LaForge were having about warp drive engines on the Enterprise. When the commercial came on, he finally answered me: "You can't understand it. You're not a guy."

"No, not all of it, but I understand enough to know that when someone admits they're afraid, that's enough to make you *not* look weak. You don't have to be like that, please."

"I can't promise you that, Haylee."

"Please, Justin."

"I'm done talking about it." He turned the volume up on the remote. There was no sense in trying to keep arguing my point; I had made it, and I could tell it got to him. We didn't say more about it then or ever, but after that conversation it seemed to me he did go easier on the guys who admitted defeat, which was most of them.

But this time, with Drew, I didn't think that would be the case. Drew had it coming, and he was about to get it—big time. The only person Justin was more protective of than me was Lizzie, and we were probably even more protective of her than of ourselves. I was pretty sure Drew wasn't getting out of the fight without bleeding. He'd be lucky to make it out conscious.

"Hey!" Justin shouted when he turned around the corner, picking up his pace even more. Sure enough, the slimeball was right where we expected him: outside Lizzie's classroom, waiting like a vulture for his prey. Drew saw Justin immediately but didn't have time to prepare for the first hit, idiot. Justin crushed his nose before he said anything else. Pablo's hand went to his mouth, making a fist and laughing with Edgar about the hit.

"Ohhhh! Yeah!"

Drew didn't even take it like a man; he squealed like a girl. The blood I was expecting didn't come. Maybe Justin's hit wasn't as hard as it sounded.

"You think it's funny to follow Lizzie around? She told you to leave her alone."

"Dude!" Drew backed away and put his hands up to the side — cowardly, in surrender, not protectively like he wanted to fight. "What's your problem?!"

"You won't leave her alone; that's my problem!" Justin answered before giving him Clayton's favorite, a sucker punch to the gut. "She told you to leave her alone. Did you not get the message? 'Cause I'm pretty sure she made it loud and clear."

The bell rang, and kids started pouring out of classes. They could smell the energy of a fight even before they saw it. Teenagers huddled and circled the two of them, while teachers sat oblivious in the comfort of their heated classrooms. They wouldn't realize there was a problem outside for several long minutes.

"Justin!" It was Lizzie; she had seen the hit.

"Lizzie, what did you tell him?" Drew asked.

"I—I didn't tell him anything." She was panicking. She wasn't trying to make Justin look bad; it just came out that way. She looked from one face to the other, pathetically at Drew, pleading with me and Justin, to the faces in the crowd. She was analyzing, processing, trying to figure out what to do or say to make it all go away, like she expected Justin to have done something differently to make Drew stop following her.

"What, Lizzie? You want this guy to keep following you around? You want him to grab you and tell you what to do?"

"No! But I don't want you to beat him up. You'll hurt him bad, Justin."

It was enough of an insult to emasculate Drew right there in front of everyone. The big bad football player was no match for the poor loser-kid, and Lizzie blurted the truth for all to hear. Even though he was scared, Drew did what comes naturally when a guy gets put down: he fought back to prove he could not be hurt by Justin.

If Justin hadn't been distracted by Lizzie he would have seen it coming, but he caught Drew's right hook square to the chin. Lizzie screamed, but Justin shook it off. He was used to taking hits, it barely fazed him, except to make him more mad.

The crowd went wild. We were loud enough to signal a ruckus was afoot. Teachers would be coming out any minute; if we knew better, we would disperse before they got there. But what do teenagers in the heat of emotion know?

Justin couldn't afford to get in trouble at school right then; he had been suspended for insulting a teacher two weeks before. But it didn't matter. At that moment he was protecting Lizzie. He would give up his life for that girl to have a good shot at hers; giving up his education was of little consequence.

To repay Drew for the hook, Justin turned around and clocked him good—three, four, five times hard in the face. Drew tried to block but was no match for Justin's speed and experience. The rest of the fight was for Lizzie.

"She doesn't want to see you . . . " Punch.

" . . . To talk to you . . . " Jab.

" . . . To have you follow her around like a freak . . . " Punch.

" . . . Or to lay a hand on her ever again!" Hook to the face. And then came the blood, like lava from a volcano—thick, slow, red, smearing on Justin's knuckles and Drew's cheek.

"You got that, bro?" Justin asked, stepping back to wait for Drew's answer.

"All I wanted to do was talk to her."

"You're done talking now, right?"

"Yeah."

"You sure about that?"

"Yeah, man! I'm sure."

"Tell her you're sorry."

Drew looked at Lizzie, "I'm sorry."

"And?" Justin asked.

"And I won't mess with you anymore."

That was it. It was over before a single teacher broke through the crowd. The students wanted more. A fight for a good cause wasn't good enough; they were in it for the blood and beating, regardless of the reason for the fight. It wasn't a grudge match for Justin; it was about making the point to let Lizzie be. Justin made it loud and clear, and Drew conceded it. The fight didn't have to continue. Drew was a coward anyway; that's why he was all rough and tough with Lizzie—he wasn't a man; he was a little baby who wasn't getting his way. He got smacked down and learned real fast he wouldn't be getting what he wanted. Lizzie would be safe.

In Justin's mind the fight was worth it because Lizzie would be free. Drew knew there would be a round two if he messed with her anymore. In my eyes it was the right thing for Justin to do. I'd seen him fight for far less noble causes before; this one was actually for a good reason. But in the eyes of the governing bodies of the school, it was improper, inappropriate, and the last straw for Justin.

Drew got suspended for three days for his involvement, but they straight-up expelled Justin. It was a death sentence. He hung up all his hopes and dreams. There was no point in coming back the following year; at that rate he would be almost twenty before he graduated. There was no point going home, either: Clayton would be pissed. My mom would do what she did best and use the expulsion as an excuse to head to the bar to gripe about having to put up with Clayton's worthless son.

I couldn't go back to class, even though I told Lizzie to finish the day like nothing happened. She was embarrassed that they were fighting over her. It really won her sympathy with her popular friends—her loser friend beating up the football stalker. The drama would be good for her high school career. She went to third period, but I followed Mr. Duncan, who walked between both boys, as they went to the office.

"What are you doing here, young lady?" the receptionist, Ms. Solis, asked.

"I'm waiting for Justin; he's talking to Sipe," I answered nodding toward the principal's closed office door.

"You need to go back to class."

"It's OK; I'll wait," I said. There wasn't much the office workers could do with us kids who lived on the fringe. I could see it in her eyes; she looked at me the way Clayton and Mom did: she saw trash, a pointless waste of the oxygen I breathed. The only difference was she didn't say the words. She didn't have to; I heard her expression loud and clear.

"Well, you can't wait here. What's your third period class?"

"Doesn't matter."

She was getting impatient, but I was starting to have fun. This would be a good way to pass the time. She looked something up in the computer and found the information I wouldn't give her. She wrote me out a hall pass to my class and held it smartly toward me between two fingers.

Fun over. I rolled my eyes with as much attitude as I could muster and jerked the thing out of her fingers. I wasn't going to class, but I left the office anyway. Cell phones would have been so nice to have back then. I had to wait in the alcove of a door for Justin because he wouldn't know where I was otherwise. It took forever. Neither of the parental units bothered to come and get him or sign him out or whatever parents are supposed to do when their kid gets expelled; he just walked out—pissed.

"That's it, Haylee—I'm done. I'm screwed. It's over!"

"What? What do you mean?" I asked catching up to him as quickly as I could.

"She expelled me."

"What?! No way. Did he get expelled too?"

"I don't know. She's sick of me ruining the reputation of her perfect school. She was waiting for a chance to nail me, and I gave it to her. She wanted me gone, and she got her wish."

On the way out the door Justin threw down a gray plastic trash can that was only half full. It wobbled and bounced in front of him, and he had to kick it out of his way. As it thudded against the wall, only one of those red and white paper French fry baskets from the cafeteria fell out; it was as sad as Sipe's expulsion was. If it hadn't been too serious of a moment to laugh, I would have. He made his point better when he slammed the old wooden door open with so much force it hit the outside wall and chinked off some of the concrete wall.

We drove. That's all we could think to do. Home would not be a welcome place to land yet. This was one of those things that could keep Clayton going for weeks. Justin was liable to really get kicked out. He was guaranteed to be clobbered good; the only thing that might save him from too bad of a beating was that they both knew Justin was almost stronger than Clayton.

"You should talk to Mr. Reyes," I said halfway through the day when we were almost to Chino. He was going to see his planes before life completely destroyed his dreams.

"Why? All he's going to do is tell me to stick it out, come back next year and graduate. I'm not graduating, Haylee; there's no way."

I knew it was impossible but I couldn't concede that his dreams were over. "You can still graduate. You can do it, and join the Air Force and get us out of here. Don't give up."

"It's not giving up; it's growing up. I can't wait around for a year. Besides, people are going to piss me off just as much next year, and by then I'm going to be even further behind. I can't do it. It's not worth it. I'm not graduating."

"What about us?"

"What about us?" He was too mad to understand my fears.

"If you don't graduate, what does that mean for us? How are we going to get out of here?"

"I can get a job again. You need to finish school. I'll save up while you're finishing; then we can take off."

"To where?"

"I don't know—Egypt? What do you want me to say?"

"You were supposed to go into the Air Force. You were supposed to fly, and I was going to follow you wherever you went."

"Stupid dreams, Haylee. That's all they were. You know what kind of person I am. That kind of life isn't for me. I'm not one of those guys; I'm going to be dead by 25 in a bar fight, not flying a fighter jet for the Air Force." He slammed his hand against the steering wheel, making the car swerve.

"Then why are we going to Chino? You're going to the museum. You're going to see the planes. It's not dreams, Justin; it's who you are."

"Was."

"Why do you have to be like that?"

"Like what—realistic? It doesn't make sense to try to fight for something that's not going to happen anyway. Sipe hates me, and I don't even have all my sophomore credits, let alone my junior and senior ones. It ain't happening for me."

"Did Sipe tell you that?"

"Pretty much. I'm done with high school. I'm done."

And he was. He never looked back after that. If he regretted it, he's never said so. It was just the way it was.

We didn't make it to the museum. A few miles farther he turned the car around and went to the only place we had: a lousy home, complete with deadbeat parents at the end of a dead-end road.

When Clayton found out, he didn't even yell. In fact, I think he was gloating: he had told us we would never amount to anything, and finally one of us was proving him right. Instead, he got Justin hammered—that was his punishment. He was puking before eleven o'clock that night. It was the first time I think I really hated my life. Justin looked enough like Clayton that I could almost picture him at Clayton's age, and our kids doing the same stuff we were doing: drinking, failing, turning into their parents, who turned into theirs.

The older we got, the more dreams we had to let go of—and now, like the last balloon in the bunch, Justin released our last hope for a better life, and we both watched our dreams disappear into a hopeless, cloudless, starless night of pitch-black darkness.

CHAPTER 7

AS SOON AS I KNEW Clayton was cool with Justin, I went to my room. I tried to cry myself to sleep and escape into make-believe dreams, but I couldn't sleep; all I could do was cry.

There were tears for everything about my miserable life. Knowing that our last hope was lost ripped through my shell of indifference, and all my sadness and despair came out.

I cried for it all, but I spent most of the night crying about Gramma Diaz's pictures. I hadn't seen them in forever; I hadn't gone to have cookies with her since AWANA gave way to youth group and they expected the kids to talk about more than Bible verses. I could handle that, but I didn't want people knowing my business—especially not church people.

That night I couldn't stop thinking about her pictures. All of the smiling faces—why were they so happy? Had anyone who smiled out from the pictures grown up like I did with alcoholic parents, or did theirs make cookies for them every Wednesday? I imagined they all had their diplomas and went into the military or college on top of that. There wasn't a loser in her bunch. How come they could smile and we got screwed? Justin could have been such a great guy.

Then I was mad. I didn't know who to be mad at, so I picked Gramma Diaz's God. I hated Him. How could that God she said loved us give us the kind of life we had and give her—an ugly old wind bag—a good life? It wasn't fair; life wasn't fair. I wanted a refund; I wanted to leave; I wanted out.

But I was stuck. I had nowhere to go. If I left, that would mean leaving Justin. And if I did, where would I go? My whole life revolved around him. If we left, we'd never get away with it. I was

14 and he just turned 18. I couldn't get a job, and he couldn't very well sign me into school and support us both while I grew up. I couldn't kill myself and leave him that way; I was pretty sure I was all he had to live for. I was stuck in a hopeless life with no way to escape. I was going to be just like my mother, like Lizzie's mom, like Justin's washed-up, strung-out and worthless one.

There was nothing to do but resign myself to become like them the same way Justin had earlier that morning. So I did.

I didn't even care what Clayton or my mom thought when they saw me come down that night. I expected them to say something, but it was as if all they had been waiting for our whole lives was for Justin and me to realize we were no better than them. Now that we were giving up our dreams of a better life, now that we accepted that our fate would be the exact same as theirs, they had all the love in the world for us.

They even smoked me out. I'd been high with Justin before, and I'm sure they knew I was smoking weed, but we never did it together until that night. They didn't shut the bedroom door and try to hide the smell; we didn't even go in the bedroom. Mom stuffed the pipe tight and passed it around and smoked me out right there in the living room.

I guess we were having a good time, but I was still wary of Clayton. It was too good to be true. How could Justin come home and say, *"Hey, Dad, guess what? I got expelled today!"* and Clayton not flip out? I kept waiting for it, and then it came.

By midnight Justin was in-the-bag-done and about ready to pass out. I meant nothing by what I did except to help him sit down before he fell down, but Justin made the mistake of touching me. I put his arm over my shoulder and walked him to our nasty old couch Mom had since the seventies and sort of let him fall into it. As he fell he grabbed my arm with both of his hands and grinned. That was all—an unsteady but too familiar touch, and a grin—and that was all it took to set Clayton off.

The yelling I was waiting for, the screaming, the beating was upon us, and there was nothing Justin or I could do to defend ourselves. Looking back, I think Clayton planned it that way. I think he knew even before Justin did that Justin was too strong for him.

He knew the only way to put him in his place was to inebriate him first, so that's what he did—and his touching me was just the excuse he was waiting for.

Justin was too far gone to stand up to him, and Clayton let him have it. He pounded on him like a rag doll right where he sat on the couch. Justin was drunk enough to forget to demur to Clayton's authority, so he bumbled back up to his feet, trying to stand up to him. He got some good hits in but they lacked strength or coordination—and to make it worse, his aim was off, so his hits didn't do anything to hurt Clayton. It was over before it started. He looked like Apollo against the Russian, and no matter how loud I screamed for Clayton to stop, Clayton kept hammering him with one blow after the other. My mom sat on the other end of the couch watching it like it was nothing more than another one of the Friday fights. She didn't flinch, even when the blood was splattering onto the velveteen floral print on the couch. I hated her for it. "Get off him! Leave him alone! Clayton, *stop*! Mom! Make him stop! Clayton, *stop*!" All she did was shrug with half-closed eyes.

"What—you don't want me to hurt your *boyfriend*?" Clayton sneered to me after clocking Justin and knocking him to the floor. His head hit hard, but he was still conscious. I was afraid to go to him.

"He's not my boyfriend, Clayton. Leave him alone!" I lied.

"What was that that I saw then?"

"What was what? What are you talking about? You didn't see nothing! He's drunk!"

"I saw the way he touched you," he said, turning from where Justin was on the floor to face me. I was relieved to have him away from Justin, but I knew that meant I was next. But that was OK—if I couldn't go to Justin, at least I could distract Clayton from hurting him anymore. I knew I could take a hit or two, and if he knocked me out, maybe he would calm down.

"You're smokin' crack! He didn't touch me! I was helping him to the couch. Look at him," I gestured. We both watched Justin, bloody and unsteady, staggering up from the floor again. "He's wasted..."

"Has he touched you?"

"No!"

"Don't you lie to me, you little slut!" Clayton said rushing me. I braced for the impact, I was so sure the hit was coming, I just didn't know if it would be to the gut or face.

"I'm not, I swear! He's never touched me. I was helping him, that's all. And you beat his face in. I'm going to take him to his room unless you want to beat me up too." I said it with all the fake bravado I could muster. I waited for the blow to the back of my head when I turned to ask my mom to help, but it didn't come.

"Mom . . . Mom, help me!"

"That boy made his own bed," she said with a dismissive hand in the air, looking away, her grey eyes unsympathetic.

"Clayton, please?" I didn't think I could take him to his room alone, and I wanted him out of there. I don't know why I asked Clayton since he was the reason Justin was bleeding in the first place, but I did. That kind of chaos made me do things that didn't make sense. And he did help—in fact, he walked Justin to his room all by himself, the same way I had tried to lead him to the couch. I walked behind them but went straight to my own room and slammed the door.

Even with the door shut, I could hear what Clayton said to Justin. I don't know whether Justin was conscious enough to hear him, but I did: "You keep your hands off her, boy. You hear me?"

The words swam in my head. Why? Why did a man who couldn't care less about me, who never had one nice thing to say about me, who screamed at me on a weekly basis, care if Justin and I had a thing between us? This wasn't the first time he got mad over it either. I didn't know where the anger came from. I especially didn't understand why that night, when he could have attacked Justin for the fight, the expulsion, or the cruise we took without permission— why that was what he chose to zero in on.

I don't know, and I don't talk to the man—haven't talked to him in years—so maybe I'll never know. How would I ask that anyway? *Excuse me Clayton, I'd like to know—did you actually care about me when I was a kid, you mean, cold jerk? Or were you jealous of your own son? Or did you think dirty thoughts about me and take your disgust at yourself out on Justin instead?* I can't picture an opening in a conversation that would lead to asking him something like that.

The next morning was pretty bad. Clayton left for work, Mom was up for a change making coffee and eating toast, and Justin and I both got up and ready like normal. The only difference was Justin had nowhere to go. Finally after half an hour of avoiding the obvious, I asked, "What are you going to do?"

"I don't know." He was bruised badly and his left eye was swollen shut. It was a deep, dark purple, almost like a make-up artist painted it. I wanted to touch it and see what it felt like. I imagined it would be hot to the touch. But I didn't dare touch him and risk my mom seeing after a night like last night.

He looked sad and lost. It made me feel sorry for him and unsure of him for the first time in my life. He had always been the one to know what to do, and now he didn't. It troubled me to doubt him; I didn't want to, but there it was, in the pit of my stomach: doubt. For once I told him what to do.

"Take me to school. Let me see if Mr. Reyes will come talk to you; he'll know what you should do."

He didn't argue or complain or come up with a better plan; he simply went along. That frightened me more than anything. Justin always knew what to do, and I followed him, and now he was taking direction from me, a stupid fourteen-year-old freshman. Why?

When we walked out the door together, Mom finally said something: "Where do you think you're going, punk?" It was her pet name for Justin.

"Taking Haylee to school, then something."

"Something better be getting a job 'cause you ain't living here for free anymore. I'll give you the rest of this month; then you're paying me and your dad rent. Three hundred dollars every month or you're gone, you hear me?"

They always said that: *You hear me? You hear me? You hear me?!* Of course we did—all they did was yell and talk and go on and on about everything. Yes, we heard them loud and clear.

In the Accord that wasn't his, he broke down and panicked.

"Where am I going to come up with three hundred dollars in two weeks?"

"They'll let it go; they always do."

"Not this time. Don't you get it, Haylee? Everything is different now. Nothing is the same."

"We can leave."

"To where? How would that work?" he asked.

"You have to get a job, that's all—just get a job, and it'll be fine, and we can go."

"How am I supposed to get a job? I just got expelled from school; I'm screwed."

"You have places you can stay."

"Maybe for a little while. But that leaves you in that house alone. You can't handle that; no one can."

"I'll be fine." I tried to comfort him even though I was petrified of being alone without him or Lizzie.

"Really? Who do you think he's going to start hitting if I'm not there? You know how many times he's come after you already; it's only a matter of time before he hits you. And trust me, you won't be able to handle a hit from him."

"Thanks—I'm not a wuss."

"I didn't say that; it's just he hits a lot harder than he slaps you."

There was a long quiet stretch where words wouldn't come, and both of us tried to come up with a good plan—unsuccessfully.

"You can't stay there alone."

It was about twenty minutes before class started when we got to the school. I went straight to Mr. Reyes while Justin waited in the Accord by Smoker's Corner. They knew the car, and he was specifically told not to be at the school, so the curb out front wasn't an option. Mr. Reyes had heard— who hadn't?—about the fight and the expulsion. He came right out with me to see Justin.

"What happened?" he asked when he saw Justin's face. "That can't be from the fight. I heard Drew only got in one good hit; that's not from him."

"Door," Justin answered looking straight into Mr. Reyes eyes with his one good one. He didn't even try to make it sound convincing. Mr. Reyes didn't buy it for a minute; I could tell that by the look on his face. But I also saw that it didn't matter. Justin was eighteen; no one would do anything. We all three knew that.

"What do I do now? Don't tell me school. My school days are over."

"How about a GED?"

"All due respect, Mr. Reyes, I need a job. I have to pay my dad three hundred dollars for rent or they said I can't stay there anymore." He paused, trying to figure out the way to say it right. He looked toward me, then at Mr. Reyes. "I can't leave her there alone. You know what I'm saying? I need a job."

Mr. Reyes sighed, lowered his head, and rubbed his eyebrow with his thumbnail like he did in class when someone was acting up.

"I know a guy who'll give you a job . . . "

A wave of relief flooded over Justin's face, and I felt it hit me the exact same moment. Everything would be OK, I knew it.

" . . . but it comes with conditions."

"Anything, I swear," Justin promised through his smile, putting his hands together prayer-style.

"No more drinking; no more weed. No matter what, or you're out. He'll take you on my word, but he won't tolerate drugs or alcohol, and he'll test you."

"I'm done, now. Won't use again, I swear!"

"And..."

"Anything, Mr. Reyes; thank you so much!" Justin said.

"And you get your GED before I give you his number."

"What?! I can't! I have to have the money in two weeks; I need a job yesterday."

"You can make an appointment to take the test at the Training Center any day this week. You can go today even—they open at nine. It's gonna cost you fifty dollars to take the test. I can call them and let them know you'll pay them for it later."

"I can't take a test today. I'm failing all my classes; there's no way."

"Justin, you're one of the smartest students I've ever had. I know what you're capable of, and I have no doubt you can pass the test no problem."

"I don't think so."

"I do, and if not, you can study there for a day or two and learn what you need to pass. Go give it a try. Do you know where the Training Center is?"

"Yeah, over on Fulton Street, right?"

"Yep, that's the place. Go try the test; let them know I sent you over, and when you've got that paper in your hand, you let me know, and I'll give you the number."

"OK, I'll try, but what if I can't?"

"You can try again next week. That will give you seven days to study, and you'll knock it out of the park on that try for sure."

"Thanks, man."

"Anytime. I gotta get back to class."

"For sure. See ya."

We watched Mr. Reyes walk halfway up the block before he turned back and pointed directly at me, then at his watch, then at the school over his shoulder. We both knew what it meant: my butt better be in class when the bell rang. I smiled at him and gave him a cheesy thumbs-up. We watched him go the rest of the way up the street to the front steps of the school and disappear inside the old wooden doors.

"Haylee, you need to go."

"I know. Are you going to the place?"

"What else can I do?"

"You'll do great."

"I don't know—I haven't passed a test since like tenth grade."

"I know, but just think—this one has a job at the end of it. You can do it. You have to; you can't leave me."

"I know." He grabbed my face and pulled it to his. "I love you so much."

"I know. We'll be OK." The kiss was quick, but the hug lasted longer than the bell. I was late. I didn't care.

Justin studied that day but failed the test. It shook him up but Mr. Reyes let him come after school and studied with him for hours every night and he aced the test the very next week just like Mr. Reyes knew he could. He reminded Justin it was no diploma and strongly encouraged him to start taking college courses too to make himself look better on paper. Justin promised he would, and I think he meant it at the time. Then Mr. Reyes gave him the name of the man with the job: Raymundo Contreras, his uncle, and owner of a local tire store franchise called Treadmore Quickly.

Mr. Raymundo Contreras, or Coffee, as he insisted Justin call him, was a short, squat man who always had a tire rag in his back pocket; a thin, high-necked muscle shirt under his mechanic shirt; and grease on his hands. He was also a multimillionaire, though few people knew it. His hair was white, a stark contrast to his coffee colored skin that got him his nickname. He wore the undershirts to cover the old, fading gang tattoos he kept around to remind himself of where he came from and why he owed God his life. Coffee was the closest thing to a dad, grandpa, or brother Justin ever had. Other than Mr. Reyes, he was the first person who ever believed in Justin the way I did. He was the man who gave Justin hope.

Justin came home from his first day and took me out to the old shack to tell me about it.

"He's the coolest old guy I've ever met in my life, Haylee. He's going to put me to work in the tires first; he wants me to stock them and sell them. He says I have charisma, and charisma sells tires! He's going to give me a dollar for every ten dollars I sell—on top of a base pay! The sky's the limit—the more I sell, the more I make!"

He looked like an angel—an angel who had just gotten his face pummeled. But he was so happy and hopeful, I could see the future in his eyes again.

"I told him I had to pay my dad three hundred dollars by the first or I was out, and he gave me the money! Look." Justin pulled three crisp hundred-dollar bills from his wallet. In all my life I had never seen that much money at once. Clayton got paid with checks, and my mom got her disability check, but I'd never seen that much cash. I couldn't imagine what they would do with it—probably stock the bar—but it didn't matter. Justin could stay.

"I told him how Clayton is," he said quietly.

"What?! Why?"

"I don't know; it just came out. I told him I couldn't leave you here alone, and when he asked why, I told him everything."

"What did he say?"

"That his old man was the same way..." Justin stopped talking. As his eyes pooled with tears, he put his head down, letting them drop out, straight onto the ground, and whispered, "and that I don't have to be like him."

I've only seen Justin cry once in my life, and it was that day. He couldn't hold in the tears. All our life, all those years, he thought no matter how hard he tried to be different he wasn't ever going to be anything but a little Clayton. He hated it, but accepted it more than I even realized, and Coffee had said the magic words even I had never said to Justin.

"I don't have to be like him, Haylee; I don't."

"I know you don't, babe. You're not anything like him—you know that, right?"

He sniffled. "No. I look in the mirror, and all I see is his face. I hear him when I yell. It scares me, Haylee. But I don't have to be like that! I can be my own man."

"I know you can."

"Coffee told me to wait to give them the money until the first, so I have to hang onto it until then."

"Don't spend it."

"No way. It's gonna keep me here, by you." As he kissed the top of my head, his smile lifted my soul. Everything was going to be OK.

CHAPTER 8

THAT WAS IT—IT WAS ALL OK. We were going to make it until I was old enough then we were going to ditch them and live happily ever after. I knew it. Life became routine and manageable, until the day it wasn't. In the mornings Justin left for work a little after Clayton did, and often he didn't get home until after dark. He was a grunt for Coffee, but he didn't mind; he liked the work and Coffee was right—he was a great salesman. I think, too, he liked being gone because he didn't have to deal with Mom and Clayton. He wanted to be there for me, and at night and in the morning after Clayton left, he was—but it was good for him to be anywhere but home. It was good for both of us.

Justin kept his word to Mr. Reyes too: he didn't drink or smoke anymore. Like everything he set his mind to, Justin decided to be done, and he stuck with it. Clayton was pissed about that more than anything. I didn't understand why. I mostly quit too, but I was a sucker for whiskey and Coke on a Friday night after a hard week at school, so I admit I still got hammered plenty of times. Justin never made me feel bad for it, but he never caved. His mind was made up, and he wouldn't change it for anything or anyone, not even me.

I think that's when I kind of knew how Mom and Clayton must have felt. I felt like he secretly thought he was better than me because he could say no and I still wanted to drink. The worst part was knowing he was saying no so he could stay with me and I wouldn't quit. I felt like a failure, like he must be disappointed in me but wasn't saying it out loud. It made me mad at him sometimes, and I don't remember being mad at him before that even once in my life. It scared me, but I didn't know what the feeling was or how to say anything about it, so I didn't.

He was also getting stronger, and that pissed Clayton off—or maybe he was scared too, and his fear—like mine—manifested itself as anger. I think if Justin hadn't been paying them rent Clayton would have kicked him out just out of spite, but he liked the money. He still yelled at Justin and took swings now and then, but I think he was afraid he might be the loser if he pushed Justin too far, so he stuck to yelling more than hitting. I knew it was bound to happen and waited for the day they would come to blows and Justin would come out on top.

The time did come, but Justin figured out a way to beat Clayton at his own game without a real fight in order to save Clayton the slightest bit of dignity. I don't know why he did that, why he cared at all. If it were me, after all the years of Clayton's fists in my gut, I'd have pummeled him and not cared about how it made him feel. But Justin had enough love for his dad to make the point—and make it well—but spare him a beat-down.

It was a normal Friday night at home: I was having fun getting smashed, and since he had nowhere better to be, Justin was down there in the living room with us. He was back to playing his guitar all the time. While we all got more drunk and high, he sat and played his guitar with the music, getting better at his craft, serenading our sorry souls. Then out of the blue when the song he was playing finished, he called out Adrian, one of Clayton's friends. It wasn't a fight he was looking for, but he was going to prove to everyone that he was stronger and better than his Old Man.

Justin's job was physical: he mounted and balanced and lifted tires all day long, which meant he was constantly building up his body. He was strong before, but in the few months he had been working he had honed his strength. He was younger than all the guys there that night by at least a dozen years, and he wasn't drunk. It was his moment to assert himself as the Alpha male, and Adrian was so wasted he walked right into it, no questions asked.

When Clayton wasn't looking, Justin flashed me a knowing look. I knew then he had a plan. I had to watch it play out. He told me later that he waited patiently for the right night, the right party, and the perfect moment. He was patient like that, never rushing anything to happen sooner than it was supposed to. His goal was to beat Clayton—to let him know once and for all who was stronger, who was the boss. It would have been too obvious if he came out and challenged Clayton outright; it would be far better to pretend it was all in fun and then humiliate him in front of his buddies. And so that's exactly what Justin did.

"Hey man, arm wrestle me!" He put his guitar down and chest-bumped Adrian.

"Think you can take me, huh boy?"

"That's right, check out these guns," Justin said pulling up his sleeve and flexing like a goober. He was joking around, keeping it light-hearted, but I was impressed with the definition and bulk. He looked good. I wanted to touch him; I wondered when he had bulked up and how I had missed it. Then I remembered, we were never alone anymore; I hardly touched him or saw him enough to know how much he was changing, inside and out.

"Alright, but don't cry," Adrian answered.

"Not a chance."

The men moved into the kitchen and took sides around our tiny table we never ate at. They pushed the bills and newspapers to the side and then the match was on. There was the grip, then the "GO!" and we all watched.

If I hadn't known Justin the way I did, I wouldn't have known he was faking it. I don't know if Clayton knew or if my mom could tell, but I could. He pretended to fight, made it look like a struggle, and slowly, slowly, his hand fell closer and closer to the table. He didn't make it a super easy fight— Adrian was straining—but I knew Justin let him win. He played it up, too.

"Oh man, no way!" he said jumping up from the chair, "No way! I want a rematch. Let's go again!"

"Fight the loser of the next match," Adrian answered, nodding to Cameron, another of Clayton's buddies, over.

It was turning into a pissing match, just like Justin wanted. He sat back and let it play out. Cam beat Adrian, but instead of letting Justin wrestle him again, Cam faced off with Luke. Cam won, and Clayton took him on. It was a tough match, Cam was a scrapper, but in the end Clayton won, as he nearly always did. He stood up and flexed, and then Justin sprang up.

"How about you and me, Old Man?" he challenged Clayton with a nod of his head. I can't explain it— the music was blaring again, but when Justin threw down the challenge, silence hung around us all. A fire blazed in his eyes—a fire kindled long ago, now stoked and raging—and it would not be quenched without a duel. The air grew thick; tension wrapped its tentacles around the room in invisible swooshing swirls that rivaled the blue-smoke haze hovering potently in the air.

"You were out first round, Son; I don't think so," Clayton answered, eyes locked into those of his grown son. He stood taller than normal, chest puffed out, asserting his dominance, but he shifted slightly to the left, then right, like the drunk he was. He was caught in his intoxication this time, too stupid to know Justin could tell he was too far gone to put up a real fight, too clueless to realize his son had planned this moment for years—the moment Clayton would lose his power, and there was nothing he could do about it. He was too drunk, too out of shape, too old to compete with Justin ever again.

"You afraid?" Justin asked back, the slightest hint of a smirk on his lips. I loved that smirk; Clayton usually yelled at him when he saw it. "Wrestle me," Justin demanded.

The challenge lingered in the air like the last note plucked on a string. By then everyone knew it was more than a wrestling match that was about to go down. Clayton was stuck with only two options, and I knew he would lose either way. He was a fighter, so to back down from the challenge meant Justin automatically won, but to take him on and lose meant his son was stronger than he was, and everyone would know his reign of terror was over. In my mind, the possibility Clayton could win was slim.

Apparently, Clayton thought more highly of himself than I did, though. He took Justin on. Venom—and maybe admiration—passed between them; neither took his eyes off the other. The years, the anger, the abuse were all on the line.

Justin's smirk twisted into a half-crooked smile; he moved to the table to sit across from Clayton when he saw the Old Man lower himself back into the chair. Justin already knew he would win. Clayton showed no fear; he didn't look like he knew it, but he was about to lose. I knew it. I felt it in my bones. Maybe the whole room knew it. Justin had to win.

The grip was hard and fierce. Justin had perfected his technique—a squeeze that set his opponent off from the start.

Adrian called the "GO!"

The match was on.

Not that it was a match at all. It was apparent in a second that Justin had let Adrian, who was out in the second round, win. He arced Clayton's hand over and almost down to the table within the first two seconds. I saw it in Clayton's eyes—shock and awe as he looked at Justin. His son had become a man, and he had missed it, like I had. I bet he wondered what happened to the boy he had beaten to a pulp just four months before.

But Justin wasn't interested in putting him down quickly; he wanted to make it clear who was the stronger man. Justin let Clayton take their arms up again, nearly perpendicular with the table, and then he pushed Clayton's hand down again, almost to touching, but up enough to give Clayton a shred of hope to come back. His arm was tired. We all saw Clayton shaking. Sweat beaded on his forehead; his left hand went to grab the edge of the table for leverage.

Justin saw the desperate move. "Go ahead," he egged on, looking down for the slightest second to acknowledge Clayton's grip on the table. "Do it. It won't help you. I'm going to win." Then he locked eyes with Clayton again. Justin wasn't shaking at all. He was putting out effort, but nothing near his father's. He even had the nerve to look over at the other guys and joke.

"How long should I hold him here?" he smiled effortlessly. They didn't answer. It wasn't funny. It never had been. It was something they all dreaded—the day their power was threatened and their own sons were stronger, faster, and better than them.

Justin let Clayton up yet again and even let Clayton tilt his arm toward the table, but then, in the flash of a second, he pushed Clayton's hand back up and over and down and SLAM!

It was over.

Justin won.

He stood up and did what any good man would do: extended his hand to the loser. Clayton was had. His dominance was over; he no longer had the power to control us physically, and he knew it. We were free. Justin had saved us.

They shook. It was a silent truce. Justin would let Clayton keep his place as head of the house as long as Clayton would keep his fists off Justin and his rage away from our faces.

It wasn't his strength alone that was developing; a lot of things about Justin changed after he started working for Coffee. He grew up, he was different. He had his dream back and more.

He was going to fly, and he had a focus and a drive I'd never seen in him before. His dream turned into a written plan he posted on his bedroom wall where he could see it every morning when he woke up. He was capable of working out the details now that he was an adult, and he started to notch them away one by one. He was going to join the Air Force, but not yet—that was like number three or four on the list. He needed to wait for that. He needed time and money to get some college credits so he looked better for the recruiter—and he needed to wait until I was older. I know there was more to it than just me; I could see it on his list. But I felt like I was the thing between him and enlisting. I felt like he put off his plan so I wouldn't be alone, but he talked about it openly in the house, and there was nothing Clayton could do to deter him now that he was beaten.

Justin pushed me to do better in school, and I really wanted to try for his sake. I gave it my best effort, but just because he suddenly had Coffee to guide him didn't mean I felt the hope too. While he was succeeding, my life was still as bad as ever, and in some ways worse. For one, I hardly saw him because he worked so much. He was never home. We used to have the morning rides to school together, plus after-school and weekend laziness—not to mention all the times we skipped school together. None of that was available now. Between work and the college classes he started taking at the beginning of my sophomore year, he was gone all the time, and I was left to take Clayton's lectures and Mom's alcoholism myself.

Lizzie wasn't a comfort anymore either. She too had taken steps to better herself. I wondered sometimes if Justin should have chosen her to love instead of me; she was obviously the better of the two of us. She didn't want to come home with me—without Justin as a buffer it was worse: the yelling and accusing and Clayton-ness of it all. Eventually we only hung out at school, then only in JAG class, and ultimately we barely spoke. It wasn't like we weren't friends; but when we talked, we didn't have anything in common anymore.

Lizzie was staying with ShamRae, her popular, rich, classy friend with soft-hearted parents who gave her anything she wanted. What she wanted was for Lizzie to stay with her, so Lizzie moved in. I was invited over a couple times, but it was too perfect for the likes of me. They mowed their lawn in pretty diagonal rows, their couch wasn't ragged or torn up, their fridge had plenty of food, and they had pictures on their walls just like Gramma Diaz, a sore reminder that I was the different one, not them. I didn't fit there, and I knew it was better for Lizzie if I drifted away, so I did. Our lives were more different than they had ever been. She was made for a house with happy pictures in shiny frames; I was made for a raggedy couch and weekend ragers.

What was worse than my two best friends making their own ways in life and leaving me in my pit of despair was that I never had anyone else. I never made even one other single friend. For a while when we were lots younger, Mom and Clayton's friends would bring their kids over, but they were never part of us. They were kids to play with, not friends. We were the Three Musketeers. It was always and only been Justin and Lizzie and me. Now that they were both gone, I was alone, and I had no one to tell about it.

If that wasn't bad enough, it got worse for me and Justin, not better. When we could be together, which was hardly ever, we had to be extra careful around the house to avoid Clayton freaking. Just because Justin proved he was stronger didn't mean we were free to let our feelings be known. There was more danger now because we both knew Clayton could kick Justin out for any reason he wanted, and then I would really be alone.

The only time we had together to be us was when Mom and Clayton went out and stayed out for the weekend, but we never knew which weekend they were going to the bar and coming back sometime in the night and which weekends they wouldn't come home. When I was a kid it seemed like their disappearing acts were few and far between, but age taught me otherwise. They were gone at least one weekend a month, and in the summer usually more. All their friends liked Cam's house—it was even more secluded than our place, and I heard they had bonfires and crazy, good adult fun out there. Only on those rare Saturdays when they didn't come home *and* Justin didn't work could we enjoy being together.

That was the only time I felt happy. When they stayed gone, Justin would come home greasy and tired but just as happy to be alone with me as I was with him. He would come in and kiss me—tall, strong, and smelling of tires and Eternity. He would shave and shower away the work of the day, and while he cleaned himself up I would get dinner ready. He usually brought home a prepackaged meal from the store like lasagna or Hamburger Helper, but other times I'd make something from scratch. I played house, pretending we didn't have a care in the world. We were too old anymore for baby make-believe adventures, but I think he liked to pretend it was still us against the world too.

We would eat at the table together like families are supposed to and wash dishes together, not because it was a corny bonding thing but so the parents wouldn't guess we were cooking fancy dinners when they were gone. Afterward, we'd sit together on the old blood and dirt-stained couch and cuddle, his arms wrapped tightly around me, pulling me right into his soul. I never felt safer than in his arms. I still don't.

Even with things changing so much, some things stayed the same. Justin still loved science and sci-fi, so we mostly watched *Star Trek* or rented videos about space and time travel. Every so often he would play the guitar all night or read out loud the way he used to when we were younger. He was always reading but I think he read even more after starting college. His taste was expanding and refining too. When we were little he only had eyes for sci-fi novels from the greats and not-so-greats, but he started to read about real things and people too: Chuck Yeager, WWII fighter pilots, NASA space missions, John Glenn, Neil Armstrong, Air Force requirements and missions. To be honest, I missed the books we used to read, but it didn't really matter because I could listen to him read a car manual and be happy. I'd lie there in his lap looking up at his perfect face while he read. Sometimes I missed the context of what he was reading, but I never forgot the way his lips moved or how his index finger, stained from his greasy work, caressed the page when it was a good part.

Even when Mom and Clayton were gone, we never spent the nights together, it was still too much of a risk. But there were plenty of times we fell asleep, locked in each other's arms, on the couch. If I woke up in the middle of the night, I stayed as close to him as I could and tried not to wake him. I listened to his heart beat strong and steady, felt his rhythmic breaths, mimicked them with my own until I fell back asleep. If he was the one to wake before morning, it was different. Justin would take me to bed, kiss me good night, and walk away to sleep in his own room, leaving me alone, waiting for what he promised would come when the time was right. It would have been easy for us to take things further, and it would have happened if Justin were any other kind of guy. But he wasn't. He insisted that I still wasn't ready. I wasn't—I know that now—but at the time I wanted him desperately. All he would ever allow was what he was strong enough to control.

We had fully clothed make-out sessions every time he was home and they were gone. They left me wondering and wanting to know what he would feel like moving inside me and not just on top. But we never dared to take anything off except his shirt—partly because of Justin's rules and also because if we did and the parents came home we'd be dead meat for sure, and we never knew when they would show up. Sometimes, when they were gone, I attacked him as soon as he got in the door. The uniform shirt he wore with his name embroidered on it never stayed tucked in for long. I would unbutton the buttons and push it off his shoulders and sneak my hands up under his T-shirt and pull it up and off and trail my hands down his sides and abs. He was toned, ripped, so good to look at by then. Sometimes he stood there letting me kiss his lips and his neck and his chest while I touched him, feeling him under my fingertips in all the ways I wanted to.

When I pushed for more than he would allow, he would take over, moving my hands, my face, my body where and how he wanted, telling me what I could and couldn't do and finding little ways to give me the release I needed without crossing his lines. I obeyed and followed his lead.

His hands, too, liked to find their way under my shirt to touch my bare flesh. He would push my shirt up and my bra down but never took them off—just in case they came home. It saved us more times than I can say. Sometimes we didn't even know they were home until we heard Clayton's truck doors slam shut. There's no way I would have had time to pull my shirt back on, let alone redo my bra. He could justify his being off if it was hot enough, but there would be no explanation to appease Clayton for mine being off. And anyway, I didn't want Clayton to have the chance to see me shirtless.

We always kept the TV on or his guitar nearby so we looked like we were doing something else, too. They were necessary precautions, but they didn't keep his hands from having their way with me. Justin especially liked the curve at my hips right at my waist and would tease me there and make me crazy. His thumbs crept down inside my jeans enough to make me catch my breath and press into him harder.

Our eyes closed when we kissed, but when we touched we liked to watch each other—eyes meeting eyes, souls intertwining, speaking our love without words. I was never timid or afraid with him, nor was he with me. We belonged to each other: he was mine to look at, to touch, to love and arouse and desire. In the same way, I was his.

I wanted him to see me and know me, know how his hands and mouth could work me into a frenzy. But whenever a groan escaped from his throat, I knew it was over. That was the line he would not cross, for if he did, all his strength to wait would be lost. Sometimes he let it out when he was touching me and I hadn't even done anything to him; most of the time it was when I pushed him too far, which I learned to be careful about. It was a primal sound I learned to love and hate all at the same time—guttural and low, the last bit of his strength to restrain our passions in one breath. It was never a harsh rejection but more of a stoic acceptance of what must be done, what he had to do. He would let me go gently, sit up or stand up, and close his eyes and breathe in deeply—inhaling reason, reality, and rationality, stretching his arms up high into the sky, exhaling the urges he would not fulfill. By then I knew better than to question or beg, but I did get good at holding him at bay as long as I could to make our time together last longer.

And that was how my life went. My worst times and best times were in that house. Other than an occasional movie or dinner at Skippers, we didn't really go out that much, even when Mom and Clayton were gone. It suited me fine because it meant Justin and I could be close and tempt fate.

I think it was more about the money for Justin than the making-out though. He had a plan for every cent of it— *our* plan—and the sooner we saved it all up the better. He said he would work and save and get me out of the house, and that's what he was doing. Mr. Reyes told him about the financial aid office at the community college, and they helped him find grants for most of his school expenses. So except for food, gas, and the rent Mom and Clayton made him pay (and books he couldn't keep from buying), he saved all his money and grew his stash in secret. He had it in a bank where Mom and Clayton couldn't touch it, and he was so proud to watch it accumulate.

In six months he managed to save over a thousand dollars. He had his bank statements sent to Coffee's house and would bring them home to show me. "I'm going to get us out of here, Haylee," he would say and flick the paper proudly. I knew he would, and I couldn't wait for the day we could walk out that door and never have to depend on Mom or Clayton ever again.

Then my mom died, and everything changed again.

CHAPTER 9

I CAME HOME FROM SCHOOL ONE DAY and my mom, as usual, was passed out on the couch. It was nothing new; I'd seen her like that a million times before. I ignored her, grabbed something to eat from the fridge, and went straight to my room.

My radio was playing Blind Melon's happily, depressing song "No Rain" when Clayton pulled into the driveway a couple hours later. I had a test the next day in my science class, and I wanted to make Justin proud with a good grade, so I was intermittently working on a study guide between painting my nails and daydreaming to my favorite songs. I can't remember what day of the week it was, but I don't think it was a Monday. It doesn't matter. The point is that my mom wasn't passed out; she was stone cold dead.

Gone, just like when Justin's mom, Karina left all those years before. No note, no goodbye, no hint she was leaving, just plain dead. The only difference was I had no hope she would ever get better and come back.

Real death isn't like in the movies. It never felt real to me when I saw someone dead on TV. I could watch the actors on the screen and feel their grief, but somewhere in the back of my mind I knew it wasn't real and that they were being paid to pretend to be dead; their lives were going to go on when the movie was over. That's not the way it was when she died. When Mom died she was dead, for real. She didn't come back; she didn't get revived. She was gone, and I knew she would never be alive again.

Clayton screamed. It's all he knew how to do. He screamed for me to come downstairs, he screamed into the phone when he called 911, he even screamed at my dead mother on the couch to wake up—which of course she wasn't going to do, no matter how loudly he screamed.

Then he cried.

I couldn't shed a single tear. I stood there like a statue with half the fingers on my left hand painted chocolate brown, staring at her lifeless body, and not one single tear came out.

Clayton's cry turned to bellowing. Somewhere deep down inside he must have loved her. I thought back on their times together. I remembered the hugs, kisses, and butt pats I had tried to ignore. I remembered that they went out together a lot. So what if it was to party and get high? They were together all the time, except for when he was working, like Justin and me. I realized Clayton had just lost his mate. The fights, the hatred they would spit at each other during their bouts, the poverty they shrouded themselves in—none of it mattered. He was a broken man who had just lost his lover.

The ambulance came, the coroner, the body bag. I saw them looking around uncomfortably when they came into the house. We tried to keep it clean for Clayton's sake, but it was not the Plaza Hotel. Our furniture—all of it—was old, beat-up, and nasty. The man who painted walls for a living made us keep them free of dirt, but the house itself was falling apart and in need of repair. We had no handy men or maids to come in and make our place look nice, and with pathetic, ungrateful kids like us who never helped out, it had slowly deteriorated over time. I was so used to it I didn't see how bad it was until I looked at it through their eyes. I was suddenly self-conscious of the filth in the same way Lizzie was of her mom's messy apartment. I thought ours was the good house, but their furtive glances told me otherwise: we were just as bad.

The coroner's report said it was a massive heart attack. They tested her system, and no surprise to us, her blood alcohol level was something like six times the legal limit. They found traces of other drugs in there. too.

I never knew how much life my worthless, alcoholic mother brought to our house until she was dead. Without her, the curtains didn't open in the morning; dishes didn't get done, and the laundry didn't either. Without her, there was no one to greet Clayton when he came home with an ice cold beer. There were no nagging jokes about how stupid we all were that we could laugh at uneasily. It was quiet, bare, and lifeless.

All that was left was Clayton. And all he had inside him was a mountain of grief that turned to anger quicker than I could get away from him when I saw it coming. He cried, then yelled; yelled, then cried. When Justin wasn't home I did my best to hide out in my room and avoid him at all costs.

I used my mom's death as an excuse to skip a week and a half of school. We had her funeral on a weekend, I'm pretty sure, but those days all blur together for me. My mom had a sister, Aerin, who lived in a town a few hours away from Seattle, Washington. All Mom had ever said about her was that she thought she was better than us. Mom said that about anyone who could hold a job. I didn't take her too seriously until I met Aunt Aerin myself at the funeral.

Mom's funeral was a sorry affair; for all the times my mom called me pathetic, she was the one who really was. There were exactly fourteen people at her funeral if you counted the director from the funeral home and the minister we got from the Diaz's church for a $50 donation. Lizzie came; so did Brenda. I still couldn't cry. My mom was gone, and I took it all in stride, like it was just another day.

At the time I thought it was because I had no love for my mom. But I know now that's not the case at all. I loved my mother; I only wish she had been a better mom. I try to remember the good times, like when she danced with Lizzie and me, and how she tried to make Justin feel better when Karina would take off. She had a beautiful singing voice, like a real star. I should have listened more when she sang. Back then it was annoying to me, but now I regret not listening to her more. I should have asked to fix her hair, too. A lot of girls do that to their mothers; I should have done that. Whatever—she's gone now, and it's too late. *Accept the things I cannot change.*

Aunt Aerin saw me and smiled. I stared at her, stunned because she was thin, she looked more like me than my own mother, right down to the straight, light brown hair, only hers was graying, and her blue-grey eyes were darker around the edges than my own. I knew who she was as soon as she walked in the glass doors. She went first to Clayton and tried to hug him. He stood stiff as a board and then started to cry again. She patted him on the shoulder and put her head to the side like she really cared. I wondered why, if she cared, she had never been to see us before. It was like my mom had said: she thought she was better than all of us. She certainly looked the part. She was wearing a knee-length, A-line black skirt with a dumb ruffly button-up shirt with three-quarter-length sleeves. She didn't fit in with our kind of people; half of us were wearing our best jeans and whatever black thing we could find. I resented her for being there and hated her before she said one word to me. I saw Clayton point me out to her and tried to pretend I didn't notice.

"Oh man, here she comes, let's get out of here," I said to Justin and Lizzie who were congregating with me in the back of the viewing room.

"Don't you want to meet her?" Lizzie asked.

"No, why would I?"

But I didn't leave. I stood there as she approached. I wished for all the world that I could hold Justin's hand. It was like he knew because he put his hand on my shoulder reassuringly but in a way that looked strictly platonic.

"You must be Haylee," she said with pity in her eyes. Her voice was too sweet and sing-songy, not at all raspy like my moms, but I couldn't get over how much her face looked like mine and what my mother's had been before the weight deformed her features. I wanted to hate her, but I wanted to hear what she had to say even more.

"Yeah, so?" I shrugged and crossed my arms.

"Oh, honey, I'm so sorry for your loss. I can't even imagine what you're going through." She hugged me in her bony arms, which were surprisingly strong for as little as she seemed.

"It's whatever; people die every day."

My answer shocked her. She pushed me back to arm's length and held me at my shoulders, looking straight into my eyes like she was searching to see if I had a soul. It was awkward. I looked away, glancing down, but then I caught her eyes again.

"Do you need to talk to someone? I talked to your dad."

"He's not my dad."

"Sorry, I thought he and your mom —"

"He was my mom's man," I interrupted. "He was never my dad. You would know if you ever had anything to do with my life, but you haven't, have you?"

All the anger in me came out at her. People stared, and I didn't even care like I normally would if all eyes were on me.

"You think you can come down here after being an invisible sister and aunt all these years and it's going to magically be OK? You think I'm going to jump into your arms and say, 'Oh, Auntie, thank you so much for taking time out of your fancy, rich life to be here with us now that my mom's dead'? It ain't gonna happen. You've never been here. You've never lived our life. You have no right to be here now. Peace! I'm out."

I looked to Clayton with a nod to let him know I was done mourning and took off out the doors of the funeral home. Justin and Lizzie followed.

"What was that?" Justin asked, pulling me back by the shoulder to slow me down once we were outside.

"What? She's got no right showing up here like that! Did you see how she was dressed? She's got money, and what's she ever done for us? I bet that BMW is hers," I said, pointing to a sleek black newer model in the parking lot next to Luke's pick-up.

"It's probably a rental, since she flew in to be here," Lizzie answered. "You should go easy on her."

"Why? She don't care. She never has."

"How do you know that?"

"Have you ever seen her in my life? Was she there when we got the power shut off when Clayton was out of work that one winter? Was she there when me and Justin stood in line at the food bank? NO! She was in her million-dollar condo, or wherever she lives, eating turkey!"

"Turkey?" Justin grinned. He was trying to calm me down.

"I don't know. Whatever rich people eat."

"You just need to chill."

"How am I supposed to chill? My mom is dead. My *mom* is dead! How do you chill out about that?"

And then they came; the tears poured out. I finally cried for my mom.

Justin took me in his arms, cradling my head in one hand while the other wrapped around me. Lizzie grabbed onto the both of us and rubbed my back while cooing to me that she was so sorry. She cried too.

It was early spring, the time of year when things come to life, and my mother was dead. It wasn't fair, and I cried out of the unfairness of it all until I was hoarse. It was still cold enough outside that I was uncomfortable without a jacket. For a while it didn't matter. I stood there in their embrace and let the tears fall. But eventually, even with the two of them wrapped around me, I got too cold to stay like that, and I was tired and embarrassed.

"I just want to go home," I said, and that's where Justin took me.

I didn't see Aunt Aerin after that until I went to live with her two months later.

After the funeral I tried to fill my mom's shoes the best I could. I became the one who opened the blinds in the morning and washed the plates and did the laundry, and I was the one who was drinking way too much. Usually I was drunk by the time Justin and Clayton came home. My mom would have been so proud. I couldn't help it; I had no reason to go on. As soon as I thought about her not being there, I'd hit the bar. In my mind, it was better than crying. I didn't think Clayton would notice, and I didn't bother to tell Justin. I screened the answering machine for calls from my school so neither of them would know I was skipping as much as I was, and I made sure I was in bed before either of them got home for the day.

After that first week and a half off I tried to go back to school, but I was so far behind it was overwhelming. I couldn't keep up—or catch up. Mr. Reyes tried to help me. He would let me come into his room to work on stuff, but I was too behind, and he was too busy to be my personal tutor.

"I'm sorry, Haylee, but I can't do this for you. You have to try."

"I am trying."

"I know you think you are, but you've let yourself go since your mother died. What work are you doing at home? This is the same place you finished working yesterday. Is everything OK at home? Is Clayton. . . hurting you?"

I looked up at him but didn't answer. I didn't want to talk about home. "No, everything's fine. He's cool; Justin keeps him in line."

It was probably too much to say to a teacher. But the truth was that Clayton wasn't a threat anymore. How he managed to keep his job, I don't know, but he and I were doing the same thing: waking, drinking, sleeping. We could hear him cry at night, and I really didn't get it. I thought he couldn't stand my mom, but apparently, he loved her and missed her.

Sipe called me into her office a little while after I started going back to school. She wanted to talk about how things were going for me at home. I had nothing to say. "We're fine, considering my mom just died and all."

"Clayton isn't your father, is he?"

"No, why?"

"I'm trying to figure out the dynamic in your home now that your mother's gone."

I didn't know what *"dynamic in your home"* meant.

"Does Justin still live in the house?"

"Yeah, but why do you need to know all this stuff?"

"Because we don't have a legal guardian on file for you anymore. Who takes care of you?"

"Me."

"When was the last time you went to the doctor, Haylee?"

"I don't know."

"How about the dentist? When did you go to the dentist last?"

"I have good teeth; I don't need to go." That was a lie—I had one tooth that hurt when I ate sugar—but I felt like I was being interrogated and something bad was about to happen.

"Has your step-dad ever hit you or Justin?"

Danger sirens were going off in my head. Principals didn't ask that stuff, and kids from bad homes didn't answer those kinds of questions.

"He's not my step-dad. Don't you even listen to your own questions? Is there even a point to this?"

"Yes. We need to have a guardian on file for you, and we don't have one."

"Then why didn't you ask me that? You were asking me if Clayton hits me. Not even the same thing. I'm out of here." I stood quickly, shoving the chair back in the process.

I took off out the wooden doors and walked home. That was a really dumb idea because we lived ten miles away. It was after five before I got home.

"Where were you?" Clayton bellowed.

"Does it matter? You're not my dad; what do you care?"

"Who do you think has raised you all these years? You better believe I am!"

"Well then, *dad*, it's none of your business where I've been. How do you like that?"

"Don't tell me it's none of my business! You been whoring around town?"

"Yeah, that's exactly it," I said.

"I see you, making eyes at everyone. I see."

"You see nothing, Old Man, nothing! 'Cause that's not what I'm doing."

"You think I'm a fool?"

I walked over to the bar ignoring him, and grabbed the Johnnie Walker—partly to drown the sorrows of another day and partly to divert him to something other than who I was with.

I think at first I enjoyed the argument. It brought back a sense of normalcy that I didn't know I craved. In a sick way, I liked it when he yelled at me—it had been weeks since I felt the warm spray of his spit on my face. It was normal, predictable, and I wanted to get back to real life, none of this crying from Clayton or questioning from Sipe.

"What do you think you're doing? You ain't drinking my liquor; what do you do to contribute around here?"

"I can drink if I want to; you can't do anything about it, Old Man."

It was a challenge. I stood up to him. Justin might be able to prove he had more power with an arm wrestling match, but I had ways of my own, and I was about to pull them out of my pocket. Clayton came toward me. "Oh, yes I can." He reached for the bottle to take it from me. All I meant to do was move the bottle out of his reach, but I was too slow, and it hit him in the face while I tried to keep it from him. Rage and anger flashed on his face. Justin wasn't home to protect me, and my dead mother wouldn't have done anything even if she was still alive. All I had were the words I had rehearsed for years in my head.

"What are you going to do?" I asked coolly. "You gonna hit me? Go ahead, hit me!" I yelled, inching into his face. "One hit and you're in jail, and you know it!"

"And if I go to jail, where you gonna go? You ain't got nowhere to go. You ain't got no one." I hadn't thought about that. I braced for the impact, but it never came. He pulled the bottle out of my hand and yelled into my face. He had me backed up to the bar as far as I could go and kept pressing into me. He was touching me, his chest to my chest, his legs straddling one of mine, he was so on me that I couldn't think of anything else. I wanted to get away, but I was no match for him. I tried to turn first to the left then to the right to get away, but he held me there and screamed out his rage and suspicions.

He grabbed my neck, squeezing and lifting under my jaw until I felt like my head would pop off—but I could still breathe, so I don't think he meant to kill me. He squeezed and pushed into me harder.

"If it wasn't for me, you'd be on the streets right now! I see you all the time; you think I don't notice, but I do. How many of my buddies you been with? How many of those boys at school?" Then his grip got tighter and I couldn't breathe. I panicked and grabbed his arm with both of my hands and tried to push him away, but he was too strong; I couldn't move him.

"You got nowhere to go, and you know it, and you think you can tell me what you're going to do in *my house*? You want to stay here? You want a roof over your head?"

I was frozen. I couldn't breathe. But mostly I couldn't get my mind off the fact that he was touching me—everywhere—and accusing me of things like that, and I couldn't get away. I turned to try to get away, but he kept me pinned beneath his weight. Finally he let go of my neck. His hand slid lower, toward my chest, but he still held me fast against the bar, the edge of it cutting into my back. I breathed in deeply—oxygen had never felt so good going into my lungs. I looked at him, terrified of what would happen next. His hand rested just above my right breast, then inched down a little lower.

"I didn't ask you for nothing after your mom died! I just let you stay. Do you want to stay here?"

I didn't know how to answer. I had nowhere else to go, and we both knew it. If I said yes, I was afraid of what he would ask for. If I said no, I was sure he'd tell me to leave in a heartbeat. I didn't know if Justin had enough for us to leave yet; I didn't know how we could do it. I was frozen with fear.

He smiled a horrible, triumphant smile.

"You ain't got nowhere else to go, do you? *Do you*?!"

"No, I don't. Is that what you want me to say? Get off me!" I tried to push him away, but he pressed against me harder. I couldn't believe it was possible; I felt like the edge of the bar was going to slice me in half as it was. I was no match for him. We both knew it. I didn't know what he would do with me. He had always called me a whore and a tease, but they were just names he used to call me until that evening. That night he was using them too much—and touching me, moving his hand lower. I was afraid, but surely he wouldn't do anything like *that*. Justin would be home soon, and he had to know I'd tell if he did. I didn't think he would dare, but that was all I could think about.

I didn't want to, but I started to cry. There were no sobs, only tears that spilled out because I couldn't control them.

He grabbed me by my neck again, I was grateful, I preferred his hand choking the life out of me to the alternative. This time, though, he twisted my face so I had to look at him. He stared at me hard. I saw the thrill he was getting from being in charge of me like that. I felt it too. I didn't look away; I stared right back, hoping my eyes showed him my feelings. I wanted him to know that I hated him.

"I'm gonna let you stay, but you're going to start contributing around here, you understand me?"

I couldn't answer. I didn't know what kind of contributions he expected. He interpreted it as insubordination and squeezed, constricting my airway again. "I said, you're going to do your part around here; you got it?"

"Yes!" The tears were pouring down my cheeks. I was shaking from the adrenaline. Then he shoved me back into the bar, rattling the glass. He stepped back and slapped me hard across my face. Spots danced in front of my eyes. It stung the tears away and split my lip. I tasted my blood; sharp and metallic, and resisted the urge to spit it on him. Relief. He was off of me. At least it wasn't a punch; he could have dropped me with one hit, I'm sure.

The first thing I noticed was that it was cold. He had been up on me for so long that his body heat had consumed me. I was cold when he came off, which did not help my adrenaline shakes.

Clayton must have felt bad about the whole thing because he gave me back the bottle. After all of that, he gave it to me like nothing.

"You owe me," was all he said as he handed it over by the neck.

I grabbed it and retreated to my room for the rest of the night. I didn't drink the Johnnie either; it was evil. If I drank it I would owe Clayton something, and I was afraid I knew what he would expect.

Justin snuck into my room later that night. Since my mom died he had come in several times like that. He would always stay on top of the covers but would pull me into his arms and hold me until I fell asleep. When he came in that night I started crying like a baby. He misunderstood at first.

"Shhhhh, I'm so sorry, baby. I know you miss her."

He thought I was crying for my mom. He was wrong, maybe for the first time.

"It's not that."

"What, baby, what?"

"Clayton. He flipped out." I couldn't keep the tears in, but I tried to whisper, even though my voice squeaked out some of the words. I was safe now; Justin wouldn't let anything bad happen to me. I cried into his chest. He let me.

"What did he do? Did he hit you?"

"I don't want to be here anymore, Justin. I can't. He doesn't want me here." I didn't answer him directly because I didn't want him to get mad and confront Clayton right then. I needed him to be here with me and keep me safe.

"He kicked you out?"

"No . . . " How did you tell your boyfriend that his father had done something like Clayton had done to me? "He said I owed him . . . and he touched me."

"What?!" He moved to get up right away.

"Not like that," I said pulling him back to me, "Well, almost . . . sort of. I can't stay. Can we get out of here yet?"

Justin was pissed. I could feel his jaw clenching over my head as he held me tighter.

"I'm going to kill him!"

"No, let's just leave! Tomorrow, let's just go!"

"I'll see."

I was dozing off but startled awake when Justin moved the covers away and got under them with me. I turned so he could scoop me up. His arms wrapped around mine, and he pulled me close to him, nuzzling the top of my head. It was astounding how he could make me feel so safe this close after Clayton made me feel the exact opposite. I wanted to melt into him and disappear forever.

"What did he do to you?"

It didn't seem like that big of a deal now that the moment was over and I was safe. "He yelled, like always, accused me of sleeping around, like he usually does, then he—"

"Did he rape you?"

"No! Nothing like that." I turned around to face him in the darkness.

"But he touched you?"

"Yeah."

"How? Where?"

"Justin, I don't want to say."

"I need to know, Haylee; tell me."

I was as humiliated as he was mad, but I had to tell him. I owed him that. Justin's grip around my back tightened but he listened to me recount the whole thing.

"He's a dead man," he said when I was finished. He moved to get up, but I tried to hold him close to me.

"No, don't! He's not worth it. Stay with me. Let's leave. Tomorrow. Let's go and never come back. We can do it; I know we can."

"We can try."

CHAPTER 10

THE NEXT MORNING, Justin called in to work and told Coffee that we and Clayton got into a fight and we had to move right away. Coffee, like always, appreciated Justin's honesty and told him about some cheap apartments up the street from Treadmore's. Justin got a hold of the landlord and rented a small (and when I say small, I mean *small*) studio apartment about five miles from the tire store on his good word and Coffee's reference. Actually, what happened was Coffee promised the landlord, Adriana Cookson, he would take the rent out of Justin's paycheck if he didn't come through.

Justin didn't tell her about me when he signed the contract. There wasn't much to move, and we weren't going to make Clayton mad by taking anything that wasn't ours. Coffee let Justin use one of the store's trucks, and we packed up our beds, dressers, and the TV Justin had in his room. We did take two plates, two sets of silverware, two cups, and two coffee mugs and hoped he wouldn't even notice those. Oh, and a steak knife—we had so many we were sure he wouldn't notice if it was gone.

It was a good thing we didn't have more to move in because it wouldn't have fit. As it was, we pushed our beds together in one corner farthest from the kitchenette area and put the TV on Justin's dresser across the room. There was about two feet from the foot of our beds to the dresser on the other wall. We used my dresser, which was longer and lower, as our catch-all.

The first thing we noticed after sitting down on the beds was darkness. There was only one overhead light above the entryway and a light in the shower-only bathroom. The kitchen had a mini-stove with a lighted hood, but it was no brighter than a nightlight.

We went to Target and bought a particle board nightstand, a floor lamp, a table lamp for the nightstand, and a hamper—because I always wanted one, and I needed something to haul our laundry to the common wash area in. They had bar stools too, and Justin thought it would be a good idea to get them so we had somewhere else to sit besides our beds.

We didn't have money for anything else but food. Justin was used to paying three hundred dollars a month for rent and was shocked to find out we would only have to pay two hundred-fifty dollars for the apartment, including water and garbage. All we had to spring for was TV and power, which would probably balance out to the same amount, but we had to be careful. He was hopeful we would still have money left over every month so he could keep saving; he liked to save. I felt like we had made the great escape.

We were free.

We lay side-by-side on his bed, exposed and unafraid, for the first time ever, of getting caught. We talked deep into the night about what life would be like, and we kissed freely, deeply, passionately between the lulls in the conversation. My shirt and bra came off but he still refused to cross the line. I straddled him and moved my hips until he groaned I hoped this time, for the first time, he would ignore it, so I kept going—but no. He lifted me up and off of him, stretched his arms up to the wall, and took in air. Then he sat up on one arm and looked down at me, playing with my breasts and dipped his head to kiss them quickly. I sucked in a breath as he raised himself back up and smiled and looked me over, his desire as obvious as my own. His hand trailed down my navel and up again, tracing the contours of my curves.

"Someday," he promised.

"Someday can be today," I offered.

"Nope, not yet."

"Always *not yet!*"

"Not always; our day will come. Just wait."

"That's all I do, Justin."

"Just a little longer."

"You suck!"

"I know, and you like it." He straddled me that time, grabbing my hands in his, pushing them up over our heads so that our bare chests touched. And we kissed until the groan escaped again. Then he pulled away for good and winked.

"Love ya, baby!" and like that he was done. He walked over to his duffel bag and pulled out some clean clothes and a book, thumbing to the page he had dog-eared, before setting it face down on my chest of drawers and heading to the bathroom to take a shower, a cold one probably.

We awoke the next morning, each on our own bed, though I had fallen asleep with my head on his chest listening to his heartbeat while he read.

To my dismay, the move didn't make me a grown up in Justin's eyes. I was still a child in his opinion, not ready for sex or managing my own life. Like a child, he told me I still had to go to school while he went to work.

Serrano was three or four miles away, much too far to walk every day, and he had to be at work before I started, which meant I couldn't ride with him. The city bus was my only option. I skipped the next day to figure out which bus to take and how much it would cost.

Two days after the fight with Clayton and Sipe's talk, I finally returned to school. It was a joke, really—I was so far behind—but I had nowhere else to go. It felt good to be in school, to have something I was used to doing, even if I didn't understand what they were talking about anymore.

I expected to get sent straight to the office from first period since I didn't have a note, but instead Mr. Pearsall called the office and motioned me away to find my seat. While the other kids talked about their night or annoying parents, I watched Mr. Pearsall talk about me to someone on the other end of the line.

He looked at me and answered questions, probably about me: "Fine . . . No, I don't see anything—well, maybe it looks like she has a cold sore, but she's wearing her jacket so I can't see anything but her face . . . No . . . No . . . She hasn't said a word . . . OK, will do, let me know when you do."

I waited for it, but he never sent me to the office. He didn't talk to me at all but kept looking at me during class. Somehow I knew if I bolted for the door he'd stop me. Someone was asking about me and didn't want me spooked. The problem was I didn't know who he was talking to or why they were asking or what they wanted. I wanted to run, but I knew Mr. Pearsall would catch me, so I waited anxiously for the bell to ring, bobbing my foot up and down until my desk shook and wishing I were sitting in Mr. Reyes' classroom instead. I knew he would have at least talked to me, not just about me to someone else on the phone. He might have even told me what they were planning.

Miguel Reyes was a first-generation American who fought for his citizenship and won it through service in the U.S. armed forces. After fourteen years in the service, he was wounded in Desert Storm, received a Medal of Honor, and retired from active duty. He used his G.I. bill to go to college for no particular degree until he found his calling: teaching U.S. history and helping kids who had a tough start to life like he did.

It happened accidentally: he noticed that he always took history classes, specifically American history, if he had an elective. He was proud to be American, proud to know what most second, third, and fourth-generation Americans didn't know about their country, and he yearned to explain American pride to anyone—especially the youth of America, whom he felt were out of touch with their heritage. A friend encouraged him to take some teaching classes, and two years later he was a certified teacher.

Serrano High School had an opening for a U.S. history teacher the year before Justin's freshman year, and Mr. Reyes was the top candidate. He had been teaching three history classes a day but wanted to work full time, and that's how he got into JAG. He told me later, with a chuckle, that the ad on the school district website downplayed the students' weaknesses and talked up the teachers' need to motivate students to obtain job readiness skills for America's job market. He was hired two days after the four-person panel interview, and a single JAG class was added to his teaching schedule. He had no idea the job he took to fill his day would make him one of the most important people in either my or Justin's life.

He said he learned quickly that the kids he was required to work with, kids like us, were labeled "high-risk." That was a nice way to say that we were one step away from disaster. He realized that most of us simply lacked hope for a better future, and he took it upon himself to give us hope along with employability lessons. Unlike our other teachers, he gave us the benefit of the doubt in most situations, an ear to listen and credit for what we had to deal with. It always seemed like he could see past our problems and straight into the heart of the issues. That doesn't mean we always appreciated him getting involved in our lives, but we liked him. He said his best times were seeing kids make it, especially the ones no one else thought would. The worst times were dealing with the problems the kids faced—problems like the one I presented that morning.

As Justin recounted to me later, I had technically become a ward of the state the moment my mother died, but they didn't know I was their responsibility until the school got involved. Ms. Sipe didn't know what to do about a truant child with no legal guardians, so after I took off, she called in a report on me, and that got the ball rolling with the state. To make matters worse, Clayton called the school after we ran away, saying Justin had taken me out of the house and he thought we were having sex. All of my teachers had been notified of my situation and were supposed to keep the day as normal as possible, but keep me in their sights if I were to show up. Because of his relationship with me and Justin, Mr. Reyes was supposed to find out where we were staying, if he could, and then report to Sipe so she could tell the state.

Mr. Reyes was livid. He knew he had to get to Justin or me before anyone else did. His planning period was the second period of the day, so he used it to track down Justin, and he knew right where to find him. I didn't know then that Mr. Reyes had left to talk to Justin, but I knew something was up for sure. It wasn't that anyone did anything; it was what they weren't doing that gave it away. They all seemed to be waiting. They were stalling, first Mr. Pearsall, then Mr. Aguilar. They were keeping me in class. I felt their eyes on me in the halls too. I knew if I went out the doors during passing time they'd be on me.

It scared me. All I wanted was to know what was going on. I didn't know why no one would tell me. I saw Mr. Reyes and a couple other teachers go into the lounge after third period. If I was big news that day, I knew they would be talking about me in there. I went into the office and asked Ms. Mora, the nurse, for a tampon and walked down the office corridor to the staff bathrooms. The women's was almost directly across from the lounge door. I ducked into the bathroom until I heard the fourth period bell ring. The teachers with classes would be clearing out and the rest would probably stay put in the lounge. I used all of my prowling skills to twist the knob as quietly as I could and listen in, unnoticed. Sure enough they were talking about us.

"We don't even know if that's the case, let alone why they ran." Mr. Reyes was saying

"He took her; that's what Kim said," DeAnna Duncan, my algebra teacher who never tolerated me, said.

"We don't know that either. You guys have no idea what those kids have had to put up with. There has been no parental involvement or cooperation from day one with Justin or Haylee since she's been here. The dad probably tried to hurt her and Justin is protecting her."

"Oh right, because that's what that kid does."

"Believe it or not, DeAnna, yes, that's exactly what *that kid* does."

"Right. He's bad news, and the sooner they can get that girl away from him, the better for her. Hopefully she's not pregnant already. They should put him in jail."

"Unbelievable, you know that?"

"Hey, I'm just calling them like I see them. I've got a hundred kids a day to deal with, and your kids make it intolerable. If they were gone, my job would be a whole lot easier."

"And that's their fault?"

"Yes, most of the time it is. They're old enough to know better. They're punks. They start problems, and then you run around after them wiping their butts and covering for them."

"No, not really; I just have compassion. You should try it on some day."

"I'll pass."

I had to get out of there. I knew it. If I could get away from them quickly enough I wouldn't have to keep playing their game, whatever it was.

My fourth-period class was just a few doors down from the office, I got a pass from Ms. Mora back to class but instead of going straight there, I took the stairs down and away from the teachers who knew me. I walked out the back doors of the school's bottom floor and around to the front. The chances of a teacher looking out a window and seeing me were slim to none; they stayed near their desks or whiteboards. I was paranoid that someone might be outside, though, if they were looking for me, so I peeked around the corner first. It was clear.

It was my chance. Three kids I knew well enough—Carlos, Giovani, and Shelby—were taking the walk to Smoker's Corner. They were a perfect cover. I caught up quickly and used them to blend in. Perfect getaway. I walked right past the state vehicle that pulled up to the curb and even made eye contact with the driver. I didn't know it then, but she was my new social worker, Clara Pike. She watched me run past her windshield to catch up with them. Luckily for me, she hadn't been given a picture of me yet, or she might have recognized me.

I forced myself to walk with the group to the corner so I didn't stick out. I kept expecting to hear Sipe or someone else yelling for me, but they never did.

"I thought you dropped out," Giovani said.

"Nah, just ain't been here much since my mom died."

"Oh . . . sorry."

I hated how people got all awkward when I said that. Their faces turned from normal to masks of pity. Then they never knew what to say; at least the kids my age didn't try to say anything to make me feel better. Mostly they tried to change the subject.

"It's whatever. Any of you got any buds?"

"That stuff will rot your brains out, Haylee. What are you thinking, you stoner?" Carlos laughed. That meant they were out or didn't want to share.

"Smoke?"

All three boys said, "Yeah," at the same time. I took the closest one, from Shelby, but we waited to light up until we were inside the tree line.

"You going back to class?" Shelby asked me, legs shifting back and forth. It looked like he was trying to keep warm, but it was his nervous habit; he did it all the time. It wasn't even cold out.

"Nah, I'm heading home. I think they're gonna bust me for something."

"What?"

"Not sure," I answered honestly. "Pearsall was acting all weird in class. He didn't say nothing about me being absent for like ever, but he kept looking at me."

"Oh, dang! You rob someone?"

"No. I ran away."

"You ran away, and you came to school?!" Carlos laughed at me and the others joined in. "Are you an idiot? Why would you do that?"

"I didn't have anywhere else to go." I smiled, realizing how stupid the plan was.

"Wow!"

"Whatever, I'm out. Thanks for the smoke. Peace!"

Teenage goodbyes are mumbled, backward, wavy kind of things, and that's what we offered each other. I never saw any of those three boys again. I made my way home, bus stop by bus stop. Home to my tiny apartment that I shared with Justin, where I relished our brand new life together. Finally we were out on our own; finally we were away from Clayton; finally life could begin.

The TV didn't work and I was bored. Instead of trying to catch up on school work, I took one of Justin's books from the stack on the floor by the wall and started reading. It was a *Star Trek* book, and in minutes I was engrossed in the story line and cuddled into bed. I must have been tired because I woke up when I heard Justin shut the door.

"Oh, hey, babe. I fell asleep reading."

"How come you aren't in school?" he asked?

"Something was up, so I jammed."

His face told me. He knew what was up. It was bad.

CHAPTER 11

"MR. REYES CAME TO SEE ME at the shop."

"Why?"

"He wanted to know if I took you from the house."

"What? No! We left together, but—we had to."

"I know that and you do. The problem is they've got a school full of people who don't. My dad called and accused me of sleeping with you. He said you're a ward of the state now, and they can press charges against me for it."

"What do you mean? We haven't done anything because you knew that."

"Look, it doesn't matter. They won't bat an eye about charging me; everyone knows we're together."

"Charging you for what? You didn't do anything."

We've talked to Mr. Reyes since, and even he still doesn't believe we never had sex back then. We've agreed to disagree on the subject: we can't make him—or anyone—believe us if they don't want to, and that was his point to Justin that day.

"Haylee," Justin sighed and ran both of his hands through his hair, "Listen to me. They're going to try and charge me with statutory rape."

"They can't!"

"They can. And Mr. Reyes said they will if I keep you from them. Child Protective Services are looking for you. They want you to go with them today. As long as they get you, they won't charge me. You understand?"

"What are they going to do with me?"

"They're going to find you a home."

"A home? I have a home. We have a home."

"It's not a home for a fourteen-year-old girl. It's fine for me, I'm nineteen now and on my own. If you were older they wouldn't care. He says you need to be taken care of."

"I take care of myself. We take care of each other."

"I know that, but they don't care. If you don't turn yourself in, they're going to find me and charge me and arrest me! No more job, Haylee. No more money. No more home. I go to jail and they still take you. Do you know what that does to our future? It ruins it."

"But we haven't had sex! We could have last night, and we didn't. They can't!"

"Haylee," he said, cupping my face in his hands, staring me down, "They can–and they're going to. It's only a matter of time before they find me."

"Mr. Reyes turned you in?"

"No, but he can't risk his job over it, he said he has to tell them where I work tomorrow if you don't turn yourself in."

"But it's not fair, you didn't do anything wrong. You were saving us."

"I moved a fourteen-year-old girl into an apartment. What do you think it looks like to everyone?"

My head swam. This was not at all what I thought would happen. It was supposed to get better away from Clayton's wrath. Losing me scared Justin as much as losing him scared me. He raked his hands through his hair again.

"I can't lose you. You're all I've got. But he's right, I can't take care of you either. You need to be in school, doing Spirit week and worrying about test scores; not paying bills and dodging CPS."

"I'm going to school. I went today; yesterday I had to figure out the buses."

"Haylee you've barely been there since your mom died."

"So? Things are hard right now. I'll go. I won't miss a day. I promise."

"You don't get it. They think you need more help than I can give you right now and they're right. I can't afford to support the two of us. I can't give you the stuff you need. And I definitely can't if they lock me up."

"What are we supposed to do then?"

"Do what they want. You have to turn yourself in. We can write—you remember you always wanted me to write you love letters? Guess you got your wish." He was trying to lighten up the mood. It didn't work. "And wait. I know you don't believe it, but you'll be old enough in no time; then we can be together and no one can stop us."

I stared at him. Later wasn't enough. I wanted him now.

"Look. Think about it this way: I'm going to enlist, right?"

"Yeah?"

"I was going to wait until you were old enough but I can do it now, and by the time my four years are done, you'll be old enough, we'll get married and no one will separate us ever again."

It was a lie. All Justin wanted was to convince me to turn myself in so he could stay out of trouble and I could get a good home, like I was a stray puppy or something.

"I won't go."

"You're killin' me! You think I want you to? Think about it. Think long and hard about it, what do I have without you? Nothing! You're my life, Haylee. Everything I've ever done is for you! But we're screwed. If you stay I go to jail and everything we've worked for is gone. We have to do this. There's no choice. Baby, believe me if there was any other way I'd do it. But there's not. Four years. That's all."

"We can leave. We can go where no one knows us."

"No, we can't run from this."

"Sure we can; why couldn't we?"

"Because, Haylee—" I could tell he didn't want to say it—"you're just a kid. You're too young."

"I'm not! We can do this."

"How? I can't pretend to be your dad and put you into school at the next place we go, even if we could find somewhere else to go. I got a job here, and only because Mr. Reyes hooked me up. If I leave, I ain't got nothing, especially if they put a warrant out for my arrest because I kidnapped you. We'd always be looking over our shoulders and if we got caught it would be ten times worse."

"But you didn't do anything to me!"

"It... doesn't... matter! Why can't you get it? It doesn't matter what we say or do. They got us nailed. We can't outrun them."

"Yeah we can. Kids go missing all the time, and they never find them."

"They get killed, that's why. I'm not going to live on the streets just so we can be together."

"You don't want to be with me?"

"I didn't say that, Haylee. Don't put words into my mouth I didn't say."

"Then what? You're going to give up on us? You're going to let go?" He was abandoning me; I felt it.

"No, never! There's no me without you; you're my heart and soul. It's just like before; it's just like with the kiss. You remember when you wanted it?"

"Yeah, but it's not the same. We were together."

"We'll still be together." He took my hand and put it against his chest so I could feel his heart. I started to cry but no sound came out. "Mr. Reyes said I could write you; I'll write you every day."

"It's not the same."

"It's exactly the same. All you have to do is wait for me, baby. Wait, and I'll be there for you."

"No. No! I don't want to leave."

Then he pulled me to him and held me while I cried. He tried to cover me from all the sadness with his strong arms, but they didn't have the power to make the mess that was my life disappear.

"Shhhhh," he cooed to me, rocking me, holding me.

The tears wouldn't stop. My life was one nightmare after another. Every time I thought things were going to get better, they got worse, and there was nothing I could do about it. I had cried so much by then I couldn't even believe I had any more tears left. I wanted to stop, but I couldn't. My life would mean nothing without him.

"Then I'll kill myself."

"What are you talking about?" As he grabbed my face in his hands I saw real live fear in his eyes. He was afraid I would do it. I didn't think I really would; I was desperate, but I wanted to live. I wanted to live with him, by his side. I really didn't want to live without him. No one could make me.

"You can't think like that, Haylee. You can't! What would I do without you? You're my everything. I can't lose you. Don't do that to me. Please, baby, promise me you won't. You think I want any of this? You think I haven't tried to figure out a way to get around it? If we could, I would take you right now. We'd get out of here and be gone, but we're trapped. One way or the other they're going to find us, take you, and put me in jail. We lose if we play our way. But if we wait, play the game their way, we can be together. What's a few years?" He smiled, trying to fake us both into believing it was the best option. "We can do this, Haylee."

"No! We can't. I can't. Where will I go?"

"I don't know."

"Exactly! I don't have anywhere to go. I won't go back to Clayton if they try to send me back to him."

"Not gonna happen; I told Reyes he was no good for you. If he tries it, I'll have him arrested for what he did to you."

"But I don't have anywhere else. They're gonna make me a foster kid or something."

"It couldn't be worse than living with my dad, right?"

I cried. It wasn't like before when he didn't know what to do or say. He had all day to think about it, and he knew this was our only option. He knew what we had to do and what the state would do if we did anything else, and I had no choice but to go along helplessly. I could walk out his door, the door of the apartment that was supposed to be our home, and never look back, but where would I go? So much for being bold.

He was right: we had no choice.

He pulled me into his lap and rocked me like a baby while I cried.

"I'll take you to the school tomorrow. Turn yourself in and let me know where you are as soon as you can. We'll make it through this. I promise."

For the longest time we sat together on the edge of the bed, rocking quietly and doing what tragic lovers do: promising the world and that we would always love each other and nothing could separate us. Then the words were all used up, the promises were all made, and we had to move on because the moment called for it.

Food and books were really all we had to occupy us. In our haste to move we had forgotten pots and pans and were now realizing it. We heated cheap chili dogs in the apartment's included microwave and ate them in silence, pondering four years of future questions. Because there was nothing else to do, we did what came naturally: he played the guitar and I listened. He read his book and I sat beside him on my twin bed reading the one I started earlier, wishing I was on the Enterprise and a million light years, or only four earth years, away from where I was. I lost myself in the story, only coming back to reality when Justin turned a page.

It was a pretty boring night for all the questions that loomed in front of us. We didn't want to go out in case someone was at the grocery store or movies looking for us. I laugh now at how we stayed holed up, like our lives depended on it, like any second someone would bust down the door and demand my release. Truth was we were minor blips on anyone's radar; when five o'clock hit, the state was done working for the day. We could have gone out and had a last night on the town without fear, but we were so young and egocentric we were sure everyone was looking for us. Nothing kept us inside but our own ideas of self-importance.

We lay down together one last time at ten o'clock after I showered the refuse of the day off my body. Time for one last intimate memory.

"Good night, Haylee," he said smoothing my wet hair down and out of my face.

I begged him to make love to me, to give me that one thing to hold on to—it didn't even matter anymore, anyway—but he refused, not in a mean way but in Justin's strong, firm, nothing-would-change-his-mind way.

"Baby, we can spend the night fighting about something that's not going to happen or we can enjoy it and be together. I want that."

"Kiss me then,"

"Now, that I'll do." He smiled, pulled me to him, lifted my chin—still slightly sore from Clayton's assault days earlier—and kissed me. Like the first, this one meant so much more than simply skin on skin. His one hand stayed propped under my head while the other held my cheek, thumb touching the corner of my lips while we kissed. I cried knowing it was our last night together, realizing I'd never spent a night away from Justin since my mom had moved in with Clayton. He felt my tears and looked at me, held me with his eyes, promising me forever but just not yet. Then he pulled me into his chest, wrapped me up, and said, "I love you, Haylee. Wait for me."

"Always," I answered him, and I meant it as much as any fourteen-year-old can mean anything.

He woke me up early the next morning before he had to be at work. I packed the clothes I could carry into my backpack along with the book he let me keep to finish. Inside the cover he wrote the address to the apartment that was not ours but his alone and the number to Treadmore's since we didn't have a phone yet.

"As soon as you know where you'll be, write me. Promise."

"Yeah."

I cried again the whole way to the car and during the ride to the school. It's so much faster to get somewhere when your heart is breaking; it felt like mere seconds between the beginning and end of the trip.

"I can't go with you or I would."

"I know. I'm afraid."

"Don't be, baby. It'll be OK." He pulled me in a sideways hug.

"I don't want to leave you."

"Haylee, don't do this again; just go. Write me as soon as you can; call me at work if they'll let you."

We hugged so hard, I was trying to disappear into him, but it didn't work.

"I love you."

"I love you too, so much!"

My hand rebelled against opening the door.

"C'mon, Haylee, you gotta do this."

"I can't!"

"You have to."

"I don't."

"Yes, you do."

He waited for five minutes before slamming his hand on the steering wheel and pulling out from the curb. I thought I had convinced him to run away with me, but I was wrong. All I convinced him to do was put his neck even more on the line for me. He peeled into the high school parking lot and jerked the car to a stop in a visitor parking space. He opened and slammed his door shut then came around the car to my side.

"Get out of the car, Haylee; you have to go."

I was hysterical, bawling like a baby and shaking my head, "No!"

He looked around, worried someone would hear and misunderstand. I was holding my backpack to my chest, but when he unlocked and opened the door I grabbed the handle with all my might to stay in. School wasn't scheduled to start for forty-five minutes, so the lot was empty, which was a good thing for us.

"C'mon, Haylee, get out!" he said through gritted teeth.

"No! I'm not going."

He fought me for the door a little longer then stopped and shook his head.

"You're really going to make me do this, aren't you?" Then he turned and walked toward the building. He was going to be the one to turn me in, which meant he would be in trouble, too, for being with me. I couldn't let him do it.

"No! Stop! Fine, I'll go!" I said getting out of the car.

"You mean it?" he shouted as he stopped and turned back to me. He was already halfway to the door.

As I got out, anger, frustration, and confusion were taking over where the sorrow had been. I would not let them see me cry. I was done with the tears.

He came to me, looked around warily, and hugged me.

"I love you," he said putting our foreheads together. "You can do this. Tell me you're OK when you can."

He stayed to make sure I went inside; then I heard him leave. I wanted to go to Mr. Reyes—he would be cool with me, maybe tell me what was going to happen—but his door was locked. I walked into the office, and Mrs. Solis stared at me like I was a ghost. I let myself get mad. I was going to be bold.

"What? I know you guys want me for something; what is it?" I demanded.

"Let me go get Ms. Sipe. You stay right here."

"Not like I can go anywhere! You people *screwed* up my *life!*" I threw myself into one of the lobby chairs and hugged my backpack again. My leg shook. I told myself to be mad, not sad, and it mostly worked.

The day was complex, confusing, and slow all at the same time. I could tell I was a headache to every single adult I met that day. Ms. Sipe was on the phone, off the phone, having me sit in the conference room, then the lobby when there was a meeting. Mrs. Solis kept calling and calling and leaving messages for Clara Pike, who must have been the person in charge of me now. She tried to make it sound all cool, but I could tell she was frustrated and tired of being my babysitter.

"I can go to class."

"No, no, you need to stay right here while we figure things out."

"What things? I'm here now; I'm not going to go anywhere."

"No, Haylee, you're fine. Just wait."

Wait, wait, wait. Justin wanted me to wait; teachers wanted me to wait. I hated waiting, and it was all anyone ever wanted me to do. I cursed that word. Then I cursed my age. My whole life was about that word and my being too young to defend myself or be with who I wanted to be with or make grown-up decisions. I swore then I would never let anyone tell me what to do again—not Clayton, not Justin, not anyone.

Finally, halfway through third period, Clara Pike made her appearance. Whether she recognized me or not, I do not know, but as soon as I saw her I remembered her from the car the day before.

"Well hi there, Missy. You're a tough one to track down, you know that?" Her smile suited her pixie cut auburn hair well, but I didn't fall for the pleasantries. She was attempting to be courteous. I had no interest in returning it.

"Well, I'm here now." I shrugged, crossing my arms like I didn't care, even though my heart was racing like crazy. I was so afraid of what was next. I wanted to ask her what she knew, but I didn't want her to think I needed her.

"Well, we've got a lot of things to figure out." She smiled.

"I'm not going back to Clayton's; you can't make me."

"No, dear, he isn't your guardian. That sounds like a good thing for you, but it complicates matters. How about you come with me and we talk about it over lunch?"

Clara checked me out of the school. I tried to be tough, I really did, but they weren't mean like Clayton or my mom; they were all being so nice—even Sipe, for once. I couldn't help the tears that rolled down my cheeks, but I tried to wipe them as inconspicuously as possible as soon as they rolled out.

Before we left, Mr. Reyes found me. That was when I lost it. I'm not sure why—maybe he was the closest thing to a real dad I'd ever had—but I crumbled into his chest and cried and cried all over again. He held me and promised, like all of them, that it would be OK. Just like Justin, he gave me a book, *The Diary of Anne Frank*, and inside was his personal address and phone number, along with twenty bucks and a little note that read:

I know things are hard right now. I wish I could make it better for you and Justin.

Have hope things will get better now and life will give you a break for once. And remember your old JAG teacher and check in with me when you're settled and life is good. Be one of the ones who makes it, Haylee. I know you can be!

-    *Mr. Reyes*

After that, Clara took me to Jack-in-the-Box for lunch. I tried to see Justin at Treadmore's when we drove past it. If I had known I would never go back to Serrano I would have left my school books, but I didn't, so I kept them with me. They made me feel a shred of normalcy, and I cried again when I had to let them go a week and a half later when we all knew I was changing schools.

The state had a hard time placing me because of my "unique circumstances," Clara said. I knew what she really meant was that no one wanted me. A week later I called Justin's work from the third house they put me at.

Clara saw me or talked to me almost every day at the first two houses because it was made very clear they didn't want me for a long time, and she was afraid I would run away. It was called emergency shelter; they let me stay there while they found a permanent solution. The lady at the first house deloused me like I was some slum kid, washing all my clothes five times, or so it seemed. Then she took me to a doctor up the street where they asked me fifty million questions about the drugs I did and the people I slept with. I told them I didn't do any drugs or sleep around.

I hate how no one believed I was a virgin. It was like just because I was a "bad kid" with a bad history I was supposed to be a slut too. They were all pleasantly surprised when the pregnancy test came back negative. I told them where they could go.

Clara kept me so busy that first week answering questions, visiting specialists, and going shopping that I didn't have time to call Justin earlier, or I would have tried to.

My first set of "permanent" foster parents were Brad and Kaylee. Clara told me they would keep me until we figured out a permanent solution. When I asked what that meant, she said the state would find me a "forever home"—in other words, Brad and Kaylee didn't want me either but were willing to put up with me for a little bit.

I was going to start school in Chino the next week, which was dumb because there were only a couple months of school left anyway. I was smart enough to know that the classes I took wouldn't count for anything. I wouldn't be there long enough to get full credit, and I sure wasn't going to do extra work to get the credit. Clayton always said school was state-funded daycare, that's another thing he was right about.

Brad and Kaylee were OK, except they looked at me with pity like everyone else did, and had annoying little kids. Even though I had been to a doctor with the other lady, Kaylee made me go to another one the second day I was there. I told her I just went, and she said she believed me but it was the state's rule. I said it was dumb, and she agreed with a chuckle but scheduled the appointment anyway. She told me about some of the things the state made them do for me, like schedule appointments for the dentist and counseling.

"I don't need any counseling."

"Well, maybe you do, maybe you don't, but we have to take you."

I was glad about the dentist though; for the first time in years my tooth didn't hurt me. I didn't even know how much it bothered me until it was fixed. That was nice.

They let me call Justin.

"Hi," I said when he came to the phone. Coffee had asked if it was me and I didn't know what to say, so I answered truthfully. It worked: he let me talk to him.

"Hey. So where are you?"

"Some house in Chino."

"Whoa, you're in Chino?!"

"Yeah, but not by the museum; it's some neighborhood."

"How do you like it?"

"It's whatever. They have a baby who cries all the time, but other than that it's OK. I'm starting school next week."

"Why all the way in Chino?" he made the mistake of asking.

"'Cause I'm a freaking teenager with problems, Justin. No one wants me."

"But they do, right?"

"No, not even. They're totally in it for the money. They're letting me stay until the state can find someone who actually wants me. Could be a long time."

"I don't understand."

"I'm an orphan, Justin. I have no parents. No one wants me."

I wanted to cry, but instead I hid my feelings under a cover of apathy. If I didn't care, I didn't have to feel sad or get mad.

"I'm so sorry."

"Really? What did you think was going to happen?"

"What about your aunt?"

"What are you talking about?"

"Your Aunt Aerin, the one who came to your mom's funeral. Can't she take you?"

"I don't know. I guess not; she hasn't so far."

"But does she know? Are they looking for her? Ask, Haylee. Ask them if they're looking for her. Do you remember where she lived?"

"No, I didn't talk to her, remember?"

"I did. It was in Washington State, I'm sure of it."

"I don't know, and I don't care. I just wanted to call you so you didn't worry."

"Cool. I'm getting a phone next week; the guy is coming out on Tuesday. I have to take the whole morning off—stupid tech can't tell me when he's going to be there; they just gave me a time window."

"Yeah, sounds dumb."

"I'll let you know as soon as I have a number. Will you write me?" he asked.

"Sure."

"You haven't yet."

"I've been busy," I lied. The truth was I was still too mad to say anything to him, even though I missed him.

"Can I write you?"

"I don't care."

"What's the address?"

"I don't know, let me check." I put the phone down and asked Kaylee for the address, but she said they didn't want me giving it out.

"Whatever," I said. Nothing worked out for me; why would they let Justin write me?

I picked up the phone again. "She said no."

"Who did?"

"Kaylee, the lady I live with."

"Well, write me at least, OK?"

"Sure."

"Haylee . . . " Justin knew me better than anyone; he knew I'd given up.

"What?"

"Hold on, OK? It's gotta get better."

"Sure. Look, I gotta go. She wants me off the phone," I lied again. I knew I was going to cry if I stayed on the phone with him. I refused to cry anymore.

When I hung up, I took out my frustration on Kaylee.

"How come you won't let me give him the address? All he wants to do is write; he's not going to come and take me."

"We've been told you're not supposed to talk to that boy."

"Looks like I just did. He didn't call me; I called him. I want to talk to him. There's nothing wrong with that."

"Honey, we can't let you . . . "

"Don't call me 'Honey,' OK?"

After that I sequestered myself in the room they let me share with their little girl. It was decorated for a preschool princess. I was not home. I lay in the bed and faced the wall, but I didn't cry. That's pretty much what I did at their house until I went back to school at a new high school the next Monday.

CHAPTER 12

THE GREAT THING ABOUT HIGH SCHOOL—any high school— is there are always stoners who'll smoke out a new kid with a sad story like mine. I made friends with a couple kids and ditched class with them more often than I went. Brad and Kaylee were mad about me skipping, so they grounded me and didn't let me go out or use the phone. I feel like they used it as another excuse to keep me from calling Justin. The only days I didn't skip were counseling days. I hated counseling days the most because the counselor was half an hour from my school, and they never had appointments in the afternoon. I always had to leave in the middle of the day and had some weird driver take me there. On those days I had to make sure I didn't skip, but I don't know why. It was more embarrassing to leave half-way through class because of "an appointment" than it was to skip. They made me see him every week. He told me I was depressed and recommended I get on medicine. Even though I was old enough to tell them I didn't want it, the doctor prescribed it anyway. Kaylee said I had to take it, but I didn't want to, so I cheeked it and spit it out in the bathroom later. I can't even remember what that counselor's name was—some guy with toys in his office. Since he knew our time together would be short he said he would give me tools to help me cope instead of having me talk about my life. He taught me about deep breathing and how it calmed down the mind. That's when I realized why Justin always breathed deeply: he must have learned that too.

The breathing came in handy when I talked to Justin next and he told me I'd be moving to live with my aunt. Once he had his number hooked up I got in the habit of calling him almost every night after

Brad, Kaylee and their kids were asleep. I was sure the scuffing sounds of my new pink slippers on their tile floors would wake Brad, but the house always stayed quiet. I never dialed until I was outside where they couldn't hear.

"Hey," I said when he answered.

"Hey," he sounded funny, I knew something was up.

"What's up?" I asked, pulling my blanket tight around my legs and shoulders so I could sit on the porch steps.

"I talked to Clara."

"How do you know her?"

"Reyes, he told me."

"She's not even looking for your aunt. Did you tell her about her?"

"No."

"Well, I did, I don't think she could find anything so I went to my dad's. Haylee, she wants you."

"Yeah, right,"

"Dead serious. I knew he had to know something. I found a letter she wrote him. She said she'd come and get you anytime."

"He never said a word about it to me." I said.

"Me either." he breathed deeply, audibly before continuing, "I thrashed the house."

"No way,"

"Yeah," he said, remorse thick in his tone. He told me how he ripped the house apart and then spit on the step on his way out. Then he said he called my aunt when he got back to his apartment.

"She sounds real nice, Haylee."

"But she lives so far away."

"In Washington, it's the best place remember?"

"For you, not for me."

"Just try it out."

What I tried out were the deep breaths, breathe in the good, deep, long, full breaths. And breathe out the bad, pushing it as far as I could away from me. The rest of that night we talked about his work, my school and the new people I had on my "team." That's what they called all the people who were up in my business.

There were so many people to keep track of. I had Clara in California, but when I moved to Washington there were even more. I had a new social worker named Krista—she was nice and saw me every month at Aunt Aerin's home. Then there was Thomas, my court-appointed lawyer; I never really saw him outside of court, but he was the one who petitioned the court to allow Justin and me to talk to each other.

Michelle was my CASA—Court-Appointed Special Advocate. I liked her best. She was older and had the most beautiful brown eyes I had ever seen. She would meet me at home with Aunt Aerin like Krista did, but sometimes she surprised me at school too, and before I gave up on sports, she even came to some of my volleyball games.

Michelle told me that our county, Chelan County, made sure every single kid in foster care had a CASA. The CASAs were volunteers who wanted to help kids. I wondered where they had been all my life. Maybe California didn't have them. She said their job was to tell the court what they thought was in the best interests of the children. She wasn't like a lawyer who did exactly what I wanted, but she wasn't like a social worker either. She was a little bit of both and would tell the court what she felt was truly best for me, no matter what my lawyer or the state said. She also promised to tell the judge what I wanted, even if it was different from what she thought was best. She was the first person I asked about being able to talk to Justin—actually it was Aunt Aerin who asked.

"It sounds like you two care about each other a lot," Michelle said.

"Yep. We grew up together."

"So, he's like a brother to you?"

"No . . . " I hesitated and shuffled to reposition myself on Aunt Aerin's overstuffed cigar chair. I didn't know what to say. I was afraid if I said we loved each other she, like everyone else, would think we shouldn't talk, but I was afraid to lose a chance to talk to him if she could help. "We're really good friends," I continued, "but not like brother and sister."

"Oh . . . " I saw a look of understanding pass between her and Aunt Aerin.

"Justin is the one who first called me to let me know Haylee needed a place to go."

"I'll have to look into it before I can make a recommendation or enter a motion. Do you have a way for me to contact him and talk to him?"

I gave her his new number and crossed my fingers that it would work out.

"I have to also tell you that you have a lawyer appointed for your personal interests. Do you know who it is?"

"Yeah, Thomas something, I think."

"Thomas Johnson. He's one of the public defenders in family court. Do you have his number?"

"Um . . . somewhere . . . maybe, I think . . . "

"OK, I'll find it for you in case you don't and pass it on. He'll be the best person to petition the court, but give me time to check Justin out too, and I'll be able to make an informed recommendation to the court. Remember, I can't promise I'll say what you want like your lawyer will, so he's the best person to petition for you."

"But you won't say no, will you?" I asked, upset that I said anything in the first place. I was sure she was just like the rest of them.

"I can't make that promise right now. What I can promise is I'll be honest and tell the court what I believe is best for you, OK?"

"Whatever . . . " I folded my arms and checked out of the rest of the conversation. I let Aunt Aerin finish up with her. Michelle was cool. The very next day she called with my lawyer's number and said she had left a message for Justin to call her. She also told me she had called Serrano and talked to Mr. Reyes and that Mr. Reyes said Justin was a great kid.

"Did you talk to anyone else?" I asked, worried that Sipe or another teacher would ruin it for us.

"I spoke with the receptionist, Mrs. Solis; she said the best person for me to talk to would be Mr. Reyes. Is there anyone else I should ask for?"

"No, Mr. Reyes probably knows us best," I answered honestly, wondering why Mrs. Solis hadn't given the phone to Sipe—or anyone else who would have said bad stuff about Justin. Maybe Mrs. Solis had a heart after all.

"OK then, you give Mr. Johnson a call, and I'll keep on researching until it gets to court. How about it?"

"Alright . . . "

"Alright."

"Um . . . Michelle?"

"Yes?"

"Thanks. He really is one of my only friends. I really need to talk to him."

"I know you want to. Keep your chin up, sweetie. Talk to you soon."

"K, bye."

As soon as we hung up, I called my lawyer and left a message. It took forever for him to get back to me, and when he did, he did exactly what Michelle said he would do: he filed a petition and got us a court date. Then all I had to do is what I had always done: wait. Only now, instead of waiting on Justin, I was waiting on the court to allow me to talk to him.

The state said they wanted to find me a "forever home," so I thought when they found Aunt Aerin they would go away, but it didn't work that way. I kept Krista and Michelle and Thomas around for a long time until the court finally decided Aunt Aerin, my own flesh-and-blood aunt, was good enough to keep me.

It didn't take me long at all to figure out she was cool. Mom lied about her—she was nice and thoughtful; she didn't like Mom's lifestyle was all, and Mom was the one who stopped talking to her, not the other way around.

Even though she was so much better than my mom or Clayton had ever been, the state made her take classes and tests and have her home studied to prove it. I didn't get why they cared so much about someone like Aunt Aerin but let me live with my mom and Clayton for so long and didn't bother. It didn't take a brain surgeon to figure out Aunt Aerin was safe, but we had to go through all their hoops. She told me we had to play the state's game too. All of us played their game.

The only thing I didn't like about my aunt after I got to know her was that she looked so much like my mom. I wanted her to have a face that was all her own. It was easier to look past it on good days— and we had lots of good days—but on the bad days all I could see was my mom, and I would take it out on her.

She was single and probably could have been called a spinster except that she had been married four times.

"Never took," she told me once, smiling, over dinner at a restaurant in town. We rarely ate at home. Aunt Aerin wasn't rich like I imagined her to be, but she lived comfortably. She admitted to being "well-off" but certainly not rich; it was just that she was single for ten years before she took me in, so she had a lot saved up. She took the money the state gave her for me—every single dime of it, until she officially became my adopted aunt-mom—and put it into a college fund.

"I don't want to go to college," I had argued when she made a point to deposit the first check into her savings account with me in the car.

"Oh my, of course you do; you just don't know it yet."

"No I don't."

"Well, I'm not going to argue with you like a school girl; we'll just leave it there until you're ready to go, or until I'm dead, and you can spend it on whatever you want." Then she patted me on the hand. I loved it when she did that, even when I was mad at her.

I wanted to hate her, and for the first couple weeks I tried. But like she said about marriage, it never took. Aunt Aerin lived in a magical little village in the Pacific Northwest called Leavenworth. It was a made-up Bavarian town at the base of the Cascade Mountains, just inside Central Washington. Most of the residents either worked in one of the hundred or so tourist shops or owned them. Aunt Aerin owned one.

Her last husband was "the one that got away," and it had been his shop. She loved him and talked about him the way I talked about Justin, and her eyes always got soft and faraway-looking when she talked about his death. I knew how she felt because I felt that way about Justin. I think that's why she let Justin and me write even before I got permission from the court.

"Just have him put my name on it until everything is taken care of with the state. Mailman's nosy, you know, and might snitch on us."

That's what we did until the court granted permission for us to talk. Aunt Aerin let me call him once. She didn't want the long distance charges to eat up her phone, so she discouraged frequent calls out, but he could call in.

I was lucky to call when I did because he was working even more hours for Coffee and finishing up his college classes too. That's when he told me he had enlisted and was almost officially an

Airman in the U.S. Air Force. He was so excited—all he had to do was finish the classes, and at the end of June he would be in.

"I'm gonna do it, Haylee! I'm gonna fly."

He told me he went straight to the recruiting office after he got done talking to my aunt. As soon as he knew I would have a place to go, he did what he needed to do to make the best life for us in the future. In our first phone call after I moved in with Aunt Aerin, he promised that four years would fly by, and then we would be together forever.

That's when I grew up and saw outside myself for the first time in my life. Until then, it had always been about me: how Justin made me feel, how my mom and Clayton made me feel, how I liked or didn't like some people, places, and things. I thought it was about them, but it was all about me. As soon as I was gone, Justin had nothing to wait for, so he started to chase his dreams. For our whole lives I thought he wanted to be with me—and he did, but it had cost him his dreams, and I never even cared about it. I wanted him there for me—to keep me safe, to be my guy—and I was willing to let him give up on himself so I could have him. I felt so bad, but I didn't know how to tell him that I realized how selfish I had been.

I was happy he was going after what he wanted, but I was afraid, too, that life would tear us apart. I worried that while I waited to be grown-up, he would leave me for some older girl or a better life than the one he could have with a pity case like me. In practically every letter I told him I was scared he would leave me. He always answered back promising that would never happen and ended every note the same way: *The best things come to those who wait. Wait for me, Haylee.*

I waited a long time, too, but it didn't take.

All of my fears about him leaving were unrealistic. It wasn't him I had to worry about; it was me—just as he had always known. That's why he begged me to wait: he knew it was me who would leave. And he was right. They all were. I was too young; I didn't know what I wanted, and I let the best thing that ever happened to me slip slowly through my fingers. It wasn't his fault—he would have waited forever for me.

I could blame Aunt Aerin, even though I know she didn't mean for anything to come between me and Justin. All she wanted was for me to have the chance to be a kid. She used to take me for walks with her Great Dane, Pepper. Pepper was huge, the size of a small horse, but she treated him like a lap dog: she fed him from the table, and he even had his own bedroom. Pepper had to be walked regularly so he wouldn't tear up the house, so we took him out every day, sometimes twice. Aunt Aerin made me go at least once a week, but at first, since I liked her company and since she didn't yell at me like Clayton and my mom, I went more often than that.

Her favorite place to walk Pepper after the snow melted was called Ski Hill, a bygone site for fancy winter-time competitions. Remnants of the old, wooden ski jumps were still erect, though disintegrating, on the western hills. Since then it had become a forested cross-country ski trail in the winter, an amphitheater where "The Sound of Music" played in the summer, and an all-around good recreational nature hike area.

An old kelly green ski lift chair, hung like a swing, sat at the top of one hill. Sitting next to Aunt Aerin on that chair lift always meant the same thing: she wanted to talk about something important. She would wander to it and motion for me to come sit with her. That's where she told me she wanted to adopt me. That's where she told me her history. That's where she told me I needed to spend more time focusing on school or I was going to spend less time talking on the phone to the friends I'd made. And that's where she told me I needed to let go of Justin—just a little. It was fall—too early for snow and too late for the sun to zap our strength completely. It was perfect walking weather for the three of us.

For a while we just sat, rocking lightly and talking about nothing important. Then she patted my hand and said it: "Haylee, I think you think about Justin too much. I'm not saying you need to break up with him—I like him, and I like the fact that your boyfriend is hundreds of miles away learning how to fly fighter planes. It means he's not having sex with you."

"Ewwww, Auntie!"

"Well, dear, I'm just telling it like it is, and you know it. I like him, or what I've heard of him from you. He seems like a nice boy, and you have all the time in your adulthood to be with him, but you'll never get your youth back. He had a chance to be a kid; you should too. Don't let your childhood waste away while you're waiting for him. Explore other avenues while you wait."

"He didn't have a chance to be a kid. He was always looking out for me. Neither of us had a childhood."

"So take the time to have one now. Be a kid! Stay out late—*just not past curfew*. Take a joy ride to Seattle—*just go the speed limit.*" She was so funny, leaning into me, reminding me to follow the rules when she really just wanted me to have fun.

"Haylee, I want you to enjoy being a kid while you still can. Don't be in such a hurry to grow up. Justin will always be there, unless it's not meant to be for either of you. You'll be grown-up before you know it."

I told Justin about it in my next letter, and he agreed with everything.

I want you to have fun too, Haylee. Just wait for me; that's all I ask. Go out and be the girl you couldn't be because of the way things were when we lived with my dad and your mom. I wish I could erase what they put us through, but I can't. Sometimes I still get so mad at my dad for what he did to us. I don't get why they couldn't be good parents and realize what they were doing. I can't take it back; neither can you. All we can do is be better than them and prove to everyone who thought we were worthless like them that they were wrong.

And so, with Aunt Aerin and Justin's blessing, I went out and tried to have fun.

CHAPTER 13

BACK THEN I ASSOCIATED FUN with drinking and getting high. I didn't see how I could have fun without the two. The first time Aunt Aerin caught me it was because I came home too late and too in the bag to be quiet.

"Where have you been?"

"Just out with friends, Auntie," I slurred.

"You're drunk! Do you want a life like your mother's?"

"My mom was an alcoholic; I'm not like that. I was having a good time. Lighten up."

"I'll lighten up next month. You're grounded."

She meant it too. I had never been grounded by Mom; all I had to do was listen to Clayton yell, and they would forget about it the next day. Being grounded meant I had to go straight home after volleyball practice, unless I went to the shop to help her sell things to tourists. No phone either. I couldn't even take Justin's calls.

That made me mad, so I complained to Thomas and Krista and Michelle that she was keeping me from talking to him. When they all said it was within standard guidelines for a guardian, I said I didn't want her to be my guardian. Thomas offered to enter a motion to the court to have me moved. Krista said she could look for other placements, but since I came from California, I would probably have to move back down there—and there was no guarantee I would be anywhere close to where I came from.

Michelle made me think it through, reminded me of how long and how hard it was to get to Aunt Aerin in the first place. She asked me if it was really that bad. It wasn't, but it wasn't fair either. All she said was, "Suck it up buttercup!" and told me if my lawyer brought a petition to the court, she would not be in favor of it.

After I got done being mad, I gave up, but I did that to Aunt Aerin a couple of other times too. I feel bad for it now, but at the time it made me feel like I kind of had some control over my life.

Getting grounded should have taught me to straighten up, but I learned nothing. Weird thing was it made me miss my mom. I had never really missed her before then, but getting in trouble set me off on a pity party. People felt sorry for me when I lamented over losing my mom too, so I played it up, and it became part of who I was: the sad little orphan girl. All of the acting sad made me believe that life with my mom had been so much better than when she was dead.

Even though I liked living with Aunt Aerin, I missed the way things used to be. The three biggest things I missed were Justin, Johnnie Walker, and the idea of my mom being alive. I was more like her than I allowed myself to believe, and I didn't appreciate Auntie pointing it out by grounding me for doing what had been normal for so long. While we lived with the alcohol and drugs all around us, it didn't seem bad or out of the ordinary to be drinking, but to Aunt Aerin it was the end of the world. She asked Krista if I could get into counseling, which I said I didn't want, and she asked about alcohol treatment, which I said I didn't need. She made it all seem way worse than what I thought it was.

Our childhoods were more similar than I realized. My mom and Aunt Aerin's parents were addicts too, but their dad molested them. Aunt Aerin said she and my mom were tied at the hip and would try to hide the alcohol or pour it down the sink. She laughed when she recalled the beatings they would take for their mischief. Only someone who's been abused could laugh about being hit upside the head because you wouldn't tell your dad where the vodka was. I laughed too because Justin and I had our own stories of sad hilarity with Mom and Clayton. I shared them with her, and she would pat me on the hand and purse her lips together and get a sad faraway look in her eyes.

"That's why I don't drink, dear. That's why I don't have kids. I was so afraid I would be just like them: my mother, who looked away when Daddy would take me or your mom to the room, and Daddy—sad, sorry soul that he was—who did the most horrible things to us then made us feel bad for it. I blamed it all on the alcohol." She laughed. "I had myself convinced if they would just quit drinking, everything would be better, like the evil inside them would go away if they quit. I was wrong, of course—that kind of bad is there with or without anything to help it along—but the drink certainly made it worse. Even though your mom and I hated it, once we tried it, we took to it like fish to water. I'm afraid you're doing the same thing."

"I'm nothing like my mother."

"No?"

"No."

"Then why don't you stop? You're not old enough to drink anyway, and I'm not going to get it for you. I don't have it around the house. Quitting should be easy."

"I can quit if I want to."

"Then do it."

"Fine, I will." My insides flipped upside down thinking about not drinking again. I refused to admit to her or anyone that I liked it too much to quit.

In my next letter I told Justin I got grounded. I wanted him to feel sorry for me for getting in trouble, but instead he said I should follow her rules and not ask the state for another home.

I couldn't get permission to drink from him or Aunt Aerin, and I knew the state wasn't OK with it, so I did it behind all their backs. I started to live my own secret life—not the one Justin wanted for us, not the one Aunt Aerin wanted for me, and not the one my mom had, even though my choices looked freakishly similar to hers. I played the game: I went to the counselor and the treatment classes, said what they wanted me to say, even came up with my "out" plans if I was tempted and needed a way out of a situation, but I didn't mean any of it.

For the first year I wrote Justin every week or more and told him about everything—except that I was still drinking and getting in trouble because of it. I told him about school, how I didn't love it but was still going. That was the truth: I was trying to stay in school, which meant I couldn't skip. Without parents who drank, I had to be in good with my school friends to find out who would have the next party I could go to. I needed friends to spend the night with who had access to alcohol. The best girl to be with was Gabriela, my volleyball teammate. Her parents had a bar equal to my parents', only they didn't let their kids drink.

Gabby and I were partners in crime—she liked to drink too—so we would sneak sips together and giggle about boys and high school drama while we got buzzed. We got along well, but their bar, not her friendship, was the motivation I needed to keep my grades up. If they fell too low, Aunt Aerin wouldn't let me spend the night with anyone, and I'd have to quit the team. I knew I had to stay close to Gabby to stay close to the alcohol I loved so much.

I told Justin about my new friend, I told him I had good grades, and I told him I stayed at Gabby's house, but I didn't think he needed to know that part of the fun we had was sneaking her parent's booze.

Gabby didn't drink as much as I did. I would wait until she fell asleep and sneak more sips from her parents stash until I was wasted. That worked until her dad busted me one night during the summer between junior and senior years. After that he wouldn't let me spend the night, so volleyball and softball and my grades didn't matter as much anymore.

I was afraid to tell Justin because he was all I had left of who I was, and I couldn't lose him. I didn't want him to break up with me or get mad, so I kept the drinking a secret. I told him how much I missed him and how I couldn't wait to see him and how I wished he had followed me to Washington instead of enlisting. I tried to make him feel bad for my misery while he was living it up. But he remained as steady and strong as ever, wanting me to hang on and wait, promising he would come for me when the time was right.

He loved to write about all of his Air Force escapades, and I loved reading about them. But sometimes I felt like the better his life was getting, the worse mine was getting—and I resented him for having so much good to tell me about, even though in reality it wasn't all good.

During basic training his letters made me feel like I was there with him: I was tired for him, and my muscles ached when he talked about all the squats and drills they had to do. I got angry with him at the drill sergeant who kept him up running in place until three o'clock in the morning. The physical challenges were endless, but he met them—every single one. I loved him for it, for how strong he was despite the difficulty. But I started to doubt his words.

In my letters I was lying by omission, not volunteering the fact that I was lifting booze from friends' houses or that I feared becoming my mother after all the years I swore I'd never be anything like her.

His letters always made it seem like his only problems were from other people. So did mine. I imagined that he was dealing with tough stuff too, or maybe he was dating other girls and leaving them out of our letters.

He would write pages and pages sometimes about the most mind-numbing things. My least favorite diatribes were about how he could assemble and disassemble the parts to his gun, or worse, how to clean them. Only slightly less boring were his descriptions of the planes, which I already knew plenty about from all the years he'd taken me on fantasy field trips (and real ones) to see them.

He told me he wouldn't be flying a fighter jet after all—he would be a plane refueler—but he didn't complain. He tried to share every detail of the plane he was learning to fly and the process of hitching and refueling—I think it was partly to have something to say and also to help him remember it better himself.

I wondered about what he wasn't sharing more than what he was.

The further down the hole I went, the more I doubted him. I stopped writing every week, and by the start of my senior year he was lucky if I put a letter in the mail once a month. I felt like there was nothing to say anymore. All the words were used up. Love wasn't enough, it never is.

He pledged his love in every letter, and I bemoaned the distance. He wrote about his career and the missions he was allowed to talk about, and I lied about staying sober and picking out a college. Like Lizzie, he was moving on to a better life, and I wasn't. We had nothing in common anymore, and I began to doubt if we ever had anything in common in the first place except a house and bad parents. I couldn't even remember what it felt like when he sang to me or held me and kissed me—not that I wanted to.

That's when I decided that even though Justin would always live in my heart somewhere, I didn't love him—maybe I never had. I only used him as a crutch to get through a miserable childhood. I wanted him to fade into my history like everything else had.

When Aunt Aerin took me in and time was ticking closer to the day I could be with Justin again, life should have gotten better, but it didn't. The only thing that helped was the soothing burn of Johnnie Walker, who had become my main man. I found a bum in our little town who would buy me a fifth for twenty bucks and a swig—which was more like half the bottle, but in my desperation I took him up on the deal more often that I would like to admit.

Over time I learned how to hide my depression and drinking from Aunt Aerin so she wouldn't ask questions or ground me. As long as I kept my grades to passing, talked about college like it was a real possibility, and threw in details about classes or other kids every now and then, she let me go where I wanted and do what I wanted. I wasn't a bad kid—I didn't get in fights or skip school—so she had no reason to suspect that I was doing anything wrong. But she took it hard when I didn't go for volleyball or softball after Gabriela's dad caught me.

"It's your senior year, sweetie; this is the one to remember."

"I already did sports, so it's not like I'm missing out, and it's too hard to study and work at the shop and play."

"You don't have to work so much. I can get someone else to come in and help. Don't use work as an excuse to miss out on all the fun."

"No, it's OK. I would rather have the money—more for college."

Eventually, she let it go. She wasn't a bad guardian; she was just too involved in other things to notice my problems if I played like there weren't any. She had her shop, which she gladly paid me to work in after school. The work kept my pockets padded—the better to pay the bum with—and kept her busy selling, ordering, stocking, and cleaning from morning to night. After work, she didn't like to be holed up at home. She had her walks with Pepper and went out almost every night: to an AA meeting, or church, or dinner, or a date (which never went anywhere because she picked apart every man she ever met). Aside from the dates, she invited me to most things, but I didn't always want to go, and she didn't usually want to spend her evenings at home. We loved each other, but we were different. She stayed busy to avoid her addiction, and I hid mine to make her think everything was OK, just as I did with Justin.

When I missed my mom, I drank to her memory. That's when I got the sloppiest drunk. I can't explain it, but I missed her most when things were really good between Aunt Aerin and me. Sometimes in the shop, when it was slow and it was just the two of us, Auntie danced to the music like my mom used to. She would twist and twirl and get me into it too, and it was fun, but all of a sudden it would hurt too. She wasn't my mom, and I felt guilty having fun with her when my mom was dead, so I numbed the guilt and loneliness with drinking.

It was easy to get away with: all I had to do was smuggle the Johnnie into my room before Aunt Aerin got home, or hide it in my backpack if she was already home. Then I'd spend the night alone in my room—no longer for safety from yelling parents, but now for the privacy to wallow in my grief over losing my mom. I would drink until I was too wasted to stay awake or until I had no more holes inside that the alcohol hadn't filled for the night. I knew then—when I bought off the bum and ditched friends, parties, sports, and being a teenager to get my fix—that I had successfully become the woman I missed and hated the most in the world. I realized that my mother wasn't dead; she was me. I was her.

On my especially stupid, drunken nights, I wrote Justin. The letters usually came out in one of a few ways. Sometimes I would profess my love for him and confess I had screwed up again and was drinking—drunk, actually—at that present moment. I would say I wanted nothing more than for him to be there with me, and if he were only there, if he would just come for me, I wouldn't have to drink every night to drown my grief about my dead mother and sad orphan life. Those letters never made it to the mailbox; I'd always tear them up the next morning.

In other versions I bemoaned my horrible life: how my aunt didn't understand me, how my mom and his dad had ruined my life, how other kids got happy lives and how I hated being away from him and missed him so much. Some of those made it to him; most didn't.

The other variety consisted of handwriting that was so ridiculously messy even I couldn't read it. Nope, they didn't make it to the mailbox either.

It was silly the way I treated our relationship back then. I wanted Justin, but only right then and on my terms. I had a hard time imagining my future with or without him. For so long he was part of me but the time and distance changed us whether we wanted it to or not.

He wrote about life in the Air Force and having to decide if he would reenlist or call it good once we were able to be back together. He wanted to know what I wanted. I dodged the question. I couldn't get past our past; I only saw what we had, and I wanted that back. He would assure me in every way he could that we still had it, and then he would use the word I hated: *Wait. Just wait, Haylee; I'm coming for you.*

I was angry with him for leaving me in the first place. I didn't care that he was doing what was best for us. I didn't care that he promised me forever. He told me to wait, but he got to go on with his life, and he wanted me to decide if he stayed in the Air Force or left. I didn't see it as him including me in one of the biggest decisions he would ever make; I saw it as him pressuring me to decide his life for him. It made me mad at him—when it didn't matter, he cared about my opinion, but back then, when it did matter, he made the decision for us. I used my anger at him as another excuse to drink.

I used anything as an excuse to drink. I had a problem, and I couldn't see it. At least I was pretty good at hiding it, or so I thought.

Aunt Aerin would talk to me often about my mom's drinking. She said Mom didn't turn into the slobbering drunk she was overnight; it took time. Mom stole alcohol from their parents and would always pressure Aunt Aerin to drink more than she wanted because Mom always wanted to drink more and more herself.

Then Auntie would ask me if I had urges to drink. I only told her about the old times with Clayton and Mom, not about now. I felt like her eyes could bore straight through me and see the truth. Once, at the shop, I lost my temper with her over it. It was better than having to admit I had a problem. Luckily there weren't any customers in the store. I had been putting shot glasses up on a revolving shelf, replacing what had been sold earlier that day, and the sight of the shot glass in my hand set her off. She started recounting when she first realized she and my mom had a problem.

"Are you accusing me of being like you guys?"

"No, no dear, it's not that at all. I'm sharing history, letting you know what to look out for so you can spot it in your own life. The chances of you becoming an alcoholic are . . . "

"I *know* what the chances are! You tell me every five seconds. I don't need this lecture again. My mom was a lousy drunk who never got sober. I get it, I get it! You've told me a million times, and if you hadn't, I would still know because she was drunk every day of my freaking life! And you're not. You got sober, and you want me to be like *you* and not her. I know this, Auntie; I'm just tired of hearing it. And she's my mom, OK? I can't take you badmouthing her all the time."

"I didn't mean for it to come out that way."

"No, you didn't, but it did."

"I'm worried for you, Haylee. When you got here you were more open, you did more with me and with your friends. Now you hide out in your room—like she did. You have to understand why I worry."

"It doesn't mean I'm up there chugging on a fifth of Johnnie Walker!" (That's exactly what it meant, and even though I denied it, it felt good to let the words escape.) "It means I want my privacy. You're so nosy; you always have to be up in my business. Can't you leave me alone? I do everything you want me to do. I help out at your stupid store and put up with your man-of-the-month dates. Can't you put up with me shutting myself in my room? I lost my mom!"

That's what I did to get pity: bring up the dead mother. I didn't cry much anymore, except when I was alone in my room, so instead of crying I chucked the shot glass across the store, aiming low for a ground hit. I wanted to make a point but didn't want to break any of her stuff. I ran out of the door and yelled behind me, "If you need me, I'll be in my room getting drunk!"

It was the truth. That's exactly what I did. She knocked on the door later that night and found me half drunk with a letter to Justin half written beside me.

"Haylee? Haylee, honey, can I come in?" It really wasn't a question she was asking, more like a statement. I was busted again. My room probably smelled like a bar, and I was in no condition to talk. "Why won't you leave me alone?"

"Oh, Haylee. You've got a problem; can't you see that?"

"I'm fine.."

"If you were fine, you could stop. But you can't, can you? You need help."

"I don't."

"What will it take to make you quit?" She sat on the edge of my bed and rubbed my shoulder. She wasn't mad; she wanted to help me. I expected her to yell, to ground me or to punish me, but it was an ear she offered, and I wasn't used to that when I'd done something wrong. Clayton yelled; Mom ignored, she grounded, Justin fixed things. Listening was a new thing.

"I can quit any time."

"We've been down this road before, and you didn't. You're obviously not drinking for the fun of it or you wouldn't be drinking alone in your room after a fight. You say you don't have a problem, so then why are you drinking?"

I knew right away.

"Justin. I miss him." I tapped the paper with my pen.

"OK, so did you drink when he was with you?"

"Yeah, but . . . "

"No, honey, no *yeah, but*. If you drank with him, he's not the reason you're drinking. What is it?"

"My mom's dead."

"But you drank when she was alive, didn't you?"

"Yeah."

"There's something inside you making you drink. It might only be that you are addicted and you need help to quit, but it might be that you're running from something: memories of the past, regret for what you've done. I don't know; only you can figure it out. But you'll need help."

"I don't know," I said trying to make my eyes focus on her. The room was starting to spin and her face was doubling up. I knew I drank too much that night; I wished I hadn't had those last couple chugs, but it was too late to take it back. Usually that was when I told myself next time I wouldn't drink that much because it felt gross. Always next time.

"Maybe I'm just an alcoholic."

"Do you want to quit?"

"Sure."

"Really?"

"Of course."

"If you want to, you will, but you can't do it alone; you need help. Are you sure you really want to quit drinking, for good?"

"Yes, I said."

"Quitting is a huge commitment. It's forever, for the rest of your life. I'm only asking because forever is a very long time to go without another drink. I can help you quit if you want to, but if you don't, I don't want to waste my time."

"Wow, thanks."

"Oh c'mon now, you know I didn't mean any harm. I've tried before to help people who don't want to help themselves. It hurts too bad, and I have never been able to get one person sober who didn't want to."

"You tried to stop your parents..."

"Yes, and husband number one . . . and your mother. Oh how I wanted her to quit drinking! She was so much like you, defensive and locked in. It killed me. I know I talk about it a lot, but Haylee, I loved her." She crawled onto the bed and wrapped me up in her arms, like she was a kid all over again. "She was my baby sister. I wanted so much for her to be OK. I tried to keep her from it when we were little, but then, when we were older, we turned into them. Your mother was the life of the party, so lively and full of energy. I drank to chase away the pain; your mom, though, she drank because she liked it," She smoothed my hair and chuckled softly, "liked it so much she never wanted to quit. It started to get in the way of everything, like it is for you. School, boys, life—nothing else mattered Our whole world turned into getting drunk one night and regretting it the next day, only to drink again. I got sick of it and wanted to quit, but I didn't want to do it alone. I didn't think I could. I begged her to stop with me. She would for a little bit, but she couldn't stay sober long."

"I can go weeks without drinking, Auntie." I said.

"Uh huh, when was the last week?"

"A while ago."

"I couldn't make her quit, Haylee. The only one I could make quit was me, and I did. We grew up. I moved on with my life and figured out how to stay sober."

"How?"

"Well . . . one way is to avoid it, which is harder than it seems. Another way is to get support, to be around other people trying to stay sober."

"That's why you go to meetings?"

"Yes, exactly. AA and Celebrate Recovery. I used to go to meetings every day, sometimes two or three a day. It's still a struggle for me, and those people are my friends now. I don't want to go back to that life, and I want to encourage others who want to live sober. I'll go until I die. If you'd like to come to a meeting some day, I would be happy to bring you; I think it might help."

"I don't think I'm ready for that."

"Maybe not, but are you ready to tell Justin you've been drinking?"

"How do you know he doesn't know?"

"Have you told him?"

"No."

"That's how. You're ashamed of it. It's a secret you're keeping, a sickness that's eating you from the inside out. Justin loves you, and you want him to see the good in you, not the thing you hate the most. Why don't you tell him next time he calls?"

"He'll be so mad; he'll hate me. I told him I was done drinking when I moved here and got busted the first time."

"You really think this boy who has done everything he has done for you would hate you for telling the truth? I doubt that. He might be upset, but I think you're being a little melodramatic, dear. Try it, will you?"

"Maybe."

"I guess I'll have to take it. And no more booze in my house. I can't be around it. My house is the one place I know I can go and not be tempted. I don't want it here; are we clear on that?"

"Yeah, OK."

"Thank you. Oh, honey, I love you so much." She hugged me hard and held me there for a long time before getting up. I knew then what a mother's love should be like.

She wanted me to move on, but I was afraid I'd disappoint her, too. Her question rang in my ear: was I really ready to be done drinking? Right then I felt like crap, so I was done drinking for that night for sure. But forever? It was such a long time.

I decided yes—yes, I wanted to be done—but not right away. Still, that was the night I started to hate drinking and finally admitted I had a problem. I only admitted it to myself, I was powerless over alcohol, it had made my life unmanageable, and I was hiding and lying to cover it up. I was ashamed.

I didn't magically get better in one night. It took a long time—years, actually—before I was finally ready to be done, and a whole lot of grief between admitting I had a problem and getting and staying sober.

I started, like Aunt Aerin suggested, to tell Justin the truth. I spilled the words out on paper because I couldn't do it when he called. In the letter I confessed everything: I told him I had never quit drinking, that I was stealing it and buying it from a bum. I told him Auntie's story about quitting and that I wanted to quit too, but that I was afraid. I finished the letter with apologies and wishes to see him. I put it in the envelope, addressed and stamped it, and almost put it in the mailbox—but I couldn't do it. I wasn't ready. I couldn't admit it to him or anyone else because I didn't want to quit yet.

Instead, I convinced myself Justin was doing the same thing. I told myself his letters were only half-truths and that he was omitting the bad stuff too. I liked that scenario better than the alternative, which was that he really was changing into a better person.

He wrote that he felt sorry for the breaking and entering and stealing we had done. And he wrote that he was sorry for the pain he had caused others, even though he didn't think fighting for what he believed in was wrong. He was growing stronger and achieving everything he had set his mind to, and I was rotting away.

I wanted him to be lying to me. I hoped he was as miserable as I was, but I didn't know for sure. All I knew after that talk with Aunt Aerin was that I was becoming everything Clayton and my mom said I would become: a lousy, good-for-nothing loser.

At least I wasn't as much of a loser as Justin: I didn't get kicked out of school my senior year; I stuck it out and I graduated. He was proud of me, Auntie was proud of me, and I was shocked myself.

I celebrated graduation the way I celebrated everything back then: with alcohol and pot. A bunch of us had a huge party at this kid named Danny's house. His parents knew what we were doing but allowed it because it was our senior party. I could tell Aunt Aerin was worried about me going, but she let me, probably because she felt bad that Justin couldn't make it for the ceremony.

He said he tried to get leave but it wasn't granted, so he couldn't go without being AWOL. Instead, as a graduation gift, he sent me a beautiful silver heart necklace with three diamonds on the side and matching earrings. I wore them to the ceremony and party and felt bad when I got a little puke on the pendant while I was heaving later that night.

I crashed at the party inside a tent full of my old sports friends and listened to them talk about their plans for the future. They all knew my life was wrapped up in Justin, and they thought it was so romantic. They talked about going away to college, getting married, living at home and going to the community college, or working in Wenatchee, a town about forty-five minutes from us. I dreamed of being with Justin, but I had no plans for myself. I talked about college to keep Aunt Aerin from worrying, but I didn't want to go, nor did I consider getting a job away from the shop. I was aimless. Listening to them, I realized how pointless my life was. Their giggles died off and I alone laid awake staring through the tent screen at the spinning stars and wondered how different my life would be if my mom or I would have—or could have—quit drinking.

Justin's letters never stopped coming, but I stopped reading them after that. I even got to the point where I stopped opening them. I got tired of reading how perfect his life was turning out. I was mad at him for it. He pretended to be there for me; he begged me to wait and said he couldn't wait to see me again, when the time was right. There was no way he could be that good, and if he was that good, there was no way he could still want me if he knew what I was becoming. It was easier to let him fade away than to keep lying to him and wonder if he was lying to me.

I stopped writing the same way I stopped reading: gradually. I didn't write back once, then twice; then eventually it was like I hadn't spent three years of my life writing to him at all.

"Haylee, honey, Justin's letter has been on the table at home for a couple days. Are you going to open it?"

"Yeah, I'll get it when I get home," I told Aunt Aerin one day at the shop.

"I remember when you first moved here how you'd rip them open the second you saw you had one."

"Yeah, I've grown up. He's moving on, and so am I."

"Doesn't seem like he's moving on to me; he's still writing as much as he ever has. Are you still writing him?"

"Wow! When did you turn into the letter police? He's my boyfriend; I write him when I feel like it. Sorry if I don't check in when I send them off."

I was angry at her for butting into my life and angry at Justin for leaving me, for forcing me to move in with her. I ran out of the shop again—only this time I didn't go back.

I took off. I left, just like Karina, just like my mother. No note, no good-bye, just gone.

CHAPTER 14

I DIDN'T LOOK BACK FOR A LONG TIME. I figured I was old enough to live my own life and make my own decisions. Maybe I wasn't old enough to meet Justin's expectations of what a woman was. Maybe I would never be old enough or good enough for him or Aunt Aerin. Maybe he told me to wait in hopes that I'd move on and he could always come out looking like the good guy.

I convinced myself that he was a jerk. I hated him that night. I hated him for leaving me, for doing the right thing, for moving on with his life while I suffered. I hated Aunt Aerin for taking me in and being the most boring and preachy person on the face of the planet. I hated my mom for being a bad mom when she was alive, and I hated her for dying and leaving me to face life alone. I hated Clayton for being himself. I hated everything and everyone. I wanted gone from them all.

I drove home and took Auntie's secret stash. She actually hid her emergency cash in the cookie jar. There was a roll of fifteen hundred-dollar bills in there and I took them all. I justified it because I knew the state had paid her way more than that for me, and that money was sitting in a bank account in her name, but it didn't help me feel any less guilty. I took my car—the one she got me for my sixteenth birthday—and drove away without a look back.

I wound up exactly where I started: at that nasty house at the end of the dead-end road. Clayton was home when I got there. I don't know why, but I went there to see him. He opened the door and extended his other hand to the top of the door frame and stood there looking at me for the longest time not saying anything.

"Yer aunt's been calling looking for you. Didn't figure I'd see you here."

I didn't want him in my business, so I changed the topic to safe territory. "You talk to Justin still?"

"Naw. You?"

"He writes, always the same stuff: guns, planes . . . you know," I shrugged.

"Uh huh."

We were standing outside; it was cold. He looked me up and down. It was not the look he should be giving a girl he practically raised as his daughter for so many years.

"You grew up. You look cold; wanna come in?"

"No, I'm good. I just wanted to come by."

"Where you heading to?"

"I don't know."

"Never figured you'd be the one to turn out this way; figured Justin for the low-life between the two of you."

"Wow, thanks for that."

"Callin' it like I see it, doll, that's all." He spit out the side of his mouth and wiped his lip with the side of his hand.

"I hate you, you know that? I always have. You ruined my life. I hate you so much." I didn't yell; it would have taken away from the point I wanted to make.

"Get off my property."

"Wouldn't want to stay here anyway."

"I'm telling your aunt."

"Good for you. You do that, why don't you?"

I left and drove all the way to L.A. It was a good place to get lost in the crowd, and that's exactly what I did: I got lost.

Without Justin, nothing made sense. Without Aunt Aerin, I had no one. But what I did have, for the first time in my life, was age on my side. I was finally old enough to take care of myself, to work, to drive, to do anything I wanted—except drink, but obviously that never stopped me from it before.

I parked in a grocery store lot and watched for someone who looked likely to help me. I settled on a group of guys a little older than me. I had become expert in picking out the willing; usually younger guys in groups or older working guys were my best bet. All I had to do was smile and flirt the slightest bit and lie about me and

some friends wanting something to drink that night. It worked most
of the time. I asked for wine coolers because they looked too busy to
bother going to a liquor store for me. Wine coolers were better than
nothing. They agreed, and I was set for the night. I spent a night in a
cheap motel near UCLA and drank all twelve coolers.

I drank a lot before I ran away—usually every weekend and
some weekdays if I could sneak it past Aunt Aerin—and though I
hid it, I didn't understand how bad my problem was. I was never
like my mom; I never had the shakes, ever, not once. I blacked out a
few times, but that had always been at school parties, where there
was way too much alcohol and I was mixing it. Even though I was
too afraid to tell Justin I was drinking, I somehow had myself
convinced my drinking wasn't as big of a problem as Aunt Aerin
made it seem.

That night it felt like a celebration: I was free, and I was finally
old enough to be on my own. How could I celebrate and not drink?

The next morning there was no hangover—no shakes or
worrying about what I'd done the night before—just lonely old me
and twelve empty bottles standing up, side-by-side, on the
nightstand. I stared at them as I laid on my side, looking through
them to the fuzzy door just beyond, and let all the lectures Aunt
Aerin gave me blur into one long streaming monologue mixed in
with memories of my mom with the empty bottles I used to see all
around her. I cried quietly—tears ran sideways out of my eyes, over
my nose, pooling into the other and wetting the pillowcase
underneath—but I couldn't bring myself to believe my drinking was
out of control.

There was a reason I made my way to UCLA: Lizzie was there. I
knew her address: she, like Justin never stopped writing me, but
unlike with Justin, I managed to keep in touch with her. It had been
a couple months since I had written her, but that morning, after I
tossed the bottles in the trash, I showed the hotel guy her address in
the return part of my last letter from her. He wrote directions on the
other side of the envelope, and I went to find the only friend I had
left in the world.

She shared a quaint apartment with ShamRae in Pacoima, a city
about a half an hour away from campus if traffic was light. When I

first heard she was going to UCLA, I was happy and sad all at the same time. I was so proud of her. Justin and I wanted nothing more for her than to see her succeed, and she had. The bitter part was knowing she came from the same place that I did, and she was making it while I was still directionless.

In her letters she told me all about how she got to UCLA. ShamRae's parents, contrary to my assumptions, weren't super wealthy or able to pay for their own daughter's college tuition, let alone Lizzie's. Instead, ShamRae's mom, Demery, made them apply for scholarships starting the summer between their sophomore and junior years of high school, the summer after I moved away. I'm not talking one or two scholarships—she made them apply for four hours a day, every weekday of the summer that they weren't working at their summer jobs. And then, when school was in, they had to apply for at least four scholarships each month.

Lizzie said Mr. Reyes was famous for finding scholarships for her to apply for and handing the packets to her on Fridays, just in time for weekend applying. They added it up, and between the two of them, by the time they graduated, they had applied for more than a million and a half dollars in free financial aid. The real miracle was they were each awarded enough in scholarships to cover both of their tuition fees to UCLA—and then some—for all four years of their school programs.

ShamRae was going to be a pharmaceutical tech, and Lizzie wanted to be a counselor, specializing in child psychology. She said it wasn't a miracle, it was hard work, and she worried about the other four or more years of school she still had ahead of her that weren't yet covered by financial aid.

From her letters I also knew they were both busy. Lizzie had a full course load at school and worked nearly full-time at a movie theater, mostly on the weekends. ShamRae had school and a job at a restaurant called Orlando's. They both had to work to cover their bills. ShamRae's parents helped with utilities, but the girls had to pay for rent, books, groceries, and any other expenses. They really did live like poor college kids. I assumed they partied like them too and Lizzie must have just left that out of the letters, but I was wrong about that.

I showed up at their apartment in the middle of the day. No one was home so I waited in my car, reading *Z for Zachariah*, a favorite book of mine that I had thrown into my bag of clothes at the last minute when I left Auntie's. Finally around four o'clock I saw her. She was grown up and not at all the girl I remembered, but I knew in a second it was my Lizzie.

"Hey!" I shouted, getting out of my car and waving.

"Haylee! Where have you been?" I saw the worry on her face immediately. Someone already told her I left. I figured it was Aunt Aerin.

I told her most of the story, but left out the part about taking Aunt Aerin's money.

"Can I stay here for a while? Just until I get on my feet?"

"Oh gosh, Haylee, I don't know. I have to check with ShamRae; we're not supposed to have anyone in our apartment."

She didn't want to help me. All those years we had taken her in and she wasn't sure if she could take me in when I needed it. It hurt, but I tried not to let it show.

"Just until I get a job and can get a place of my own. I swear it won't be long."

"Shouldn't you let your aunt know where you are?"

"It doesn't matter."

"She's worried."

"She's overprotective. I needed to get out of that town. It's too small, and I'm too young," I lied. "You're starting your life; you're on your own; what's wrong with me doing the same thing?"

"People know where I am. I didn't run away."

I was getting mad, but I couldn't get in a fight with Lizzie; she was all I had left.

"Look, I don't want to fight about it. I need to do this. I just need help for a little bit, that's all. Please?"

Surprisingly, ShamRae was easier than Lizzie to convince. She had no problems with helping me out, even recommended I go to Orlando's and see if I could get a job there since they had an opening. I did, and on ShamRae's recommendation, I got the job.

Because I didn't go to school, they scheduled me for the morning and lunch shifts during the week, and I had nights and weekends to myself. My first weekend off I found out exactly how boring Lizzie and ShamRae were. I went out and got some Johnnie Walker and figured we'd listen to music and wind down together when they got home. I imagined it like old times, only Lizzie and I were the grown-ups now, and we were the hosts instead of my parents. I had a couple drinks before they got there and had Queensryche playing on the stereo—not too loud the way Mom and Clayton played it, up just enough to set the mood. ShamRae came home first; her shift ended at eleven.

She looked uneasily at the bottle then at me. "Where did you get that?"

"Some guy."

"You had some guy buy you alcohol?"

"No, not *me*, *us*. It's the weekend—time to let the stress of the week roll off our backs. Want a drink? There's Coke in the fridge to mix it with."

"Um . . . " She breathed deeply before agreeing and poured herself a drink. I laughed at her mix; there was barely any Johnnie in with the Coke. One drink was all she had and she fell asleep on the couch before Lizzie even got home. Lizzie had even less than her.

"Sorry, I can't. I have to study, I have a huge paper due on Monday, and I have to work all day tomorrow. Anyway, you shouldn't bring that here; we could get kicked out."

"They won't kick you out. Who's even going to know?"

"What if my landlord comes to the door?"

"At twelve-thirty in the morning? For what? It's fine, lighten up!"

"I wish I could, but there's so much pressure. I have to keep my grades up to keep my scholarships, and I don't have any time to do homework. I wish this paper was due on Wednesday—then I could have worked on it Monday and Tuesday when I'm off—but it's due first thing Monday. I can't afford to drink this weekend. Another time. When the term ends there will be tons of crazy parties."

"When the term ends? When's that, December? You need to lighten up. We'll celebrate on Monday after it's turned in!" I finished, and with it I chugged down the rest of my glass.

Monday night came and they both had another excuse not to drink, so I drank alone and watched the two of them hunker down over their books. I read my book to feel like I fit in but was self-conscious of how small it was in comparison to theirs.

Lizzie kept pushing me to call Aunt Aerin, but I couldn't. I felt bad about leaving the way I did, and the longer I went without talking to her, the harder it was to make the call. The guilt was horrible. It gnawed away at my insides. I imagined Aunt Aerin calling all my friends in Leavenworth and Lizzie, Justin, and even Clayton, frantically asking if they knew where I was—or being so mad that I took off the way I did that she never wanted to see me again. It didn't matter how she was taking it; I couldn't stomach a call to her.

I spent three weeks with the two prudes until I found a place I thought I could afford on my own. And then, for the second time in my life, I was completely alone—only this time I didn't even have a social worker or CASA or strange foster parents.

I was one hundred percent alone in the world.

Nothing was like I imagined it would be. It wasn't that it was bad; it was just different than I expected. I didn't keep up with Lizzie—or rather I couldn't, because she was always too busy with work or school. I didn't have any other friends and wasn't going to talk to Aunt Aerin or Justin. I was alone.

For months I lived a quiet, empty life, but I wasn't really sad—at least not like when I used to cry all the time. It felt good to be on my own. I was making it. I could do what I wanted without anyone yelling in my face, or telling me what was best for me, or pushing me to be a better person. I was in charge of myself, and I was doing it.

I had everything I needed: food, clothes, and a place of my own—granted, it was a tiny studio, in an old weathered four-plex, with a bathroom I had to share with another apartment, but it was mine. Of course, I had all the alcohol I could possibly want, too, and I didn't have to hide how much I was drinking from Clayton and my mom, from Justin and Aunt Aerin, from Gabby and her dad, or from Lizzie and ShamRae. I didn't have to hide it at all. I found an old decanter table at an antique store and refinished it in a teak stain after watching a do-it-yourself show on a decorating channel. I built up my own alcohol collection and kept my bar stocked up and looking sixty's chic with all my crystal decanters.

Without anyone to hide or limit my alcohol consumption from, I started drinking more regularly. I drank almost daily, but never before work, and I never let it get in the way of working–at first. I liked to work double shifts and covered for people to earn extra money. I liked having money to spend, but I wasn't a very good saver.

I found I enjoyed decorating and turned my place into a retro-sixties kind of scheme to match the bar. I spent most of my extra money on pieces I'd find at thrift shops and antique stores. It wasn't like I was getting wasted every day; but I liked to unwind after a long, hard day of work. I'd usually mix myself a drink when I got home to relax before going out for a walk.

There was a trail called the Milla near the Hansen Dam Park that I walked if I got off early enough and it wasn't too dark yet. It was a private road covered with graffiti and tags, but everyone used it. I thought about running once or twice, but it wasn't really for me. I liked to walk slowly and let the families pass me by and watch people, it was almost like looking at the pictures on the walls when I was a kid. Most everyone was happy or at least not sad or mad. They had lives with purpose, husbands to hold hands with, friends to run with, babies to push in strollers and little ones to call back to them when they ran a little too far off, or said hi to the sullen looking girl with the stick straight hair. The trail made me feel tall; upon it I could see the surrounding city and landscape and watch the day fade to evening and the street lights replace the sun. It was beautiful. It was a good place to get lost in my thoughts—and most of my thoughts seemed to circle back to Justin.

I tried to convince myself I liked being on my own, but everything felt wrong without him. I wanted to write him or call him and tell him I was OK, but I was too far gone. My life had taken a turn down a road I didn't want him to know about: I'd left my aunt and stolen her money, and I knew he wouldn't approve of my drinking habit or my choice to not pursue college. Someday, I told myself, I would quit drinking so much; someday I would make something of myself and make them proud—then I would go back. But I wasn't ready yet.

That didn't mean he wasn't ready to find me.

He came for me.

I'm pretty sure Lizzie told him where I was—that, or Lizzie told Aunt Aerin and she told him. But somehow he found out and, he came for me.

My apartment was a cramped studio, maybe even smaller than the one Coffee had helped him get. He was waiting outside my door one day when I came home from work with two bags of groceries hanging from my arm. He looked so much older. He *was* so much older: four and a half years had passed since I last saw him. All the boyish features I remembered were gone. He was a full-grown man: handsome, strong, broad, and perfect. There were traces of Clayton in his freshly shaven face and form, but his hair was lighter, and his eyes, piercing as ever, were uniquely his. I couldn't look at him; I was so ashamed. I put my head down and pushed my key into the door.

"Haylee, it's me, Justin."

"Yeah, I see that. How'd ya find me?"

"Searched. You're a hard one to track down." I could hear the smile in his voice; I didn't have to turn to see it.

"You ever think maybe I didn't want you to find me?" I asked but motioned for him to come in.

I was embarrassed of my apartment. It wasn't dirty—I was fanatical about keeping it clean—but it was messy: I had clothes on my bed and a couple dirty dishes in the sink.

"Why, what happened? You stopped writing."

"I changed; that's all," I said depositing the bags on the counter.

"Doesn't look like you've changed all that much. You're still the same old Haylee." He smiled and reached to pull me to him. He meant it to be a compliment. I didn't take it like that.

"You're right," I said backing away and crossing my arms, "I'm the same worthless loser I've always been, and you're Mr. Perfect flying his airplanes up in the stratosphere."

He was confused. "I did what I promised you I'd do. I made a life for us. I did it, Haylee!" He was so proud, so sure of himself. "I'm set up. Come with me; I'll show you."

"No, I'm good right here. I work too; I'm set up; I can take care of myself. You see, while you were out there doing *your* thing—not ours, Justin, yours—I was left to figure out life on my own."

"You were safe, you were with your aunt."

"You didn't know I was safe! *You left me! You went off and did your own thing and left me alone.*"

I didn't mean to yell at him; it just came out before I could catch it. "And now after all these years you're going to come back here and pretend like we were never apart. I don't think so. I don't need a hero anymore. I needed one once—and you left!"

"I couldn't do anything, Haylee! We were kids. I couldn't take care of you; they wouldn't let me. And I did know you were safe. After you said you were in Chino, I was the one who told them about your aunt. I was the one who went back to the house and found her address, remember? I called her, I made sure she was OK. And I came back for you as soon as I could, and you were gone."

"Because it was too late. You're too late. I've got my life now, and you're not in it. You left me."

"Is there someone else?" he asked, my heart broke seeing the look on his face.

"What? No," more than anything I wanted to reach out and touch him, but I couldn't. Everything was different, "I just... I... want to be alone."

"Don't do this. Come with me." The tables were turned at last. He was the one begging me.

"I don't want to go anywhere with you. I'm fine here." I said.

"I know you got problems; we can work through them. I'll help you."

"Problems? You don't even know me anymore!"

"I know you drink too much."

"You've been talking to my aunt?"

"I wouldn't have to talk to her to figure that out. There's a fifth on the coffee table—" he swung his hand toward my latest vintage find—"and two others in the trash."

"Whoops, my bad; didn't think it was illegal to drink in my own house."

"Actually, you're not 21, so it is."

I stared at him, searching for traces of the Justin I used to know, but he was gone. The man in front of me was a complete stranger. "What happened to you?! Just leave!"

"I don't want to go without you. I can't. You're the reason I've kept going."

"You're living in the past! I feel sorry for you. Move on . . . I have."

"Haylee, don't do this. Please!" He reached for me again. I knew if I let him touch me, hold me, I would remember who he was. I could fall in love all over again and be hurt worse than before when he left, because he would leave—there was no way he could want me once he got to know who I was now, what I had done, all the lies I had told. I didn't have it in me to lose him again, so I dodged his embrace. But I didn't want him to leave either.

"Fine. Come in. Sit down; let's catch up."

He moved to my loveseat and shuffled a puce-colored corduroy pillow to the side to sit down. He told me he couldn't imagine his life without me, told me that all those years he was telling me to wait he had been telling himself the same things too. Then I stopped writing and taking his calls, and Aunt Aerin told him I completely disappeared. She told him about my drinking, and that I took the money and took off, and that Lizzie told her where I was. He said he didn't care what I had done; he just wanted us to be together.

Even though I avoided the responsibility, in the end, I had made the reenlistment decision for him. Instead of reenlisting, he came to find me. The girls told him that I worked at Orlando's waiting tables during the day and that I smoked like a chimney and that I still preferred Johnnie Walker.

"Oh, so Lizzie ratted me out too. Nice!"

"Haylee, no one ratted you out; they all care about you."

"Uh huh! That's why she didn't even want to let me stay there."

"She was worried. It's hard to overcome what we all went through; she didn't want to fall back into it."

"How about you? Did you *fall back* into it?" I asked, sickly hoping he would say yes so that I wasn't the only one of us to fail.

He swore he hadn't touched a drink or a pipe since starting at Treadmore's. I believed him. I was the only one of us to fail.

He said he owed it all to Coffee: the man loved him like a son and gave him eyes to see life for what it really was. Justin admired him and wanted to make him proud. It was Coffee who went with him to enlist, not his Old Man. It was Coffee who invited him to church with his family and was there standing with him when he got baptized. He invited him over for Thanksgiving and Christmas before he left for basic training, and he even flew out for his graduation.

Coffee had become his family and had given him a reason to change and stay on the straight and narrow, and Justin wanted to do the same for me. He didn't care how far down the wrong road I had traveled. He said I was meant for him, and he wanted me now as much as he ever had.

Hearing it infuriated me. He was acting so good and perfect, but he was no better than I was, and worse, he wanted to fix me, like I was broken or something. He wanted me to see him and run into his arms like the last few years never happened. He wanted us to kiss and head to the first church we could find and get married. He wanted to pick up where we left off, only now it would be for real and forever, and no one could keep us apart. All he wanted to do was keep the promises he made to me. But it was too late.

"You're believing in a fairy tale, Justin. It can't be like that. Everything is different now."

"It can be, Haylee; you're all I've ever wanted." This time he wouldn't be deterred; he took my hands in his and tried to pull me into him.

"Let me go. Don't touch me, please!"

"Whoa, Haylee; what did I do?"

"Just stay away from me! I stopped writing you for a reason, OK? You're not the same. I'm not the same. You make it sound like my life is so terrible, but it's not! I'm happy, OK? Do I regret some of my decisions? Yes, but who doesn't? I'm not perfect, and neither are you, but you know what? Your life turned out OK, and so did mine. I'm happy, but I've moved on. I don't want to be with you anymore. I wanted to, but that was a long time ago, not now."

"You don't mean that." He still knew me too well.

"I do," I said, even though tears were betraying me.

"I don't understand. Give us a chance, please? We can start new. We don't have to pick up where we left off."

"Let me make it clear. I'm not interested," I lied. "I've been over you for a long time. There is no 'us' to give a chance. What we had was a traumatic childhood, and we did what we had to do to survive it. Now you have your life and I have mine, and they're too different for us to get back together. I got tired of waiting. I moved on; you need to too."

"I don't believe you."

"That's your problem. It won't work. I'm sorry; please leave."

I don't know why I was so cold. All I ever wanted was for us to be together, and now that we could be, I was pushing him away even after he had come so far to find me.

He left dejected and deflated but came back day after day for two weeks. The next day I let him in. He had a bucket of KFC and biscuits, which went well with my rum and Coke (I had given Johnnie the day off). *COPS* was on TV, and for the longest time we sat quietly watching together on my burnt orange loveseat like we had done so many times before in a lifetime long ago. This time, though, he was just a visitor — not my salvation from a nightmare life.

We made small talk for a while; then when my drink was empty, I got up to fill it. He watched me mix it, pouring the rum from a crystal decanter I'd picked up at a thrift store months before. I think he looked sad, but I couldn't read him the way I used to when we were younger. I thought maybe he wanted a drink too, but he politely declined my offer to make him one. I ignored the shame within myself when he tried to psychologize me about my drinking. I told him if he didn't like it he didn't have to be around me, which, I reminded him, is what I wanted anyway. We didn't really have anything else to talk about, but he tried to keep the conversation going for more than an hour before finally giving up and leaving.

After that I ignored the knocks, but he kept coming by. He came to my work and tried to talk to me there. I told him that he needed to leave me alone and I was serious. He told me he would wait for me until I realized we were meant to be together.

The more he was around, the worse I felt about myself. I hated the person I had become and that he loved me so much and wanted so badly to fix me. His goodness reminded me of how pathetic I was. I couldn't quit drinking, and in my heart I couldn't imagine life without alcohol. I knew I had a problem, and I knew there was nothing he could do to make me quit if I didn't want to. The only thing to do was push him away. At least if he wasn't around, I wouldn't feel as bad about being such a washed-up loser. But he wouldn't leave me alone. So I called him a stalker and told him I was afraid of him.

"You've got nothing to be afraid of, Haylee. If you want to stay here, fine! Let's stay. I can find a job; we can live here."

"You don't get it! I don't want to be with you. You're the problem. You need to leave me alone."

"I can't Haylee; you're part of me."

"Well then, I'll make it easy for you. Leave me alone or I'll call the cops."

"You don't mean that."

"Watch me."

He stepped back and looked at me, searched through my eyes deep inside my soul, and I made sure he found nothing.

"What happened to you? How did it come to this?" He was so confused. I watched him crumble in front of me. I felt so bad, but I could never be good enough for him. The best I could do was push him away, and I did—and I convinced us both I didn't love him anymore.

He didn't come back after that but went back to writing me regularly. The first letter came two days after I threatened him. I tossed it on the coffee table and left it there.

It took me two weeks to open it.

My one and only love,

Haylee, I don't know what I said or did to make you so mad at me. I know you're angry about me leaving, but you have to believe me—I did it because I love you. It was our only option. There was no other way. I had to do it for us.

I've always loved you, and I always will. I'm going to reenlist, but I'll leave my contact information with your Aunt and Lizzie. I will wait for you, like I always have, please come back to me.

All my love,

Justin

I thought I wanted him gone, but when the knocks ended, I felt miserable, and for the first time the emptiness of my solitary life made me feel truly sad. I hated myself for pushing him away. I couldn't understand why I even did it. All I ever wanted was him, and he came back for me just like he promised, and I sent him away.

I was tempted to write him and tell him I was sorry and I changed my mind, but I was too proud, stubborn, and ashamed.

Instead, I shut everything and everyone out—not that there were that many people in my life. I saw only the day I woke up in. I went to work, put on a pretend smile everyone supposed was genuine, and went home to my hole in the wall. At the end of every shift, every good day and bad one, at the end of every walk and every rare night out I came home to a lonely apartment and good ole Johnnie.

I should have gone out more and lived the party life. Maybe if I had, the emptiness wouldn't have haunted me like it did, but I was a reclusive drunk. I liked the comfort of my own place and the safety it provided—besides, I still wasn't old enough to be legal.

I changed the décor over the course of a couple months to match my insides. Whereas before I looked for quirky vintage pieces that popped with color, I moved slowly to clean, cold, sharp lines in gray and black monochrome. Once when Lizzie and ShamRae came over to drop off some mail from Aunt Aerin (she at least respected my right to privacy and sent correspondence through Lizzie), ShamRae remarked that I should go into interior decorating and said she loved my eye for design. I thought she was trying to be nice and made a point to say most of the pieces were just refinished second-hand pieces. I couldn't accept the compliment; I felt worthless. My life was quiet and safe, but it was edged in a hopelessness that was creeping in on me, drowning me, and I was helpless to fight against it. All I could do was give in.

I stopped reading because the sight of books made me think of Justin. I quit walking because the smiling couples and happy families made me beat myself up for pushing him, and our future together, away. That's when I really started to drink too much. It got so bad I even missed a day of work because I didn't get up from my stupor in time to make the shift. Somewhere in the back of my mind I knew I was getting worse. I justified it, but I was sinking fast.

And then came Jordan.

CHAPTER 15

HOW CAN I DESCRIBE JORDAN? He was everything Justin was not. Justin was hardcore, heavy-metal and guitar jams like Santana and Jimmy Hendrix. Jordan was a country boy through and through.

He came into Orlando's one crisp autumn morning for breakfast and ordered the Lumberjack Special. He was alone, which wasn't entirely unusual. We didn't talk much; I took his order and brought his food. He came back the next day, and the next as well. That's when the banter started.

"Lemme guess," I said coming up behind him, "Lumberjack Special, coffee, extra cream, and a three-dollar tip at the end?"

He tilted his head to look up at me from under his ball cap. There was a glint in his eye: he was noticing me for the first time, even though I'd served him before.

"Let's do it." he said with a smile that light up the blue in his eyes.

"Alright, it'll be up in a bit," I smiled.

He nodded and looked back over his shoulder to watch me leave; I know he did because I looked back at him, too. We locked eyes; his mesmerized me and drew me in. They were a bright, beautiful blue—not at all like Justin's, serious, contemplative green eyes that I had once known so well. They were new, fresh, unknown territory that intrigued me, made me wonder what kind of thoughts swam around in his head. I liked them very much and blushed when I realized I was staring. I looked down quickly and smiled like a school girl, but I kept looking at him—and kept getting caught.

He didn't say much else to me that morning but left a five instead of three ones and winked before he walked out the door.

"Someone's sweet on you!" Kody, the cook, said from behind the counter. Again a stupid smile erupted on my face. I liked him.

I thought about him all day long. I went home that night, had a drink, and went out for a walk for the first time in weeks. Instead of being depressed by the couples holding hands, I thought of the man from the restaurant. I still didn't know his name but couldn't get my mind off his eyes. I hoped he would be there the next day.

All at once I realized that in my whole life I had never been interested in any guy but Justin. Not one. Justin had been it since I was seven years old. Several boys had asked me out over my high school years in Leavenworth, but I turned them all down. I was Justin's, and he was mine.

I wondered if I would give the boy in the restaurant a chance if he asked me. I knew I would, and he did.

It took him long enough to ask me out, but before too long, it was obvious to everyone he liked me. He was young, no, not young, just not Justin's age. He was my age, a year out of high school and working for his uncle on a construction site a block away. His uncle came in every now and then, and other guys from the site started eating at Orlando's as well—sometimes for breakfast and lunch, sometimes only one or the other.

They came in for a month before one of the guys eating breakfast with Jordan asked me if I had a boyfriend one morning.

"Nope, no boyfriend." I smiled, looking quickly in Jordan's direction as I refilled their coffees. There were four guys at the table: Jordan, his uncle, and two co-workers I had also gotten used to seeing.

"A husband?" Jordan's uncle asked.

"Nope, no husband either." I grinned holding up my left hand.

"A date for Friday?"

"Not even a date," I said trying not to look at Jordan, but my eyes darted to his again before I could help it.

"How does a pretty thing like you not have a man in her life?"

For a split-second I thought of Justin, then said, "That's about the sweetest thing anyone has ever said to me." I patted the older man on the shoulder kindly before walking away.

When the plates were cleared they all got up to leave, Jordan lingered uncomfortably. I hoped I knew why he was there, and I made my way over to wipe down the table—something I would normally wait to do until all the customers were gone.

"You need something?" I asked, my heart fluttering inside like a hummingbird's.

"Yeah, um, ah, you wanna go to dinner sometime, or something?"

"Sure, dinner sounds nice. Here," I said writing my number down on the end of his receipt, "my number..." I hated my face for smiling the way it was, but I couldn't help it.

"Friday?"

I breathed in deeply. "I don't know . . . then I'd have to tell your uncle I lied about having a date."

"Yeah."

"Fine, Friday it is. I . . . gotta get back to work," I said, motioning to the table.

"Oh yeah, sure. I'll call you."

"I hope so."

And that was it. He came to pick me up, took me to a nice dinner, and dropped me off. It was nice to spend time with someone who didn't know my past. I didn't want to ever tell him who I really was or where I had come from. I wanted to be someone new. He could make up his own story about how I grew up and what my life had been like.

The next weekend he invited me out to a movie. At the end, Jordan brought me back to my place and followed me to my door. I knew he was going to kiss me. I wanted it, but I was nervous. It was like the first time with Justin all over again—only completely different.

"This is me," I said pointing to my door and turning my back to it so I could face him.

"Nice door." He reached over my shoulder, stepping closer, and tapped it. He was nervous too; I could tell.

"Thank you." I looked up, anticipating.

He nodded, his eyes, blue and brilliant as ever in the porch light, only more intense. It was time. He was tall—much taller than Justin—and closed his eyes as he leaned down to me. I reciprocated and prepared myself for the first kiss I'd had in five years.

The feelings were all there, the anticipation, the thrill of the unknown, the attraction and butterflies, but it was different: his lips were too soft, his tongue too slow, his cologne too musky. None of it was bad, but none of it was familiar. He wasn't Justin.

I opened my eyes and pulled away and stared at him in shock. I didn't want his kiss; I wanted him to kiss me the way Justin did.

"What?" He smiled. There's no way he could have known what I was thinking, and I knew it, so I lied, which was so much better than the truth.

"I'm not . . . ready."

"OK . . ."

"I'm getting over someone. I need to go slow."

"So, I'm the rebound guy?" He let out a breath, took a step back and lifted his hat off his head momentarily. Something about the way he said it made me think this wouldn't be the first time.

"No, it's not like that; it's been a long time. I just . . . I want to go slow is all."

"So what you're saying is there's no way I'm getting inside tonight?"

"The door's all you get." I smiled apologetically, knocking on it with the back of my hand.

"How about tomorrow?"

"I have to work early."

"Next week then? Scout's honor, I won't try anything; we'll do dinner in, that's all."

"And a walk?"

"Where?"

"The Milla. I like to walk there; it's nice."

"It's freezing."

"Then bring a jacket!" I teased.

"It's a deal." He smiled. "Until tomorrow then . . . " He came back, cupped my face in his hands, and kissed me again. It was his kiss, not Justin's, but this time it didn't shock me because I was expecting it to be different. I tried to stop comparing him to the only other boy I had ever kissed, but it was always there in the back of my mind.

It never went away, either: every kiss, every touch I let him get away with, was compared to Justin. I liked Jordan—I learned to like the way he smelled and held my hand and how he would twist my hand this way and that inside his to guide me on our walks. He wanted to be a contractor like his uncle and eventually own his own company; none of that was like Justin. I had to remind myself it was OK to like him and it was OK that he didn't want the same things in life that Justin did. I could tell he was falling for me, and I wanted to feel the same way, but he couldn't quite fill the emptiness inside me.

Once spring came we were always outside. We went to dozens of pee-wee league ball games to watch his uncle's kids play. It seemed like there was a game almost every day after work. He was the best kind of big cousin, and my favorite part was when the kids would look up into the stands and wave at us. The smiles on their faces were priceless. I knew Justin and I could never have had anything like that: neither of us had any cousins—or uncles, for that matter— who cared about us. I did have an aunt, though, I would remind myself before pushing my memories of wooded walks with her and Pepper out of my mind.

Jordan liked to keep busy, and his energy kept my mind off my mistakes—most of the time. We would take long drives up into the Angeles National Forest and walk for hours alongside the forest service roads. He said he felt at home and at peace in the woods. In a lot of ways I felt the same, and I loved him for exposing me to the raw and untamed beauty of nature. He showed me waterfalls and animal dens, and we climbed rocks and trees and stayed out late to watch the stars. But even as I walked hand-in-hand with him, I would find myself wondering what Justin would think of forest walks.

Things got serious that summer, and it was getting harder for me to hide my past from him. I let it slip out one time that my mom died and I went to live with my aunt when I was fifteen. When he wanted to talk about it, I told him it was too painful, which was the truth. It was harder to keep his passions at bay, too. He wanted me, but unlike Justin, his patience had definite limits. In June he took me for a drive up into the mountains to watch a meteor shower. He loaded the bed with an air mattress, and we were lying on it, listening to Tim McGraw and Faith Hill sing "It's Your Love" and watching the stars and meteors. He pointed out all the constellations he knew and I parroted their names back. I had just enough of a buzz to make me nostalgic, so when he took my hand in his and pointed to Ursa Minor, it reminded me of the day Justin had taken me to the museum and shown me the planes. I let my hand go from Jordan's and slid it down his arm, reminding myself that this was not Justin. Jordan propped himself up on his side and looked down at me longingly. He kissed me but stopped abruptly.

"What is it?" he asked, staring into my eyes, digging for what I kept hidden inside.

"What?" I asked, feigning to be perplexed.

"Why won't you let me in?"

"You are in."

"I'm not; you're holding back."

"I'm not," I said, and pulled him down to kiss me again. I wanted to let him in, to tell him about Clayton and my mom and how Justin sheltered me from them and how the world tore us apart and how no matter how much I loved him I'd always, always love Justin—but I couldn't say any of that. What was worse is I knew I didn't want him. I wanted to want him, but I didn't, I couldn't, I belonged to someone else. I knew then that if he were Justin, this would have been the perfect night. We weren't hiding from anyone; I wasn't too young; everything about the night would have been just right for our first time. I think Jordan expected it to be our night, his hand reached up under my shirt and caressed my belly. He moved it slowly up, and up ever so gently, then finally cupped my breast in his hand. His thumb teased my nipple taut, my insides tensed and my hips started to move of their own volition as he fondled me. It felt so good, I wanted to give in to him, but I couldn't. I pushed him off gently and sat up, resting my back on the cab and curling my knees to my chest.

"And there it is: the shut-down."

"That bad, huh?" I smiled, leaning into him after he sat up too and pulled me into his chest.

"Yeah, I mean I'm all for going slow, but it's been months–months, Haylee."

"Some people wait until they're married."

"You never said you were one of them."

"You never asked," I answered.

"Maybe I should have."

"Would that have changed your mind about me?" I asked. I was actually offended at his innuendo.

"No . . . I don't know . . . maybe." He retrieved his hat from beside me and snapped it, out of habit, before fitting it back on his head with both hands and a big sigh.

"Wow, that's harsh."

"Yeah, but it's honest, would you rather I lie to you? Is that what it is? Is that what you want? To wait until you're married?"

"I don't know." I honestly didn't. If he were Justin, I wouldn't have wanted to wait—but if he were Justin, he wouldn't be pushing me for more; he'd be the one putting on the brakes. "It's hard, you know."

"Yeah," he said, moving my hand between his legs, "I know. You're a tough one, do you know that?" he asked, squeezing me in his arms before kissing me on the top of my head.

"Hand me the Jack, will you?" I asked. I took two huge swigs and handed it to him.

"Nope, someone's gotta drive us out of here."

I shrugged and swallowed another gulp before twisting the cap back on.

It was different from then on: we still dated, but I felt him pulling away slowly the way I pulled away from Justin—not because he wanted to but because being hurt would be worse than walking away on his own terms. I knew it was only a matter of time before he left me too. My drinking started to get heavier again. Jordan drank with me often enough but preferred beer and kept it in his truck. He never judged me, but sometimes when he came over I could see him look suspiciously at my bar, like he was measuring the amount of liquor in each bottle, or maybe I only thought he did because I was so self-conscious of it.

Then he found out about Justin, and everything between us changed.

Early one morning, a knock on my door woke me up from a particularly bad binge the night before. My alarm clock was screaming five fifteen in glaring red LED digits across the room by my bedside. I was still the slightest bit drunk and had to shake the fog from my head to remember that I was on my couch, not my bed.

I had come home from work the day before to find another letter from Justin in my mail slot. He never stopped writing and made every kiss I shared with Jordan feel like I was somehow cheating on him. I never wrote him back, but I was compelled to read them, and that night I wanted to reminisce. I wanted to miss him and remember what his kiss and touch felt like. I was afraid I was forgetting him because of Jordan. The two of them were getting jumbled up in my mind. I knew their kisses were different, but I couldn't really remember how anymore because Jordan's was the one I knew. I didn't want to lose my memories of Justin; he was too much a part of me to let go, and I was afraid I was forgetting him. I pulled out all his letters, and I mean all of them: the letters he sent when I was living with Aunt Aerin and all the ones I had collected since moving to California. There were probably close to a hundred of them, and I read them, reliving, remembering the unique and painful love I shared with their author. I must have fallen asleep or blacked out right there on my couch in the middle of my memories because my glass of Johnnie and Coke still had some left in it. I never would have left a drink un-drunk.

"Coming!" I shouted, wobbling a bit when I stood. I was drunker than I thought. I opened the door, unaware of the mess I was. "Oh hey," I said, turning so Jordan could come in. He stood there, staring—at me, then beyond me—concern and confusion flashing in his beautiful baby blues. It dawned on me in an instant what he was looking at. I stared at him in shock and horror. I couldn't let him see Justin—or the proof of him.

"You have a party or something last night and not tell me?"

"No," I said, ambling to the couch to collect the letters as quickly as I could, "just me by myself."

"It smells like a bar in here."

I followed his eyes to the spilled bottle of Johnnie lying on its side next to a case of Coke by the couch. I must have knocked it over during the night.

There was no time to fold and re-envelope the letters, so I tried to collect them, page by page, into one big pile before he could see them. It was no use; Jordan came in and picked up one of the more recent letters and read it. There was no point in trying to hide anymore, so I stood there with the pile of letters clenched in my hands and watched him read one side, then flip to the back side.

He lifted his hat by the bill and scratched his forehead with it before replacing it and looking at me.

"Who is this?"

"Just a guy I grew up with."

He flipped the page back over and looked at the date. "He wrote this two months ago. We've been together for nine, so tell me how come I didn't know about this?"

"There's nothing for you to know."

He looked around—at the letters left to be picked up, at the letters bundled in my hands—and picked another one up and read it as carefully as the first. "Who is this guy?"

"I told you—someone I grew up with, that's all."

"That's not all, Haylee. This guy is in love with you. He's begging you to take him back. And—" he held up the letter he just finished reading—"he's been doing this for a long time. I knew you were holding back. I knew it. I thought maybe you really did just want to wait until we were married, but it's not that. You're still in love with him. Aren't you?"

He said *wait until we were married.* He was looking at my letters from Justin. I didn't know how to answer. I didn't want to admit the truth out loud to him or to myself. "You don't understand. We had a really tough life."

"Haylee, I want to understand; I've asked you to tell me before. Tell me! Get it out now, or we're done."

And even though I knew I didn't love him or want him, I was afraid to lose him too, so I told him everything... well, almost everything. I told him about our horrible parents; about Justin, Lizzie, and me; Justin and me; how my mom died and how I moved with Aunt Aerin; how I ended up at Orlando's; and how I pushed Justin away after he came back for me. I cried some, and when I did, Jordan folded me up in his arms and held me. He asked questions along the way, but in the end it came right back to his first question.

"Haylee, you still love him, don't you?"

I had to say it. "I'll always love him. He's as much a part of me as my arms or legs. I'm not me without him."

"Then why are you with me?"

"I didn't want to be. It was your eyes. I couldn't stop staring at them, and I wanted to know who you were—and I thought maybe I could forget him if I fell in love with you."

"But you can't?"

"Can't forget him... but I do love you! I do—but... I love him too." I looked down ashamed before reconnecting with his gaze.

He looked down and shook his head and chuckled, "It happened again. I can't believe it."

"What do you mean?"

"I'm the guy who's destined to love the girl who will never love him back."

Then he told me about Maria. He met her at a wrestling meet his junior year. She was in the away team's bleachers cheering for her brother. She was a senior, and was three months pregnant. The baby's dad was in jail for stealing a car, and she was afraid and alone. Jordan said he fell head-over-heels in love with her and the baby, Miguel, who was born at the beginning of his senior year. He was even there for the boy's birth. He wanted to be Maria's knight in shining armor, the way Justin wanted to be mine. They got engaged his senior year of high school on Valentine's Day and were planning their wedding as soon as he graduated. His parents were nervous and kept warning him about getting involved with a girl with a child and an ex-lover in jail. But he didn't care; he loved her and wanted to be with her forever. Then out of the blue she broke it off to go back to Miguel's father, Daniel, who had apparently learned his lesson and swore he realized his mistakes and wanted another chance with Maria, a chance for them to be a family.

"The worst part," he said, "was that she didn't just leave, and he didn't beat the crap out of me for dating his girl while he was locked up. He thanked me for taking care of her. They wanted me to be their friend and to still see Miguel and pretend like everything was cool. I couldn't do it, I loved her. I suppose there's a part of me that still does. So, "he said with a sigh, "I moved out here to work with my uncle—and I fell in love with the wrong girl all over again."

"You didn't fall in love with the wrong girl. I love you."

"I know you do. But you said it yourself: you love him, too. I'm not going to spend the rest of my life competing with his ghost, especially one that could come back and take you from me. I should have realized that's what was happening a long time ago. I want the girl that wants me the way Maria wanted Daniel and you want Justin. I don't want to be second. I want a girl who wants me more than anyone else. You're not her; you're already used up."

"I'm not used up! I'm still a virgin... he wouldn't..."

"No, he wouldn't, but yeah, you are. You're waiting for him, or to figure out if you're done with him. I thought you were waiting to see if I was for real, not for another guy. I can't do this, Haylee. You can't either. Make peace with your past. Call your aunt, and for God's sake, call this guy and figure it out."

I should have begged him not to break up with me, promised him I could and did love him more than Justin, but I couldn't. I just cried, and he held me while I did. And then, just like that, we weren't together anymore, and I was alone and empty all over again.

Life went on, and my apartment changed again—this time to a rustic, woodsy theme—I think to remind myself of Jordan and I spent more time in nature, but always alone. I missed Jordan's company more than I imagined I would, but I longed for Justin. Still, I resisted the urges to reconnect with him. It had been too long. I knew he still wanted me, but he wanted an idea of what I had been, not the bona fide lush I had become. And I was, by then, a lousy drunk: I was late for work at least once a month because I slept too late after drinking alone too much the night before. I was officially spending more money on booze every month than I was on groceries, and I knew it was getting worse. But still I held out.

I met another guy, Jon, who was nothing like Jordan or Justin. I think that's why I said yes when he asked me out—because he was everything they were not. They had goodness inside them; there was very little good in Jon.

I met him in the bar part of a restaurant one night—there were a handful of bars I could sneak into without getting carded, and I began to frequent them to avoid the loneliness. Jon liked Johnnie Walker too—and my lips. After I ordered my drink, he commented on it: "Not many girls your age go for Johnnie Walker."

"I'm not most girls, I guess," I said with a little flip of my hair.

I didn't mean to flirt—I wasn't much of a clubber, and I wasn't looking to get hit on; I just went there to be around people. But when he asked me to dance, I obliged, and I didn't resist when he kissed me. This time it was no surprise his kiss was different from the others. They all had different kisses, and I compared his not to both, but to Justin's. His was the kiss that all others would ever be compared to. He said we would make a cute couple and asked me out.

We made a miserable couple. We hung out for a few weeks then he dropped me off one night and didn't take the hint at the door; he wanted in, and he wanted me.

"Hold on, cowboy! You're not getting in here." I said as I turned the key and felt him pushing his way in behind me. I meant it, but he wouldn't accept it or thought I was joking or something.

"You better believe I am," his whiskey breath said headily at my ear, "You invited me up, and now you're shutting me down?"

"I'm not. You said you'd take me home. I didn't agree to anything else."

"Oh, I think you did." He pushed me into my apartment and was turning me toward the bed.

"NO! NO! Get out of here, you hear me?" I demanded, digging my feet into the carpet and fighting off his hands, holding me tight at my hips. If he made it to my bed I was planning on grabbing my clock and hitting him over the head with it, but instead he spun me around and slapped me hard across the face.

"No?! You're a worthless tease!"

Thankfully he let me go, turned and slammed the door hard on the way out. My heart was pounding in my chest, adrenaline and fear coursed through every vein in my body. The metallic taste in my mouth reminded me of Clayton and the life I once knew, and didn't want to know again. I went into the bathroom and looked at my face. I had a huge welt, clearly the shape of a hand, across my left cheek, and a little crack at the edge of my lips. I stared at a spinning reflection of myself and cried; afraid, humiliated and ashamed of what had just happened and who I had become. And I called the only person I could think of…

*　*　*

"Hello?" His voice was gruff, raspy. I woke him up; I was sure of it. I felt terrible, but I had to.

"Hey. It's Haylee." I couldn't help but cry.

"Haylee? What's wrong? Are you OK?"

"No, I'm so sorry."

"Where are you?"

"At my house. Please come. I'm so sorry."

"I'll be there as soon as I can; wait for me."

Before I opened the door I checked the peephole to be sure it wasn't Jon, though I didn't think he would actually come back. It was safe, so I opened it.

"What happened?" Jordan asked, turning my face in his hand and leaning the welt to the light.

"Ouch!" I winced when he tried to touch it. It was going to bruise; of that I was sure. "Some stupid guy dropped me off then tried to get me to bed. When I said no, he belted me."

"Who is he?"

"I don't know—just some guy I met. His name was Jon." I was mortified.

"Why did you let him in?"

"I didn't. He pushed his way in."

"That's not good, Haylee. You can't be letting guys know where you live."

"It wasn't 'guys'; you and he are the only guys I've ever had here—except Justin."

"And we're probably the only two guys you've dated since you lived here."

"So?"

"So," he said going to the freezer, "you can't bring guys here. They're not all like me."

"OK, fine," I said. He wrapped some ice in a towel and handed it to me.

"You haven't called Justin yet, have you?"

"No."

"How about your aunt?"

"No."

"You need to. You know that."

"I don't want to... I'm not ready."

"That's not what I said. I said you need to. You're tearing yourself up inside; you're going downhill."

"Wow, thanks."

"Look, I care about you; you need to hear it. You drink way too much. You're running from your past, and it's killing you! You think something like this won't happen again? You keep going out drinking and it's only a matter of time until something worse happens."

"Don't come in here and tell me I have a problem."

"First of all, you called me, remember? And second, I never said that. If you think you have a problem, that's your deal. What I'm telling you is if you're going to be going out, you need to be careful—and face your demons, you know you need to deal with them. Stop running. What's it going to hurt to call your aunt and apologize? What bad can come from calling Justin? Just do it. Look, I gotta go."

"Please don't," I begged, pulling on his arm.

"Haylee, I can't stay. I'm not who you want; I'm the one who was closest. I told you, I'm not going to be second. Call him." He kissed me on the forehead and left, turning to say "Lock your deadbolt" before twisting the handle and shutting the door behind him.

Jordan told me to call Justin, to make peace with Aunt Aerin. He was a good man. Why couldn't I have loved him and left them in my past? I knew whoever finally fell in love with him would be well taken care of.

After what Jon did I didn't leave home much at all. I got sucked into Facebook. I could stay safe in my apartment cocoon playing stupid games with "friends" and taking silly personality tests. I'd come out for work, shopping, walking the Milla, and the occasional jaunt into the Angeles mountains, but otherwise I was content to hole up in my apartment.

But my apartment wasn't my home. Justin was home.

I knew his address from his letters, but I wasn't ready to fully engage, so instead I found him on Facebook—I could never forget that face even if it was now the face of a man and not the boy I once knew. I clicked. Just a quick look was all I allowed myself, but I looked every day. He was always there, perfect as ever.

In Justin's Facebook picture he was muscled and shirtless with a fighter jet in the background and had the most beautiful smile I had ever seen. His status said he was single.

I wanted to be his again. I knew then how much I had thrown away, but I was afraid we couldn't get it back. There was nothing else I could see because of his privacy settings, and I wasn't ready to friend him, so I clicked away. But, he found me.

He would friend request me regularly, and I denied him, but it made me smile. He would send me messages, just like the written ones he still wrote, only these were more frequent, and he opened his profile so I could see it without accepting his friend request. He still loved me and waited for me after all this time, and he still wanted me. But I wasn't ready to believe it or admit I had a problem, so I ignored him.

Then I woke up in the alley.

CHAPTER 16

I MISSED MORE DAYS OF WORK because I was drunk or hungover than ever before, but I knew cheap jobs were a dime a dozen, and I was a cute girl who could easily get another one if Orlando got sick of my excuses.

I spent more money on booze than anything else but rent—even more than my beloved décor— but I justified it: I had expensive taste in liquor, and I had no family, no obligations, so I could spend my money on anything I wanted. I blacked out at least once a month, but I was always at home, so it didn't scare me anymore. I could justify it all, and I did—every day and week and month.

Lizzie told me to get help and stopped talking to me until I did. Jordan, ever the good guy, told me every time I called him in a drunken stupor—even after he found a new girl, some famous reality adventure show personality—that I was ruining my life and needed to face my past. Orlando and the girls at work even tried to do an intervention on me. It didn't work, and there was no meat to Orlando's threats to fire me—he couldn't fire me; he worried over me too much. Everyone knew I was drinking my life away, but I still wanted to justify and deny it.

Then the alley woke me up or rather, I woke up in it.

I had no idea where I was, how I got there, or what I had done. My purse was gone and my shoes, too. The last thing I remembered was the previous day, after work. I talked a guy into buying me some of my favorite Scotch whiskey and that was it.

That's when I knew my life had become unmanageable and I was powerless over my addiction. Johnnie wasn't my friend; he was ruining me. I didn't know how to quit, but I really wanted to that morning. I was freezing, embarrassed, and afraid. I still, to this day, don't know what happened that night. I have absolutely no memory of it. No flashes, no guesses—I do not know.

Being that afraid and vulnerable and lost gave me a reason to want to quit, but I wasn't strong enough to do it alone.

It had been almost two years since I spoke to her last, but I finally I called Aunt Aerin and bawled on the phone. I didn't tell her about the alley, only that I was sorry and ready to get help. She sounded so much older, and I ached for the time I missed with her. I had someone who loved me, and I left her.

She wasn't upset; she was glad to hear from me. She reminded me about the AA and Celebrate Recovery meetings and this time I found one that was close, and I went. They helped me too. The first one scared me but I stuck it out. I was not a churchgoer—hadn't been since Gramma Diaz took the neighbor kids and us to AWANA—but the one I found was in a church. I can't say it any other way: walking in there terrified me:

"God...," a man said, and then the rest of them joined in, like it was some kind of cult,

"Grant me the serenity to accept the things I cannot change,
The courage to change the things I can...
And the wisdom to know the difference.

Living one day at a time;
Enjoying one moment at a time;
Accepting hardships as the pathway to peace;
Taking, as he did, this sinful world
As it is, not as I would have it;
Trusting that He will make all things right
If I surrender to His will:
That I may be reasonably happy in this life
And supremely happy with him
Forever in the next."

It was so simple, and the hardest thing I ever had to do.

I couldn't change my past, my mom, Clayton, or how we grew up. I needed to accept.

But, I could change my future. I just needed courage, and they were there to help me.

And ... I missed Justin.

I didn't deny his friend request after that, but I couldn't tell him what I had become. His pictures, like mine, had no mom or dad or spouse or child like other people had; he had friends, there were guys from his base and a girl named Tatum with dreadlocks tagged in several of them but for the most part, he was like me: alone in the world. We were alone together. And he still wanted me; I still wanted him. Would knowing what I had become change his opinion? I was afraid it would, so I still avoided real contact.

I went to meetings, relapsed, thought about the old times, and clicked on Justin's wall. He messaged me and I ignored him, sent letters and I never wrote back—no longer because I was mad at him, but now because I was afraid he wouldn't want me after all I had done to him and the mess I was. I wanted to get better first, then maybe, maybe it would work out.

"I know you're there. I still love you. I just want to know you're OK. Call me, message me, something.

Hello.

Haylee?"

I couldn't.

I couldn't tell him.

Then all at once I realized I could.

I had nothing to lose. This old guy at my Wednesday meeting confronted me on it after I shared my fears about talking to him again; cross talk was discouraged when we're sharing during the group so he came up to me right after the closing huddle.

"The worst he could do is not want you, right?"

"Right."

"So how is that any different than what you've got now?" he asked, hands splayed wide open.

"I don't know."

"You do too know! It ain't no different. You're torturing yourself worrying and wondering, kid. Just talk to the guy."

I had only seen him twice in the last five, almost six years. The old guy was right: I had nothing to lose.

So I did it. In one gigantic message, I poured it all out to him: where I'd been, what I'd done, Jordan, Jon, the escalating drinking, the alley, and my slow walk to beginning recovery. I told him I knew he only meant to help me back then. I told him I knew that he loved me and I hoped he still wanted me. But I also said I'd understand if he didn't want to have anything to do with me. He had a great life, and I had made a great big joke of mine.

He only had one thing to say to all of that:

"It's about time! I'm coming for you right now."

"Justin, you don't have to."

"I want to."

"I'd rather meet you somewhere else."

"You name it."

"I don't know yet. I'll figure it out and let you know when I do."

"Let me come get you, Haylee. I don't care."

I was broken. It didn't matter, so I said "fine" and panicked. I went to four meetings in a row to keep myself from drinking from the anxiety. I talked to my sponsor, a lady named Jeanell who had been sober for eleven years for hours while I waited.

He came the next day, and this time I let him take me in his arms while I cried and apologized and cried more. He was an angel, more beautiful than I remembered, strong and steady and everything I was not. He listened to me blubber, then wiped my tears with his thumbs.

And there it was—the kiss all others had been compared to: his kiss, his lips, his taste, tongue, and smell, the one that was made for me, who had always been mine, who I doubted for the stupidest reasons but who had never doubted me.

He wouldn't let me go for the longest time after that except to pull me away and look at me to be sure I was real. Then he reached into his pocket and pulled out a ring box, got down on one knee, and proposed to me.

"Haylee, I've waited since we were kids for this." His eyes were bright and full of joy. "You are the love of my life. I have loved you for as long as I can remember, and I want nothing more than to spend the rest of my life with you. Will you marry me?"

My hands went to my mouth just like in all the movies, and I started crying all over again. I couldn't understand how he could still want me.

"I'm not well," I cried.

"I don't care."

"I want to quit drinking, but I can barely make it one day. I try— I'm going to meetings, and I'm avoiding it, but I keep slipping."

"I don't care."

"I've been so angry at you."

"I don't care.

"I..."

He stood up and covered my excuse with his lips. The kiss took my breath away.

"I don't care about any of it. We can work through it. You want to quit, right?

"Yes, but it's so hard."

"Then, we can work through it, like we always did. All I want to know is if you'll marry me. Be with me forever Haylee."

"You're sure?"

"Never been more sure of anything in my life," he said, and I remembered the boyish grin that came with the wink. "C'mon, girl, say yes."

I nodded, biting my lip. I was afraid to say it.

He hollered and spun me in the air.

"Pack your things; we're out of here!"

"Where are we going?"

"To get married and go home."

"Washington?" His envelopes had been from the McChord Air Force base since he reenlisted. "You live in Washington now?"

"Yup, they might station me somewhere else before my term is up, but I like it there. They've got planes and Sasquatch too."

"I know. I lived there, remember?"

"Of course."

"So have you had a chance to prove he existed?"

"Not yet, but I will."

We laughed; then he got serious.

"You know I never meant to hurt you?" He said and ran his fingers through my hair.

"I know, it all hurt so bad. I needed to blame someone. None of it was your fault. You were the only one really there for me and I took it out on you. I'm so sorry."

"I've got you now; you have nothing to be sorry for."

"Except the lost years. I wasted them."

"We'll move on from here, OK? Accept the things we can't change, right?"

"You know that?"

"Mmm hmm." He winked.

He put the ring on my finger, and in less than two hours, everything I owned—which wasn't much—was crammed into a rented U-Haul.

Our wedding was quick—I think he wanted to be sure I wouldn't take off again or change my mind. We didn't go straight back to the base since he was granted an extended leave, so we went to Aunt Aerin's. There she was waiting for me, with open arms. I couldn't see how she could forgive me either, but I accepted it when she said she did before I even asked her to.

There was a little church in the mountains Aunt Aerin knew well—it was her own. She asked the pastor to marry us, and he did, on the condition that we take marriage classes when we got back to the base. We agreed—Justin said he had a pastor of his own. I never thought of Justin going to church before then even though he'd told me plenty of times in his letters.

I chose a dress from one of the boutiques in town, and Auntie was my maid of honor. We made Justin find somewhere to occupy himself while she dressed me up and put baby's breath in my hair. There were no other witnesses at the wedding but Aunt Aerin and the pastor's wife. Quaint, quiet, mountainous, special.

We honeymooned overnight in town, strolling the old-world themed streets and dancing to accordion music near the gazebo in the town square. The night ended in a lovely luxurious cabin rental with big glass windows that looked over the Icicle River. It was the most beautiful place I had ever seen in my life. I didn't know that kind of opulence existed.

Then it was time: after all the years, I was finally a grown woman of nearly twenty-one.

I was the woman he had waited for.

I had come home to him, and the moment was ours.

I came out of the bathroom in a beautiful, knee-length burgundy nightgown. He was on the bed, with his guitar. He grinned at me and shook his head in awe as he looked me up and down. He was impressed. He serenaded me with our song, *More Than Words*, and I was impressed, his voice was even more magnificent than I remembered. That time, I wasn't teleported back in time. When he sang it for me I stayed right where I was, in that moment, in that cabin with him. There was nowhere else I wanted to be—especially not back there.

The song finished, and he rested the guitar against the nightstand. The silence between us hung heavy.

"Come here," he said walking toward me. "No more waiting."

"Nope."

"It feels weird after all the time we couldn't. Now we can."

"Did you wait for me?" I asked.

"You didn't ask me before."

"I didn't want it to change my mind."

"Would it have?"

Ahhh, the tables had been turned on me. I didn't want Jordan there in this memory, but he crept in, but only for a moment.

"I'm sorry, no. I love you, no matter what."

"Well OK then, I have to tell you something."

My stomach knotted up. I said it didn't matter, but it did. Whether I intended to or not, I had waited for him, and I wanted him to have waited for me. It was wishful thinking, I knew it was, but I wanted to believe it, and now he was going to reveal that there had been another woman—or maybe more than one. I breathed deep and remembered the prayer: *Accept the things I cannot change.*

"You're it for me, Haylee. No one else, ever. Only and always you. Just you."

"Really?"

"Really. My whole life. You would not *believe* how hard it is to be this hot and say no to all the ladies."

We laughed; it was just what we needed to ease the tension.

But he got serious again really fast. "But they weren't you, Haylee. When you shut me out, I tried. I tried to let you go, to move on but I couldn't do it. Almost … once…"

"The girl in the pictures?"

He nodded, "Yeah, Tatum. I cared about her, probably always will in some way, but I loved you too much to let her in."

"I loved you too much too." The relief that washed over his face warmed me more than any shot of any alcohol ever had and I knew then why I'd waited.

We kissed, and his hands slid from my face to gently trail my collar bone. He slipped the straps of my nightdress over my shoulders and it fell to the floor. I stood there exposed in front of him like never before and shivered in anticipation and uncertainty. He looked at me with desire, lust, and love all mixed together. He was hungry for me. I was no longer sure of myself, not that I ever was. He held me at arm's length and took me in.

"This is the moment I've waited for, Haylee." He nodded his head slowly, "You are... so beautiful." His hands went to me, to touch me. He made me feel as beautiful as he said I was. He made me feel like I belonged in his embrace. Then he lifted me into his arms and I wrapped mine around his neck. Our lips met again and our tongues mingled in their lovers game. I thought he would lay me down on the bed and make love to me right then and there. Instead he took me to the bathroom and turned the shower on.

"What are you doing?"

"Shower. Trust me."

I did trust him, and I was too aroused to question him. I wanted to touch him the way he had touched me. Together we took off his

clothes while the water warmed. It was a luxury shower—I wouldn't
expect less from that hotel—and the water was warm by the time we
were finished. He stepped in and then extended his hand to me. I
tried not to look at him; I didn't know why, but I felt silly. We
weren't kids anymore, but I was shy—and he was obviously excited
about the moment.

"What?" He smiled.

"Nothing." I smiled back looking at him, eyeballing the thing
that was not nothing.

"Oh, it's something!" he said taking my hand in his and leading
me to it. It was hard and warm and he took in a breath when I
touched him.

"Oh!" Was all I could get out. It was all so new and exciting, and
even though I'd known him forever, I barely knew him now—and
certainly not as a grown, naked man facing me. My stomach was
flipping and fluttering, and I was forgetting to breathe again. I
couldn't not smile or look at him or laugh.

Then he pulled me close and held me in his arms, the water
flowing over both of us, warm, cleansing, inviting. He lifted my face
to his and kissed me again. The water sprayed, pouring down
between us and beside us. I didn't think it would work at first,
especially after he tried to wash my hair and the soap got in my eyes.
We laughed as I rinsed the shampoo out; the joyful echo must have
struck us both at the same time because he quit laughing as
suddenly as I did. It wasn't funny anymore; it was time. The water,
like warm rain, made everything seem somehow desperate. Now
was our chance to disappear from life as we knew it, from the pain
of the past and my runaway mistake. Now it was us—for the first
time, we didn't have to pretend to be anywhere but here.

We washed each other. I marveled at his self-control and his
form. His body, fit and maintained from years of military discipline,
was perfect. Maybe there were flaws, but to me, Justin was pure
perfection. All I wanted that night was for him to take me and make
me his, but he took his time instead. He wanted me, that much was
obvious, but he wouldn't have me there. It was a shower—the most
arousing shower of my life, but just a shower. He soaped me up
from neck to toe. It was maddening how he made my body feel

things it had never felt before. His touch sent shivers over every inch of my skin; I had to force my mouth shut and my eyes open.

With strong, calloused hands, twice the size of mine, holding me, covering me, thrilling me everywhere, he touched me and he made sure to explore every inch of my frame. White streaks of lather cascaded down my breasts, back, legs, and torso, caressing me. He was learning the curves of my body, knowing me, falling in love with me all over again. I turned, rinsing my front in the water, and he trailed his hands from my shoulders, into the ridge that led to the small of my back, then around my hips.

He pulled me into him, and I felt him hard against me as he kissed my neck right behind my ear, water flowing into both of our faces. My knees weakened, and I turned back to face him, wrapping my arms around his neck for support. I wasn't afraid of how I looked in his eyes, and even if I had been, all I saw was wonder when he looked at me.

I let him wash me as the water mixed with my tears. It was more than people in a shower together: he was washing the years of abuse, sorrow, regret, anger, addiction and sadness away. He was making me clean, giving me a chance to start over fresh and new, with him, with the one who loved me with an everlasting love and who had never given up on me. He still would not take what I wanted to give; he saved it for the right time—I had to wait just a little longer and knew then why my whole life I had been waiting on Justin. He was all I ever wanted.

Then it was my turn to know him, to touch the places I'd imagined and never had permission to enjoy. He was as hard as he looked—everywhere. I traced the lines of his muscles in his shoulders, fanning over their sides, down his biceps—the curve, the strength, the power that was him. I touched his nipples too, doubting, but wondering all the same if it made him feel the same way it did me–and then lower, to explore the mystery that stood between us.

"Not yet; wait."

"You said we didn't have to wait anymore."

"You have to wait a little longer or the night's going to be all about me. You touch me and it'll all be over right now."

"Really?" I questioned and reached for him playfully. I didn't think I would mind the night being all about him. He grabbed my hand and pulled it away firmly.

"Wait, Haylee."

It was a command I was not allowed to disobey.

We rinsed the suds away and turned the water off. Our kisses deepened in our desperation, but a man who waited that long for the woman he wanted didn't give into passion until the precise moment he waited for. He wasn't finished with me. He toweled me dry, then lifted me and carried me to our bed in his arms like I weighed nothing more than a feather. He kissed me and laid me down on something more like a cloud than a bed and climbed up to nestle beside me, holding me so close to him we could have been one and not two bodies lying together. He growled low. I remembered that sound all too well, but this time there was no stopping him.

"Oh, you were worth it," he said. His lips were on mine, then moved away to my neck, my breasts, cupping them and teasing them taut. I had never felt anything like it before in my life.

"You know why I waited, don't you?"

"Because you love me?"

"Because we were meant to be us. Forever, Haylee. This is it."

He was on top of me, then eased slowly into me. And then, just like that, he made us one. I pushed up to meet him, hoping it wouldn't hurt.

"It'll happen; don't rush it." He whispered the words softly into my ear as I relaxed and he pushed inside. We were one.

In all my life I had never experienced anything as beautiful and glorious as that night. Every first with Justin was the best. He was worth waiting for, and I guess I was too. When he was sure he had brought me to my first orgasm, he was finished waiting and convulsed over and over again inside me. His groan was so loud I covered his mouth as my body tensed again in response to his.

"Shhhh! People will hear!" I laughed at him, letting the waves of pleasure simultaneously ripple away and build again.

"I don't care. I just got what I've always wanted."

We lay together, naked, connected, and at ease. I realized it was the first day in a lifetime that I hadn't wanted a drink, hadn't even thought about one until that moment. I didn't want one then either. I wanted him to be my drink and forever to be mine.

The honeymoon was over the next day. Justin's leave was only a week. He had told them it was a family emergency. He didn't know how he would explain coming back with a wife, but it was a risk he was willing to take.

I moved in with him, and his place became ours. We made the former bachelor pad our home. He let me decorate with "foofy-girlie" things, as he called them, and only protested a little—it would have been wrong if he hadn't complained at all.

I didn't think I could love him any more than I already did, but I fell in love all over again when I saw the picture of me on his dresser the day I moved in. It was old and ratty; he must have carried it in his wallet for years. It was of me my sophomore year of high school, just after I moved with Aunt Aerin. I was walking through a low spot in the Icicle River when the picture was taken. I looked happy, but I couldn't remember the day—the only thing I remembered were the almost-too-short, frayed cut-offs. Aunt Aerin had probably given it to him. But that wasn't what did it: it was the folded paper under the picture, even more worn and tattered because of its age. I unfolded it and the words caught me by surprise. It was the paper he'd written and folded up into his pocket all those years before when he rescued me from Brad. The words were few but the promise was eternal:

I promise to love Haylee Howell for the rest of my life, so help me God.

It was the night of the party, the night he saved me and took Lizzie and I out to our secret place... the night I had fallen in love with him. He was the man every woman wanted to call hers. And he was mine.

THE END

EPILOGUE

I'D LIKE TO TELL YOU that we lived happily ever after and this was just the beginning of our wonderful life together. I'd like to tell you that just like Cinderella and Prince Charming, our troubles were behind us, but that would be a fairy tale, and I didn't start the story with "Once Upon a Time," did I?

The truth is Cinderella and Prince Charming probably didn't live happily ever after either. I imagine like Justin and me, they had disagreements. Like us, they probably fell in and out of love a million times over stupid things like bills and babies, the reality that sneaks in and sucks the dreamy part of the story away. But also like us, they always came back to their commitment and promise. We promised forever to each other, and as God as my witness, we will forever be together.

I still battle the raging alcoholic within me, pushing it back with strength from a higher power I know as Jesus Christ—and with the reminders of that morning in the alley and all the nights of misery with my mom and Clayton.

We both still have nightmares that wake us up in the middle of the night and scars from our youth that will never be erased. Justin had so much guilt about the breaking and entering we did that when I got to the step where I was to make amends, he made his own amends. He tried to find everyone on the block but couldn't reach them all.

"What's past is past; it's all forgiven," Gramma Diaz had said when we knocked on the door of the much older, much more wrinkled version of the grandmotherly cookie lady she once had been. She shuffled to the door and opened it to us like we never grew up.

She was happy to hear we were OK and she admitted she always worried over us but didn't know what to do—and that the Mister had caught on to our break-ins, which is why the cookies appeared in the mudroom. I pretended to need to use the bathroom only so I could see the picture wall once more. It was smaller than I remembered—only eight or ten feet, hardly the mile long hall of my childhood—but still they smiled. Now I knew why: there was happiness to be found in the world. There was healing. There was good.

It's my job, and Justin's, and yours to rage against the darkness, to fight against the monsters of our past and to become who we are meant to be.

I was meant to be Justin's, and to feed my own neighborhood children cookies on Wednesdays, and to become an interior designer who brings color and structure and style into the lives of my clients.

I was meant to be a mom—a good mom who dances with her children, Zach and Vasi, sober, and meets their bus at the top of the road every afternoon and gives them a kiss and hug every night before bed.

Justin was meant for a greatness I cannot even express. He was made to love someone as unlovable as I had been and never give up on those he believes in. He was made to fight for those who are weak and teach punk kids how to play the guitar. And he was made to fly—only instead of teleporter machines or fighter jets, he's been flying Med-evac helicopters since getting out of the Air Force. He's spending his life saving lives every day, just like he saved mine so long ago.

We survive, accepting what we cannot change. We are courageous to make our life and the lives of our children better than ours was.

Nope, not a fairy tale, not a happily-ever-after, just one day at a time. Easy does it.

SONGS THAT INSPIRED WAITING ON JUSTIN

I love music and frequently listen to playlists to suit the mood of the story I'm telling. This book was partially inspired by the words and melodies of the sound track of songs listed below. I believe Waiting on Justin will be best read in their company. If you feel so inspired, make up your own playlist and listen along while you read. I hope the story speaks to your heart the way these songs speak to mine.

La la la –Naughty Boy feat. Sam Smith
Opening scene, if there is such a scene for a book, and during all the times the kids ran to their forts or rooms to hide from their parents parties.

Pride and Joy – Stevie Ray Vaughn
I mean no disrespect to the master of rockin' rhythm and blues, he just happened to be in my ears when I was first writing the part where Brad took Haylee into the bathroom and the song got stuck in that scene.

More than Words – Extreme
Of course during Justin and Haylee's long awaited first kiss … and first time.

No Rain – Blind Melon
No particular reason on this one, just like it and it gives a little flavor to the melancholy tone of the story.

If this was a Movie – Taylor Swift
When Haylee is taken into foster care and is alone, waiting on Justin.

Let Her Go – Passenger
I was a little obsessed with Mike Rosenberg during the first and second drafts of the book so he managed to double inspire me. This is for when Justin, back against the wall, pushes Haylee to turn herself in.

Sad but True – Metallica
In moments, unwritten, when Haylee would look in the mirror and see her mom looking back at her and in the times she did share when she knew she was becoming the woman she didn't want to be.

It's Your Love – Tim McGraw & Faith Hill
Jordan's song, don't worry he gets his happily ever after in *Finding Jordan*.

Demons – Imagine Dragons
When Jordan gets close and Haylee pushes him away.

Everything – Lifehouse
For all the times Haylee was mad at Justin or tried to replace him with anything or anyone.

Patient Love – Passenger
For all the times, in the book before called *Catching Tatum*, where Justin Parker patiently waited for Haylee.

Fix You - Coldplay
When Justin comes for Haylee after all the time she's pushed him away. When they rush to the church to get married and during the shower scene! I listened to it over and over again during the last chapter of the book.

JAG AND CASA

The JAG and CASA organizations mentioned in *Waiting on Justin* are actual organizations actively working to keep high-risk youth safe. Please use the information listed below to learn more about their organizations and contribute in the way that is easiest for you. And if you suspect child abuse make a call: 1-800-4-A-CHILD. You can remain anonymous and the state will investigate if the allegations warrant it. And remember tough kids usually have tough lives, let them talk and when they do, listen, you can change their life.

Jobs for America's Graduates (JAG):

JAG is a state-based national non-profit organization dedicated to preventing dropouts among young people who are most at-risk. In more than three decades of operation, JAG has delivered consistent, compelling results – helping nearly three-quarters of a million young people stay in school through graduation, pursue postsecondary education and secure quality entry-level jobs leading to career advancement opportunities.

http://www.jag.org/

Chelan-Douglas CASA organization:

Imagine the experience of children who are removed from their homes because the people responsible for protecting them have not. These children find themselves in a world filled with social workers, lawyers, judges and courtrooms where life-altering decisions are made on their behalf. **A CASA volunteer is a court appointed, trained and committed adult who ensures that each child's individual needs remain a priority in an over-burdened child welfare system.** They get to know the child while also gathering information from the child's family, teachers, doctors, care-givers and anyone else involved in the child's life in order to make independent and informed recommendations to help the judge decide what's best for the child. CASA volunteers come from every walk of life and share a commitment to improving children's lives, a willingness to learn, and an open mind towards life experiences different from their own. **For children who have been abused or neglected, CASA means having a home instead of feeling lost, of being a priority instead of feeling invisible. For volunteers, CASA is a life-changing experience that makes our community a better place.** If you are looking for a meaningful and enriching volunteer opportunity in the Chelan-Douglas area and want to do something about child abuse, CASA is right for you. **Our case load is up year over year, and we have an increasing need for CASA volunteers. Our vision is to provide a trained volunteer advocate, a safe home and a promising future for every child who needs us.** In 2013 we had 193 children taken from their homes requiring assistance. We hope you decide to join our community of volunteers and help ensure that every child has an adult they can rely on. To learn more about your commitment.

For more information on how to get involved please visit:
National CASA organization:
http://www.casaforchildren.org/site/c.mtJSJ7MPIsE/b.5301295/k.BE9A/Home.htm

Chelan/Douglas CASA: http://cdcasa.org/

Made in the USA
Middletown, DE
08 April 2024

52622151R00120